"Ho ... dly.

George looked ... dly.

"It would appear so." She gave the little boy an affectionate look and, once again, George was struck by how readily she opened her heart to a child who needed it.

Pierre tugged at his hand. *J'enseigne!*

George looked at Flora for translation.

"He said he will teach you." Her words came out with a slight giggle, like she found the prospect delightful.

Fortunately, almost every child probably knew the familiar folk song, or at least that was what George thought. "I don't sing as well as you, but I think I can manage."

He began to sing the first few bars, then Flora and Pierre joined in.

Maybe it was wrong of him to think so, but as they strolled through the crowded area of the mine, holding hands with Pierre, who was exuberantly swinging his arms, probably in hope that they'd pick him up and swing him between them again, this felt like everything he'd always hoped for in a family of his own.

Danica Favorite loves the adventure of living a creative life. She loves to explore the depths of human nature and follow people on the journey to happily-ever-after. Though the journey is often bumpy, those bumps refine imperfect characters as they live the life God created them for. Oops, that just spoiled the ending of Danica's stories. Then again, getting there is all the fun. Find her at danicafavorite.com.

Books by Danica Favorite

Love Inspired Historical

Rocky Mountain Dreams
The Lawman's Redemption
Shotgun Marriage
The Nanny's Little Matchmakers
For the Sake of the Children
An Unlikely Mother

DANICA FAVORITE

An Unlikely Mother

HARLEQUIN® LOVE INSPIRED® HISTORICAL

Recycling programs
for this product may
not exist in your area.

LOVE INSPIRED BOOKS

ISBN-13: 978-0-373-42524-2

An Unlikely Mother

www.Harlequin.com

Printed in U.S.A.

I am not saying this because I am in need, for I have learned to be content whatever the circumstances. I know what it is to be in need, and I know what it is to have plenty. I have learned the secret of being content in any and every situation, whether well fed or hungry, whether living in plenty or in want. I can do all this through Him who gives me strength.

—*Philippians* 4:11–13

The Harlequin.com online community has been a part of my writing journey since day one. You guys are not just my job, but a second family, and I love you all dearly. I've been waiting to write the perfect book that encapsulates what a precious part of my journey you've been, but I've finally come to the conclusion that I'd need at least a thousand books to tell each of the very wonderful stories I've gotten to be a part of. Thank you all for the role you play in my life, each other's lives and in the books you've brought and will bring to the world.

And, Rae, your time is coming!
Keep the faith. Love you!

Chapter One

Leadville, Colorado, 1883

Stark raving mad. If Flora Montgomery had to describe herself in this latest scheme, that's what she would say she was. Oh, she'd done some crazy things in the past. Horrible things. But nothing so insane as agreeing to spend the summer in a mining camp helping the less fortunate.

Like everything else in her life, it had seemed like a good idea at the time.

The baby's wail pierced her ears again.

She stared at the little creature in her arms. "I'm sorry. They should have asked someone else to hold you. I've never held a baby before, and I know I'm doing a terrible job, but could you please have a little mercy?"

Unfortunately, her words only served to send more tears rolling down the baby's cheeks, making Flora want to cry herself. *Please, Lord, I know I've done a lot of bad things in my life, but surely this poor child doesn't deserve to suffer because of it.*

Why had the other women thought that leaving Flora

alone with a baby was a good idea? When they'd gone
to unload a wagon, Mrs. Willoughby handed her this
baby and told her to stay at the cabin with her.

Flora sighed. It wasn't that they'd thought having her
take care of a baby was a good idea, but that none of
them wanted to be stuck with Flora. Which left Flora
here with this tiny creature she knew nothing about.

Surely the other ladies would return soon.

Glancing down the well-worn path the women had
taken only left Flora feeling more miserable. If they
returned and saw what a terrible job she was doing
in minding the baby, they'd have one more crime to
throw at her feet.

That was the trouble with being the most hated
woman in town. Once people found an excuse to hate
you, it seemed everything else only served to validate
that opinion. She should know. Not too long ago, Flora's
words were the ones the women hung on, her opinions
dictating everyone else's place in society. But she had
been cruel in her judgments of others, shunning women
who were now the ones everyone else looked up to. When
Flora had hurt one too many people with her actions,
they'd turned on her. And rightly so. But no matter how
many times Flora said she was sorry, or tried to show
that she'd changed, it didn't seem to make a difference.

How, then, was Flora supposed to redeem herself?

Surely it wasn't impossible. After all, Emma Jane
Jackson, once tormented for being poor, uncomely and
awkward, was now one of the most respected women in
their group, married to one of the handsomest, wealthi-
est men in town. A man Flora had once hoped to marry.
Virtue over beauty. Apparently that was what men val-
ued in women these days. And since Flora had little of

the former, and a great deal of the latter, she'd finally begun to accept that unless she changed her ways, she'd never find a husband of her own.

Since the baby had yet to cease its crying, Flora walked toward the nearby stream. Maybe the sound of water would soothe the poor thing. Not finding a husband was the least of Flora's worries. After all, a husband meant children, and clearly, from the way this one carried on, Flora would make a terrible mother.

Prior to the great social revolution in Leadville, Flora would have been confident in the idea of motherhood; after all, she would hire the finest nanny from New York, or London or perhaps even Paris. But now, the women in her circle all chose to raise their children themselves, bringing even the smallest babies to help out at the mission, tied around them in some sort of apparatus to hold them against their bodies, leaving the women's hands free to work.

One more reason Flora didn't fit in. She'd had a nanny growing up, as did all the girls she'd known, but she'd also had no siblings, no babies to tend. Which was why she had no idea what to do with the squalling creature in her arms.

"Is everything all right, ma'am?" A miner, dressed in work clothes that were shabby but clean, approached.

"I…" Flora looked down at the baby. "I don't know what's wrong with her."

The man reached for the child. "Let me see what I can do. I've been told I have a way with little ones."

Glancing toward the path the women had taken, Flora's stomach dipped. What would the other women say if she handed the baby over to a strange man? It didn't seem possible that they could hate her any more, but they always seemed to find a way.

"I shouldn't," Flora said, trying to ignore the way the baby's face turned redder and redder. "Her mother might not like me letting a stranger take her."

Smiling, the man took a step toward her. "A wise decision. I'm…" He paused. "George. George, uh… Baxter."

The man, George, looked nervous. Flora had learned that many people came to these parts to escape a past they were ashamed of. Unfortunately, when one's past was in a place where everyone else came to hide, there was no hiding it.

So this George Baxter, probably not his real name, well, Flora wasn't going to judge his secrets. But she wasn't going to simply hand him someone else's baby, either.

Even if she wasn't sure her ears would ever recover from the high-pitched screaming.

"Flora Montgomery. It's nice to meet you, Mr. Baxter. I do appreciate your offer, but I'm afraid it wouldn't be proper."

Another smile filled his face. "Could I make a suggestion, then?"

"It would be most welcome. I'm sure it couldn't hurt at this point." Flora sighed, looking at the wailing baby once more.

"You're holding her wrong," George said. "Cradle her gently next to you, like so."

He bent down and picked up a large stick and demonstrated.

Flora shook her head. "I tried that, and the baby cried even worse."

"Does she need to uh…" George shifted, looking more uncomfortable than he had at saying his name. "…belch?"

She wasn't allowed to say that word in polite company. Let alone discuss those particular things with a man. But she did need to find a way to get the baby to quiet down.

"How am I supposed to know that? The baby doesn't talk."

If he sensed her irritation, he didn't show it. His face held a look of kindness and gentleness. Patience. The kind of man Flora would like to get to know, were he not so far outside her social station. A pity, since the harder Flora had worked on improving her character, the less appealing those in her social station seemed to be.

Eyes twinkling, George held the stick to his shoulder. "Put the baby against your shoulder, like so, and gently pat her back."

George reached forward and tapped her arm lightly. "Like this."

What sort of man would be so…kind…as to go so far to help a woman in distress when it was a matter in which most men would never be involved?

Flora had seen mothers pat their babies like that. She imitated the action. The baby obliged by letting out a large belch. Then another.

And then she promptly emptied the contents of her stomach on one of Flora's best dresses.

But at least she finally stopped crying.

With a smile, George untied the kerchief from around his neck and handed it to her. "I'm sorry. I should have warned you. You don't know anything about babies, do you?"

"I've never held a baby in my life." Flora brushed at the mess with the handkerchief with one hand, while trying to balance the now-happy, squirming baby with the other.

The handkerchief did little to mop up the mess. No wonder so many of the women of her acquaintance wore such unsightly aprons. At least their dresses could be salvaged. "Do they all expel such…"

George chuckled, and reached for the baby again. She shouldn't let him, but she had no idea how she was supposed to not drop the baby and get the foul-smelling liquid off herself. How did other women manage? Surely it wouldn't hurt to let this man help her for just a moment. If he didn't look like a miner, she'd think him a gentleman for sure. Hadn't he already demonstrated a level of civility that went beyond what most people would do?

Giving her a charming smile as she relinquished the baby, he said, "I believe they do. Though this little one seemed to be more enthusiastic in her efforts."

Flora used her now-free hand to finish cleaning herself off, but it seemed like she was only making a bigger mess of things.

"There's water in my canteen." George pointed to an object resting against a tree. "Feel free to use it all. The creek's not too far."

So many rules of propriety were being breached in this situation. But as Flora used the water to cleanse the remaining mess, she found she honestly didn't care. With only the water and handkerchief to clean up, she knew she was doing a fair job, at best.

Flora watched as George cuddled the baby, chattering at her and pointing to things. She would never have imagined that a man would be so good with a baby. She shook her head. One more reason she shouldn't judge by appearances. The same way people would have assumed that as a woman, Flora would know what to do with one.

"Do you have children of your own?" Flora asked, handing him back the handkerchief.

"No." George gave her a warm smile, and for the first time, she realized that the man was quite handsome, indeed. He had blue eyes that crinkled at the edges, and though his dark brown hair was unruly, she found the way it curled at his collar quite attractive. Even the stubble on his chin made him seem…well, masculine, adding to his charm.

"But I have a nephew, and I've always gotten on with children. Even now, when I attend church, no matter where I go, the children seem to congregate around me."

He tickled the baby under her chin, making her giggle. "Babies aren't so hard, really. They just need to know that they're safe and loved. The reason you're having so much trouble is that you're nervous. Babies can sense that."

Flora sighed, watching how comfortable he was with the baby in his arms. "I suppose. I just don't think she likes me much. Most people don't."

The sound of chatter in the distance reminded Flora of her duty, and that the returning women would not appreciate the fact that she'd allowed a strange man to hold the baby.

"Thank you for your assistance," Flora said, holding out her hands. "I should take her now."

"You are most welcome, Flora Montgomery," he said softly, his breath a whisper on her cheek as he placed the baby in her arms. "And if it's any consolation, I like you just fine."

Her face heated as she shifted the baby and stepped away. Unfortunately, it hadn't been soon enough for the returning women.

"Flora Montgomery! How dare you canoodle with a strange man while watching my precious Ethel!" Mrs. Willoughby marched up to her and snatched the baby out of her arms.

"I didn't—" Flora couldn't finish her sentence as her gaze drifted to the other women standing around, staring at her like she was some fallen woman.

Was this how others had felt when Flora had lashed out at them for what Flora had considered improper behavior? Oh, how she wished she could go back and change the way she'd reacted to situations she'd known nothing about. Accuse first and make apologies never, that had been the way of things. How wrong she'd been.

"Ma'am, I can assure you, there was nothing improper between myself and Miss Montgomery. Little Ethel had a slight accident on Miss Montgomery's shoulder, and I was helping her clean up the mess." He held up his soiled handkerchief, as though proving his case.

"Ethel was ill?" Horror flashed across Mrs. Willoughby's face as she examined the baby.

Flora was nearly concerned herself, except for George's chuckle.

"I'm sure it's no cause to worry, ma'am. Looked to be a typical baby spit-up to me. Just a lot of it."

"And what are you, a doctor?" Mrs. Willoughby glared at him. At the negative shake of his head, she turned and marched to the cabin.

Feeling the gazes of the others strongly upon her, Flora turned to him and smiled. "Thank you for your assistance, Mr. Baxter. Your kindness is much appreciated, and I will remember it always. I should get back to work. After all, that's why I came."

She directed that last comment at the other women, forcing a smile despite the sinking feeling that, with even this small task, she'd once again failed to meet their standards.

George smiled at her. It was a shame the man was a miner. He'd been kind, helpful and he was the first man in a long time who'd treated her like she was anything but the disappointment everyone else saw her as. A smile tugged at the corners of her lips, despite her less than joyous mood. He was also quite pleasant to look at.

But even if they could find something in common, her family and the rest of society would never approve of her marrying someone so far removed from their world.

Still, it had been nice to have someone treat her like a human being for a change. If only she could get the rest of society to do the same.

Flora Montgomery. As he lived and breathed. George Baxter Bellingham would never have expected to run into her in the mining camp. For a moment, he'd been afraid his former nemesis would recognize him, but then he remembered that he was no longer the pudgy little boy all the kids tormented. Besides, Flora had moved from Denver to Leadville several years ago, and they hadn't seen each other since. Part of him felt bad for deceiving her about his identity, but he hadn't exactly lied. He'd given her his first and middle names, but not his last. Fortunately, his middle name was his mother's maiden name, so it sounded like a real name.

Right now, he couldn't afford to have anyone, most of all Flora, know his real name. Flora's father was once George's father's best friend, but the two men had had a falling-out years ago, shortly before the Montgomerys moved to Leadville.

Though George didn't know what had happened, he did know that John Montgomery was considered an enemy of the family. With George's father now gone, it was up to George to figure out what was going wrong at the family's mine, and he wasn't sure if the Montgomerys could be trusted. A young lady of Flora's station would obviously know nothing about her father's business, but all it would take was a careless mention of running into George, and his carefully crafted plan would fall apart. John Montgomery most likely wouldn't recognize George for the same reasons Flora hadn't.

He watched her retreat, noting that the years since their childhood had been kind to her. She'd grown into a graceful young woman, and he'd heard tales of her beauty long before this meeting. The tales had not done her justice. No longer the knobby-kneed, freckle-faced brat who once poked fun at him for sport, Flora had acquired not only beauty, but a gentility that drew him.

Back in his debutante-chasing days, Flora would have been exactly the sort of woman George would pursue. But those days were over, thanks to his father's death and subsequent rumors that the mine was having financial troubles. His former fiancée, Shannon, had given him back his ring with the sickeningly sweet suggestion that he might need the money from selling it.

No more debutantes or any other kind of socialite for George.

Even if he found a way to straighten out his family's finances, he didn't want a wife who could only love him in the "for richer" part of their vows. Women like Flora expected a certain kind of life, a life he wasn't sure he could provide. If he'd learned anything from this experience, it was that a man's fortune could change more quickly than anyone could imagine, and regardless of how things turned out for him financially, he needed to know his future wife would be happy in any circumstance.

Still… Flora Montgomery. Tempting. He'd liked the way she'd taken on caring for a baby when she had no idea what she was doing. Even though she'd been utterly disgusted with the baby spitting up on her, she still had a sweet smile for little Ethel. The last thing Flora had wanted to do was take care of a baby, that was obvious, but he'd seen her genuine concern for the child.

Of course, he had to remember that he wasn't George Bellingham, welcome in parlors of the finest families, but George Baxter, lowly miner, and from the way Flora had recoiled at his acquaintance, he wouldn't be invited to tea anytime soon. As tempting as it was to get to know her better, he wasn't going to go down that path. The likes of Flora Montgomery were only interested in men who could advance their social standing. Even if George's plan worked, he wanted no part of a woman who couldn't love a man for who he was. Call him sentimental, but his parents had married long before they'd had money, and theirs was one of the best marriages he'd ever seen.

Shannon had done him a favor, giving him his ring back. And he wasn't planning on giving it to anyone else who could only see a man for his bank account or social standing.

Neither of which would amount to much if he didn't figure out who was sabotaging operations at the mine. A couple weeks ago, an entire tunnel had caved in, narrowly avoiding killing several workers. His brother-in-law, Arthur, had told him that it was the cost of doing business, and these things happened sometimes. But that wasn't how George's father had done business, and had it not been for a runaway carriage, he'd still be here to make things right.

Which left the task up to George.

His mother had been badly injured in the carriage accident, and her medical bills and treatments were costly. Arthur was busy handling the family's other business interests, which were also inexplicably losing money. Though Arthur had insisted that George remain at Harvard, pursuing his studies so that he could eventually take his place in the family businesses, George couldn't sit back and watch his family lose everything.

Arthur might be too busy to get to the bottom of the troubles at the mine, but George wasn't. How could he continue spending money that the family might not have much longer? His mother needed the medical care. His sister was expecting another baby. No, the answer was not to bury himself in the books, but in this mine.

Folks used to say that Elias Bellingham was far too generous in his dealings with others, and that it would someday send him to the poorhouse. Which was why, Arthur had told him, the family business was nearly bankrupt again.

Didn't George owe it to his father's legacy to see if he could turn things around at the mine?

A faint whimper on the other side of the tree where he'd laid his canteen caught his attention. As George rounded the tall pine that hadn't yet been claimed by the camp for fuel or building material, he spied a little boy sitting in the hollow near a boulder a few yards away.

"Hey, little guy," George said softly as he approached. "Are you all right?"

The small boy couldn't be more than three or four years old, the same age as his nephew, Sam.

A tear-stained face stared up at him, longing thick in the child's eyes. He spoke rapidly, but the words were foreign to George. All he could understand was, *"Père."*

Father. George had taken a few French lessons, but he'd been terrible at it. Many of his peers had had French nannies, learning the language as part of daily life. But the Bellinghams had gone with a more traditional English nanny. Which did him little good now.

Since the boy looked like he was about to start crying again, George knelt beside him. Maybe the boy spoke English. *"Parlez-vous Anglais?"*

The little boy shook his head. Great. That was about the extent of the French he could remember, other than a few words that didn't seem helpful here.

Pointing to himself, he said, "George."

Then he pointed at the little boy.

"Pierre," the boy said.

Then the boy began speaking again in rapid French.

George shook his head and pointed to himself again. "No *parlez Français.*"

Hopefully it was enough to convey to the boy that he didn't understand. The boy nodded slowly as tears continued rolling down his cheeks.

George pointed to himself again. "George...help... Pierre." Wait. What was the word for help? "Aid?"

That seemed to get Pierre's attention, or at least stop the flow of tears.

Pierre pointed at George's canteen.

"Are you thirsty?"

Silly of him to ask, since Pierre probably didn't know the word. George held out the canteen, mostly empty from Flora's use, but there was a little water to spare.

Pierre drank the water quickly, then pointed to his stomach.

What was the word for hungry? Back when George was pudgy, everything had been about food. *"Faim?"*

Hopefully he wasn't telling Pierre something awful. But Pierre nodded, so George took that as a good sign.

Judging by the fact that the little boy was alone and crying, George was going to assume he'd somehow gotten separated from his father. But how was he supposed to find a little boy's father when he'd barely arrived at the mining camp himself? He'd been here just long enough to pitch a tent and gain employment at the mine.

Flora. She was here with the church mission. Perhaps the people at the church mission would know of anyone who spoke French who could... George smiled. Flora had a French nanny when they were children. She used to brag about how her nanny was superior to everyone else's because of it. She and her friends would speak in French, giving themselves airs and using it as a means to exclude the other children. Back then, he'd found it annoying.

But now, it just might save this little boy's life. Flora could help him care for the boy and translate so they could find Pierre's father.

George gave Pierre a smile. "Pierre come with George. *Manger.*" At least that's what he thought the word for *eat* was. He held out his hand.

Clearly the love of food that had led to George's torment as a child was helping him now. Pierre smiled back and took George's hand.

George had never imagined he'd be so grateful for Flora Montgomery. When they were children, she'd teased him and tormented him mercilessly. Who knew that Flora's annoying affectation from the past might very well be the thing he needed most right now? While pursuing his newfound attraction to her was still out of the question, he'd be lying if he said he wasn't looking forward to seeing her again.

George ruffled the little boy's hair. He wished he could convey something more to him, to make him feel comfortable, but at least Flora could do that. Despite the complication of meeting Flora so early in his quest, knowing that she could be the one person to expose him, she would also be a great asset. People might say that Elias Bellingham's weakness was his concern for others, but George was grateful his father had passed on that trait to him. He wouldn't feel right leaving Pierre until his father had been found, and Flora's help would make it easier for George to help Pierre and accomplish his own mission. As long as he could keep Flora from learning his real reason for being in the camp.

Though he hoped to find Pierre's father quickly, George was going to enjoy every moment he spent in Flora's company until then.

Chapter Two

Flora was able to slip away to the creek to wash after her baby-minding disaster. Though how she was going to accomplish a good cleansing and change her dress out in the open, she had no idea. The place was private enough, or so some of the other ladies had said. But was this another of their tricks, like Lindsay Carmichael goading her into bringing her best dresses instead of work clothes?

Not that she had anything that could be considered work clothes. Flora sighed. Perhaps it had been a mistake to think that redemption would come to someone like her.

"Flora?" Rose Jones walked down the embankment carrying a bundle. "I heard you'd come this way."

Of course it would have to be Rose. Flora sighed. Of all the people she'd injured with her thoughtless words, Rose had been hurt the worst. And though Rose had said she'd forgiven Flora, and was polite, if not kind, to her, Flora always wondered if she could truly count on Rose as a friend.

"I was hoping to wash up. My dress smells." Flora

pointed at her soiled silk gown, a yellow stain spreading across the pale pink fabric. It was probably ruined.

Rose looked around. "It's private enough with most of the men at work, but I wouldn't come here much later in the day. And you shouldn't be here alone. As much as Uncle Frank has done to keep us safe, you have to remember that many of the people here don't have the same regard for the law and civility as we do."

Flora stared at the ground. She'd only wanted to clean up, but it seemed there was fault in that as well.

"It's all right," Rose said softly, stepping forward. "You haven't been up to the camp before, and I suspect that Lindsay didn't give you good instructions. I'd hoped to orient you myself, but Milly was ill, so I've only just arrived."

"What's wrong with Milly?" One of Flora's many mistakes, and ways she'd wronged Rose, had involved Rose's stepdaughter, Milly. Before Rose married Silas, Rose had been Milly's nanny, but because Milly's grandparents disapproved, Flora had assisted them by trying to take over as Milly's nanny. When Milly's grandparents took Milly away without Rose's permission, Flora helped them, thinking she was doing the right thing. During that time, Flora had developed a genuine affection for the little girl. Still, what Flora had done was wrong, and it was only the mercy shown by Rose and her now-husband, Silas, that had kept Flora out of jail.

Flora turned away. "I'm sorry, I don't have the right to ask."

"Of course you do." Rose stepped in front of her and smiled. "I'm grateful that you care so much about her. It was just a little cold, and she's fine now. She remained behind with Maddie, our housekeeper, but when I see her again, I'll pass on your good wishes."

Another friendly smile. Rose held out the bundle to Flora. "I brought you a dress. The one you're wearing is too fine for being up here, and from the giggling I heard from the others, I suspect everything else you brought is just as nice."

Flora gaped at Rose. Why was she being so kind to her? True, after the situation with Milly's grandparents, part of Flora's restitution was to help with the ministry. And Flora had worked side by side with Rose several times in the months since.

But that didn't mean Flora deserved any sort of kindness from Rose.

"I also brought a blanket. I'll hold it up so you can have privacy to wash up and change. You'll have to wash quickly, but it's better than the alternative."

Another bright smile.

"Why are you being so nice to me?" Flora made no move to accept the dress Rose held out.

"Why wouldn't I be?"

Flora shrugged. "I could list a thousand reasons. I've been horrible to you since you came to Leadville. I don't deserve your kindness."

With a long sigh, Rose sat on a nearby rock. "You're right. You've made my life difficult in a number of ways. But you've apologized and I forgave you. I've seen the change in your behavior over the past few months, and I know that you've let the Lord work in your heart. The Lord has been kind to me. How could I not be kind to you?"

"You sound a lot like Pastor Lassiter," Flora said,

meeting the other woman's eyes. "He's been telling me the same thing."

"And now I know why he specifically asked me to come on this trip." Rose smiled again, and because Flora was observing her eyes, she could see the warmth lurking there. "After my scandal of having my son out of wedlock, I thought I'd accepted the Lord's forgiveness. I did my best to hold my head up high, knowing that God didn't hold my sin against me. But it seemed like there were so many who were constantly reminding me of my sin."

"Like me," Flora said, hating the way she could still remember how she smiled as she gossiped about Rose's misfortune. One more thing Rose should hate her for.

Rose shrugged. "You weren't the only one. But that is exactly my point. I've forgiven you. It's time for you to forgive yourself."

She made it sound so easy. Perhaps because she didn't know all the details of what Flora had done. Things only Flora and God knew. Even so, everyone else in town made certain to remind her of all the reasons she didn't deserve forgiveness.

"The rest of the town doesn't seem to agree with you."

"It doesn't matter. Chasing after their approval is never going to bring you happiness. What matters is that your heart is aligned with God's, and that you live out the forgiveness He's offered you."

Flora let out another long sigh. What Rose said made sense, but she didn't understand how hard it was to put into action. "But people aren't actively shunning you or laughing at you."

"Not in our church." Rose stood and held out the

bundle. "But there are still homes I'm not welcome in, people who make snide comments in the mercantile. Just the other day, I was at the milliner's, and one of the ladies there noticed me and said that if they were catering to fallen women, she wouldn't shop there anymore."

"But that's ridiculous. You're a respectable woman."

Rose shrugged. "I still had a child out of wedlock, and for some, that's a fact they can't get past. But I've dealt with my sin. God forgives me. And if others can't move on, that's their problem, not mine."

Rose continued. "Now let's hurry and get you washed and changed. I'm sure they're missing us."

Doing as Rose asked, Flora quickly hid under the blanket provided, cleaning up the remaining mess. When she was ready, she emerged from the blanket and held up her soiled dress.

"Is it so terrible that all I want to do is burn this dress I once begged Mother for?"

Rose smiled. "When we get back to town, we'll have Maddie take a look. If anyone can salvage it, she can."

As blind as Flora had once been to Rose's warmth, she couldn't ignore it anymore. "You really are trying to be my friend, aren't you?"

"I know what it's like to be the most hated woman in our circle. And I know how hard it is, once you've realized the error of your ways and are trying to make up for it, to be free of the stigma. If I can help you through your pain, then everything I have endured will have been worth it."

They started back up the hill. Flora tried processing Rose's words, but all she could think of were the wrongs she'd committed.

"But I hurt you."

Rose stopped and stared at her. "I forgave you. So let go of the past. Until you can, you're never going to be able to move forward in freedom."

The cabin came into view. Flora's stomach knotted at the thought of having to face all the others, to listen to their laughter and mockery.

"What about them?"

"If there's someone you haven't offered an apology to, then make haste to do so. But if you've sincerely gone to those you've offended and asked forgiveness, you've done your part."

As part of her restitution, Pastor Lassiter had told her to speak with the others she'd hurt and seek forgiveness. It had been hard, and while many said they forgave her, they still didn't treat her any differently.

"What if it doesn't make a difference? No one believes I've changed."

Rose shook her head. "Then you keep living your life with the integrity of a woman whose heart has been changed by God."

Stepping in line with Flora, Rose linked arms with her. "But you, my friend, have got to act like you've moved on with your life. Shame keeps us buried in the past, and your future is with people who love and care about you."

Flora could tell the move was deliberate on Rose's part. After all, Flora had done the same many a time. By walking with her arm linked with Flora's, Rose was telling everyone that she considered Flora a friend.

Looking up at Rose, Flora realized what she'd been missing out on by fearing retribution instead of accepting friendship. "Thank you for not giving up on me.

I'm grateful for your willingness to guide me during this difficult time."

Rose gave her a squeeze. "I was fortunate to have family who refused to give up on me, so I could never give up on you. Now, let's go see about that handsome gentleman I see standing beside the cabin. I'm not one to give credence to gossip, but I am wondering if he's the same man you were seen with earlier this afternoon."

Flora's face warmed at Rose's words. A year ago, Flora would have been the one to spread the tales, and the unfortunate young woman's reputation would have been in shambles.

"N-nothing happened," Flora stammered. "He was just helping me. It was all proper."

Rose gave her arm another squeeze. "Of course it was. But with all those closest to me happily married, nothing gets me more excited than a handsome young man in pursuit of one of my friends."

Friends. As many times as Flora had thought of others as friends, this was the first she'd seen genuine interest and compassion in one. Rose's comments weren't about trying to get a juicy little tidbit to share with the others, but about...caring.

Then Rose smiled at her. "I think you have a suitor."

Finally following Rose's gaze, Flora noticed George waving at them. A young boy stood beside him. The nephew he'd mentioned?

"Come on!" Rose tugged at her arm. "I do wish to be introduced to this heroic man who came to your rescue."

Flora hung back. "I don't think..."

"He's heroic and handsome. What do you have to lose?"

Flora let out a long sigh. "I've lost everything, I suppose. But that's just the problem. I'm trying to gain back my old friends and their respect. I know I hurt them with my words, and I've apologized, but it hasn't kept them from continuing to shun me. What will people say about me if I allow a miner to court me?"

Frowning, Rose looked at her. "I think you have it all wrong. It's like I said earlier. Worrying about what everyone else thinks is only going to bring you more misery. You won't be able to satisfy everyone, so live your life. Be the woman God made you to be, and let people say what they're going to say. It's the only way you're going to find lasting contentment."

George waved at them as they came closer, and though Flora kept her free hand firmly pinned to her side, she couldn't help but smile. How long had it been since someone was so glad to see her?

Would it be so bad to pursue a friendship with him? Perhaps friendship was all George had to offer, as well.

George smiled at the ladies as they approached. Flora had changed, and there seemed to be a new lightness about her. "I see you found a new dress. Though the silk was lovely, I do like how the green in what you're wearing brings out the color in your eyes."

"Thank you." Flora stepped forward, smiling. She did have a beautiful smile. He supposed it was wrong to flatter her in such a way, but he'd been telling the truth. And it seemed just as wrong to ignore what was staring him in the face.

Pastor Lassiter joined them from around the side of the cabin. "Ah, Flora and Rose. You're back."

"Rose was good enough to help me clean up at the

river, and to lend me a more appropriate dress." Flora smiled at the other woman, and George couldn't help but notice how it lit up her eyes.

Pastor Lassiter smiled. "Yes, I heard about your unfortunate incident with the Willoughby baby. Good practice for when you have some of your own."

"My own? They all do that?" The horror on her face made George want to chuckle. Only he didn't think Flora was ready to laugh at the joke. Something in him wanted to protect her, even though she'd spent much of their childhood teasing him. He could sense that she'd changed since then.

Rose laughed. "And then some. But you'll find it's worth every mess. I'd forgotten you have no siblings or experience with babies. You can work with me, visiting the mothers and children. From what I've seen at the mission, you're a fast learner, and by the time this month is over, you'll be an expert at caring for children."

"That's actually why I'm here," George said, indicating Pierre. "He doesn't speak English, but I remembered—" He stopped himself. He couldn't admit that he knew Flora spoke French. For his plan to succeed, he needed to pretend this was the first they'd met.

George took a deep breath. "I remembered that Flora was connected with the mission here, so I brought him to you in hopes that you might know someone who speaks French and can help him."

Pastor Lassiter stepped in beside him and ruffled Pierre's hair. "George told me about the situation with the boy, and I told him he's come to the right place. However, I don't speak French, so I'm at a loss as to how to help find this boy's family."

Though George had already promised himself he was going to keep his distance from Flora, he couldn't help but notice the sympathy that lined her face.

"Oh, the poor dear," Flora said, kneeling beside Pierre, then breaking into French as she spoke to him.

George looked over at Pastor Lassiter, who wore a broad smile.

"Did you know she spoke French?" George asked the older man.

"I thought I'd heard at one point that she did," Pastor Lassiter admitted. "But I wasn't certain if she knew enough to converse with the boy. I see that she can do so, very well indeed."

Flora smiled at them as she stood, holding Pierre's hand. "This is Pierre, as I'm sure you know. He is four years old. His father works in the mine, but he hasn't come home for several days. Pierre went to look for his father, but he got lost. When George found him, he'd come to the creek for some water, but he got scared since it was moving so quickly. So it was a good thing George happened upon him when he did, because as I explained to Pierre, the creek is a very dangerous place for little boys."

She pulled Pierre closer to her, genuine affection shining in her eyes. Flora had definitely changed from the bratty girl he'd known as a child. So much warmth radiated from her, it was hard to imagine that people didn't like her.

"Pierre tells me that you gave him something to eat, so now all we need to do is find the poor boy's father. I told Pierre that his father is probably just as worried about him as Pierre is about his father."

Once again, George was struck by Flora's gentility and warmth. Though she addressed George, Pastor Lassiter and Rose, she kept smiling down at Pierre and giving him reassuring touches.

"I can't imagine we have too many Frenchmen here," Flora said. "Could you ask around to see where his father might be?"

Pastor Lassiter nodded slowly. "Of course. I haven't run into anyone from France up here, which is why I'm grateful we have Flora to translate."

"Me, too," George added. "I know you're not comfortable around little ones, but I only know a few words, and they aren't very helpful."

Once again, the smile George had grown to love so much filled Flora's face. "Oh, I like little ones. I had a brief opportunity to be a nanny to the most darling little girl." Her face darkened briefly, and she looked at Rose, but Rose smiled at her, chasing whatever clouded Flora's thoughts away, and happiness returned to her face. "I just don't know anything about babies."

Pierre tugged at Flora's skirt and she bent down to him, once again speaking French. Her words were melodic, almost like poetry. George could listen to her talk, even not knowing what she said, and remain enraptured for hours.

She turned her attention back to them and said, "I think Pierre is overwhelmed by all of this. Is there a quiet place where we can take him?"

"Of course." Pastor Lassiter gestured toward the cabin. "Why don't you and Pierre stay in the cabin until we can find his parents. Did he say anything about his mother?"

Flora asked the boy, whose expression became even

more despondent as he answered. "She recently passed away. That's why it was only him and his father."

Pierre started to cry, and Flora hugged him close. "Apparently his father is all he had left," she said, looking up at the others. "We simply must find him."

The expression on her face made George want to cry himself. Though he hadn't lost his father until adulthood, George couldn't imagine what it would be like for this little boy, who'd already lost his mother, to also be missing his father.

"I know I'm new here," George said, "but what can I do to help? Can we make signs?"

Pastor Lassiter shook his head. "Many of our miners can't read, or don't read English, so that would be futile. Besides—" he let out a long sigh "—it wouldn't be unheard-of that the father simply left his child. There's many a man who finds himself overwhelmed with the prospect of raising a child on his own, and without a relative to take over, sometimes he abandons him."

"I won't believe it," Flora declared hotly. "Not Pierre. He's too dear a boy." She bent down to him, whispering something in French.

Amazing. She barely knew the boy, and already Flora protected him with the fierceness of a mother. Though George had sworn off chasing after the pampered young ladies of his class, he had to admit that were it not for his uncertain financial future, and the people counting on him, he might be willing to consider the idea of Flora Montgomery. Someone with such compassion was worth taking a look at.

George shook his head. What was he thinking? He had a mystery at his mine to solve, and now this child's father to find. It was crazy to think that he could pursue a romantic relationship, even if he was free to do so.

"I can't believe someone would simply abandon Pierre, either," George said, smiling at Flora. "If you'll be so good as to continue caring for him, I'll do my part to find his father. I start work at the Pudgy Boy Mine tomorrow, but I'm at your disposal tonight. If we can't find Pierre's father, I'll be sure to ask the men at the mine if they know him, and in my free time I'll join in any effort to locate him. I know it's a big place, but surely, with all of us working together, we'll have Pierre reunited with his father in no time."

The delight on Flora's face was almost worth the time it would take away from George's own investigation. Except…the two weren't mutually exclusive. It would be a lot less suspicious if people saw George poking around, knowing he was looking for a missing man. Hopefully they'd find Pierre's father soon, so the excuse might not last long, but at least for now, it would give George the ability to look around and ask questions and have a good reason for doing so.

"Wonderful," Pastor Lassiter said. "Let's get this boy settled with Flora in the cabin, and then I can show you around, introduce you to some of the other men, and we can come up with a plan for finding Pierre's father."

Pastor Lassiter clapped him on the back, and for a moment, George almost felt guilty for not being completely honest about who he was and why he was here. This was a man of God, after all, and it somehow seemed more wrong to maintain his charade. But how else was George supposed to get to the truth about the accidents at the mine? People had been hurt in two separate incidents, and George couldn't countenance the idea of someone being killed.

He followed the pastor, Rose, Flora and Pierre to the cabin, watching how the little boy clung to Flora's hand. What if something happened to Pierre's father and George could have stopped it? As the mine owner, he was responsible. Suddenly his quest to find out what was happening at the mine and prevent further accidents became much more personal.

Pierre turned to look at George, and George gave the little boy a smile. Yes, he would help find Pierre's father. But he would also make sure Pierre's father continued to be safe when he worked.

Chapter Three

Not only had the previous night's search for Pierre's father been a waste of time, but George had never experienced such a fruitless day at work. The mine manager who'd hired him wasn't in, and George had spent the entire day hauling rock, backbreaking work that left little room for idle chatter.

Which wasn't the answer he wanted to give Flora when she gave him that sweet smile as she asked how his day had been. Pierre played nearby, drawing pictures in the dirt with a stick.

"I'm afraid I don't have much to report," George said slowly, shading his eyes from the sun to watch the pastor approach.

"Sit for a spell," Flora said, gesturing toward the log she sat upon. "I'd still like to hear how your day went, even if you didn't have any success in locating Pierre's father."

"I'm sure it's nothing that would interest you. We certainly didn't discuss the latest fashions from Paris." George grinned at her, and she smiled back.

"No, I don't imagine you would have. The only thing

I'm interested in from Paris right now is Pierre's father." Flora smiled as Pierre came running toward them, holding an earthworm he'd dug up.

Flora visibly cringed at the sight, especially as Pierre held the worm out to her. She'd never been one for anything creepy-crawly—worms, spiders, frogs, fish and even birds had always terrified her. As children, when she'd been particularly annoying, George would find a worm or insect to toss in her direction. Flora would go running into the house, crying to her mother about what a horrible boy that Pudgy Bellingham was. George couldn't help but grin. Even though she'd teased him mercilessly, he'd own that he'd been just as bad at times.

George held out his hand to the little boy. "Can I see?" Then he looked over at Flora. "How do you ask him to let me see what he's got?"

Relief washed over Flora's face as she spoke to Pierre, then turned back to George. "You say, *Qu'avez-vous?*"

She spoke slowly, clearly. George repeated her words, then looked at Pierre, speaking them again.

The little boy's face lit up as he ran to George, holding out the worm. *"Ver!"*

George glanced at Flora. "Did he just say *worm*?"

"He did." Flora shuddered slightly. "Nasty little things that they are. I'm so glad to have a man around to deal with all this disgusting boy stuff. I'd forgotten that boys like playing in mud, and with bugs and all those other horrible creatures."

"Ver. Worm," George said, touching the worm. Pierre grinned and repeated his words.

She let out a long sigh. "But he's such a little dear, I

can't really deny him, now, can I? Still, why can't small boys like things such as dolls and lace?"

Looking up from examining the worm Pierre had presented to him, George smiled. "I'm sure many a mother has asked that question. Have you asked the other ladies for their advice on less disgusting ways of occupying Pierre?"

Flora looked in the direction of the cluster of tents where most of the women were congregated. "Most of them are put out that I'm in charge of Pierre's care. I suppose I could ask Rose, but I hate to bother her, since she's already done more than enough to help me." She shook her head. "It doesn't matter. None of them, including Rose, speak French, so they really can't communicate with him. When they try, he runs and hides in my skirts. It's not my fault that I had a French nanny growing up."

She sighed again, and an expression of sadness crossed her face. "I suppose it is my fault, in a way. I spent years acting superior because I'd had a French nanny and I was fluent in the language. Why would they be kindly disposed to me now?"

The resignation in her voice twisted George's stomach. "Maybe because we all do things we regret as children."

He'd liked to have told her that even though she'd given him a horrible nickname, one that he'd found humiliating, he knew she wasn't that same little girl anymore. He wanted to tell her about all their childhood escapades, and how he regretted his own meanness toward her. But he wasn't ready for the world to know that George Bellingham was here at the mining camp.

Pierre tugged at George's pants leg and pointed to

the worm. George handed it back to him, trying to divide his attention between Flora and the little boy.

"But I wasn't a child. I was practically a grown woman, and many of the things I said to hurt others was as a woman, an adult responsible for her actions. They have every right to hate me."

Before George could respond, Pierre nudged him, holding up the worm and a stick, using words he didn't recognize. Except one.

Poisson. Fish.

"Is Pierre asking to go fishing?"

Flora nodded. "It seems you're a quick study. He's been asking all day, but as I'm sure you can imagine, I have no experience with fishing."

"I can't imagine you do. I'll have to take him sometime." George grinned. "But I'm sure you have many other fine accomplishments any young lady would be proud of."

With a smile that seemed more bitter than pleasant, Flora said, "Yes. I am quite the accomplished young lady. The most accomplished, according to many. But a fine lot of good that does me. What good is it to move people to tears with my songs, or paint a picture, or embroider a tapestry, in a place like this? It certainly hasn't won me any friends."

She turned her gaze in their direction, looking longingly at the other women. They laughed at a joke someone must have told, and Flora lowered her head.

"I don't blame them. But I do miss having friends who care about me." Shaking her head, Flora turned back to him. "No, they didn't care about me. They feared me. They knew that if they crossed me, I'd make them regret it. Until they finally got sick of me pushing everyone around."

Genuine regret sounded in her voice. Not the kind that said she was sorry she'd been caught, but that she wished she'd behaved differently. Wanted to be different now.

"Why did you do it?" George asked. He had no right to dig into Flora's personal affairs, but something about the sadness surrounding her drew him, made him want to help her see that things were not so hopeless.

"Why does anyone do bad things? I thought it was the right thing to do at the time." Flora sighed. "I hated it when my father moved us from Denver to Leadville. He was never content to be a silent partner in his various mining interests. If he invested his money, he wanted to know it was being used wisely. Leadville is much less civilized. So much lawlessness, and it seemed to me that people, even those from good families, paid far less attention to the rules than they ought. I thought that if I exposed everything I thought was sin, then the people would be punished, and they would finally start living properly. I thought it was my duty to make things right."

The rise and fall of Flora's chest as she looked at the ground told him she'd thought a lot about this topic. "To be perfectly honest, I thought I was better than all of them. That my virtues were far superior, and it was my duty to make them rise up or be shunned forever."

Green eyes shone with tears as she looked at him. "But when I finally started listening in church, instead of judging everyone who walked through the door, I realized that I had been the one in the wrong. My way was not Jesus's way, and I had been foolish in putting myself in the place of God."

"Those sound like the words of a woman who's gained an incredible amount of wisdom," George said, smiling at her. "I'm sorry the others don't see it, but perhaps they have their own faults they must grow past first."

Some of the sadness in her eyes disappeared as Flora smiled. "Now you sound like Pastor Lassiter. He says we're all sinners, and we all have our own things we need to work out with God. But enough about me and my problems."

She gestured at Pierre, who'd gone back to digging with the stick, presumably to find more worms. "How do we help him?"

George watched the little boy who had managed to capture his heart in such a short period of time. Even without sharing the same language, he felt a connection to the child. And somehow, with Flora sharing that same connection with Pierre, it brought him together with Flora in a way he hadn't expected. They wanted the same thing for a little boy they barely knew, yet cared for deeply.

If only George had a better answer for her.

"I don't know," he said slowly. "I tried talking to the men at work to see if they knew anyone, but there wasn't much time for idle chatter. Pastor Lassiter and I haven't had any success with the people we've spoken to. I suppose we just keep looking and asking."

Pierre returned, carrying several more worms, speaking animatedly in French. George wished he could communicate better with the little boy, especially since Pierre gravitated toward him and seemed to want to connect with him. But how did he connect with a child he couldn't converse with?

The little boy said something that made Flora laugh. Her laughter warmed his heart, and though she'd spoken disdainfully about her many accomplishments, George was grateful someone with her particular skills could help Pierre.

George looked around for the pastor, wondering where he'd gotten off to, since he'd thought Pastor Lassiter had been heading in his direction. Finally, he spotted him, standing in a group of women, shaking his head at whatever they were saying. From the way the women kept glancing in their direction, it seemed like they somehow disapproved of what George and Flora were doing with Pierre. But how could anyone be upset that they were helping a poor child who'd lost his father?

"They're angry because I got to sleep in the cabin with Pierre instead of a tent," Flora said softly, nodding in the direction of his gaze. "They think I'm just being lazy, not wanting to participate in the work, but they keep shooing Pierre away."

Her brow was knotted in frustration, marring her pretty features.

"Why would they do that? What about the other children? Can't he play with them?"

Flora's frown deepened. "Pierre can't speak the language. They teased him and wouldn't play with him. He came running to me, crying. Every time I intervened, the other ladies got mad at me for stopping work, until finally they asked me to leave. But I couldn't just let them torment poor Pierre like that."

A dark look crossed her face. George wondered if

she was thinking about how she bullied all the other kids when she was younger. But he couldn't talk to her about it, couldn't say that he'd been just as cruel to her as she'd been to him. Even though he'd spent a lot of years hating her for sticking him with the moniker of Pudgy, he'd come to a place of acceptance. He'd outgrown the silly nickname, and as much as he used to say that he'd get revenge on his childhood nemesis, he found he had nothing but compassion for the delightful young woman in front of him.

"I'm glad you can be there for him," George said instead.

Flora shrugged. "I know what it's like."

He hoped it didn't look like he was staring. Sure, she said now that people didn't like her, but he couldn't imagine her experiencing the levels of torment he had. After all, he *had* been pudgy. More than that, actually. The boys had been teasing him, calling him a corpulent whale, and Flora had looked at them with those big green eyes and said, "No he's not. He's just pudgy." From then on, everyone had called him Pudgy, a far sight better than if the corpulent whale idea had stuck.

In some ways, she had done him a favor.

Could he help her now?

"Were you tormented as a child?"

Flora nodded slowly, her gaze on the others still obviously talking about her. "People think I'm just a mean person. But everything I've ever done has been about self-preservation. I suppose I thought that if the negativity was directed at everyone else, no one would have time to turn the cruelty in my direction. I couldn't have been more wrong."

Flora looked over at Pierre and smiled at him. The

little boy came running back toward her. "Flora!" He chattered at her, smiling.

George didn't have to understand the words to understand the genuine affection between the two. If only he had paid better attention in the few French lessons he'd had. Then he could join in their merriment.

"Teach me," George said. "You're good with him. It's not fair you get to have all the fun."

"Basically, Pierre was telling me that his father promised him they'd go fishing when he returned from work. He wanted to ask you if you'd take him fishing, but then he thought it might not be fair to go without his father." Flora gave him another pretty smile.

"I told him that perhaps when we find his father, we could all go fishing together."

"Somehow I don't think you fish." George winked at her, grinning.

Flora's cheeks flushed pink. "No, but I would try for Pierre's sake. I can't seem to refuse him anything."

Once more, George found himself captivated by Flora's genuine kindness and gentility.

Her confession about how she'd been treated—and how she'd reacted—only made him want to reach out to her more. To tell her the truth about his past and that he could see how she'd managed to overcome her previous failings to become the kind of woman any person would be honored to know. But his reasons for remaining quiet were so much greater than a woman's hurt feelings over the petty actions of a few others. As soon as he figured out who was behind the sabotage at the mine, George could tell her everything. Hopefully it wouldn't be long.

* * *

Flora tried to focus more on Pierre's chattering than on the women complaining about her to Pastor Lassiter. Would their words finally convince him that he'd been mistaken in giving Flora a chance?

She stole a glance at George, who'd been watching her. What must he think of her, confessing all of her misdeeds like that? Flora wasn't herself around him. For some reason, she seemed to blurt out the most ridiculous things. Who was he to her that she could speak so freely?

But who else did she have?

Sarah Crowley's shrill laugh reached her ears. Flora knew that laugh. The satisfied sound of achieving victory over one's rival. Once, she and Sarah had been the best of friends. They'd worked together to bring down the girls they thought threatened their carefully organized social structure. Only, in the end, the only person who'd been brought down was Flora. Now Sarah led the group that had once turned to Flora for guidance.

Pastor Lassiter approached, the women trailing him. They giggled and whispered behind their fans.

Flora stood, smiling at him. "I hope you're here to share good news about Pierre's father."

She'd spent many years perfecting the art of deflection, keeping any negative attention off herself. While it seemed almost wrong to do so now, Flora lacked the strength to face what was bound to be another litany of criticisms.

Besides, whatever they considered her bad behavior, wasn't it in the service of another? Not that she'd done anything wrong, of course, but by the way Sarah smirked, they all thought they were really going to get her.

Pastor Lassiter shook his head. "I'm afraid not. Some folks said that they thought they might have seen a Frenchman living in a tent on the other side of the camp, but I couldn't find any sign of him. I was hoping you and George would come with me to do some asking around. Maybe if Pierre was with us, someone would recognize him."

"Of course," George said. "Since I was the one to find Pierre, I feel responsible for reuniting him with his father. Besides—" George ruffled the boy's hair "—I've become attached to the little guy."

Flora couldn't help but smile. She, too, had become attached to Pierre. Truth be told, she was becoming attached to George, as well. He was the only person besides Pastor Lassiter and Rose who didn't judge her, who listened to what she had to say as though he cared about her answers. But she couldn't imagine her family condoning her involvement with a man so outside their social class.

Not that she was interested, of course. While she felt comfortable in his presence, he often made her stomach feel…funny. It was a most unusual sensation. Like the time her father had left her alone in the carriage for just a moment, and the horses had taken off on her. Absolutely terrifying. And yet, when the dust settled, she'd been secretly exhilarated. With George, there wasn't so much terror, and not nearly the level of exhilaration, and yet something in the area that felt like there might be. But this was a man, not a pair of spirited horses.

Though she supposed it could prove to be just as dangerous.

But she couldn't keep herself from smiling as she said, "You know I would be happy to accompany you. I love Pierre dearly, but he deserves to be reunited with his father."

The pastor smiled at her. "I'm so glad. I appreciate the time and care you've taken with him. As I was telling the others, you are uniquely qualified to watch over Pierre."

"Yes, but she's doing a terrible job of it," Sarah said, stepping forward as she glared down her aristocratic nose at Flora. "That child stole my favorite shawl, and when I yelled at him, he threw it in the mud and ran away."

Flora hadn't witnessed the incident, but she had seen Sarah screeching at Pierre. She'd stopped her supper preparations and run after the little boy.

"Pierre was terrified," Flora said calmly. "As I've told you before, he doesn't speak English, and therefore couldn't understand what you were saying. Imagine how you would feel if a stranger yelled at you in another language."

Pierre came closer to Flora, wrapping his arms around her leg and hiding in her skirts.

"Well I'm not a thief, and I'm quite civilized, so strangers have no reason to yell at me."

"He's four years old," Flora said firmly. "There are many things he hasn't learned yet."

She rubbed his back, then pulled him off her skirts so she could kneel in front of him. Very gently, she asked him in French what had happened.

Tears started flowing down his face before the words came out. Finally, Flora understood.

"He didn't mean any harm." Flora held Pierre close

as she spoke to Sarah. "According to Pierre, you'd tossed aside your shawl and it fell off the bench and into the dirt. Pierre thought he was being helpful and went to pick it up. He said it smelled exactly like his mother before she passed away, and it made him miss her. He misses her dreadfully, and now with his father having disappeared, he was feeling lonely. So he wrapped himself in your shawl and used it to feel close to her. When you saw him and started yelling at him, it scared him. He didn't mean to drop it in the mud. But he was terrified, and you didn't even bother to find out what had happened. Pierre meant no harm."

Despite her explanation, Flora could still see the steam coming out of Sarah's ears.

"My shawl is ruined."

"I'll gladly replace it," Flora said.

Sarah only glared at her. "It's irreplaceable. I added the lace myself." Then she grunted. "Smells like his mother. That is the most ridiculous thing I've ever heard. My shawl would never smell like a…peasant." Spittle flew out of her mouth in a most unladylike manner. Derision curled her lip, and Flora hated that she'd once been a party to such behavior.

"I believe you wear French perfume, do you not? His mother was French. It's not such a stretch to imagine that you might share the same taste in fragrance."

Before Sarah could issue another retort—and from the expression on her face, it looked like she was working up a good one—Pastor Lassiter stepped forward.

"Ah, yes. I knew there had to be a reasonable explanation." He smiled at Flora, then down at little Pierre. "But that does lead me to something I'd like to speak to you all about. Part of why I invited you all to come

up with me is that I've noticed a great deal of dishar-
mony amongst you young ladies, and my hope is that
our time in the camp brings you closer together and
gives you a deeper sense of community."

He turned to look at Sarah and the other women.
"While what happened to your shawl was unfortunate,
Pierre was trying to help, but got carried away. But as
you see, Flora is accepting responsibility for the situation and has offered to make it right."

Sarah opened her mouth to argue, but the pastor held
up his hand. "I won't tolerate any more squabbles. We
need to think more in terms of how we can love and
serve one another, instead of being loved and served.
Sarah, now that you know Pierre took your shawl because it reminded him of his mother, perhaps you could
find another shawl or blanket to offer him? Spray it with
some of your perfume so he has that comfort. Imagine
what it must feel like to have lost a mother and now
have your father missing."

The words sounded strange to Flora. Usually the
lectures were always about how Flora had been wrong
and what she needed to do to rectify the situation. Part
of her waited for the chastisement to be turned toward
her. And yet, it didn't come. Pastor Lassiter smiled
broadly at her.

"I know you are all frustrated and angry because you
think it is unfair that Flora gets to sleep in the cabin
instead of in a tent. And that I've reduced her duties
so that she can care for Pierre. Ordinarily, I'd ask for
you all to take turns helping with him, but since Flora
is the only one who speaks his language, I want him to
have consistency of care. Our hope, and our prayer, is
that we would find Pierre's father quickly."

As Pastor Lassiter explained his plans for finding Pierre's father, Flora felt George move to stand behind her, close enough that she could feel the comfort of his presence emanating in her direction. He wanted to be a friend to her, to stand beside her. But he seemed to understand that though they shared a bond because of Pierre, he couldn't get too close. He couldn't be everything Flora could imagine him being.

She shook her head quickly, trying to banish those images from her head. They came too easily, but it was impossible to think that there would ever be anything more than a casual acquaintance between the two of them. Even if her parents were to accept such a match, as selfish as it sounded, Flora wasn't willing to trade her life in their well-appointed home for rusticating in a cabin in the middle of some smelly mining camp. Stealing a glance at him, she noticed a smile at the corners of his lips. Would he still smile if he knew what she was thinking? That despite their shared love of a little boy, and their easy way of talking, there was no hope for anything else between them?

Flora sighed. Whatever he thought, it was none of her business. The only thing that mattered right then was helping the little boy clinging to her skirts. And maybe, if the other women could see that she truly was trying to be the woman God created her to be, maybe everything in her life would finally be back to normal. She'd have friends, eligible bachelors would start calling on her again, and then she could get married and start a family of her own. A perfect plan.

Only the weight of George's gaze on her didn't make it feel so perfect at all.

Chapter Four

A week later, they hadn't come any closer to finding Pierre's father, Henri. It was as though the man had never existed. Except there was a little boy missing him who said otherwise. Today, George found himself walking through the mining area itself, hoping that someone would recognize the little boy happily swinging between him and Flora.

The mine was no place for a child, but George had no other ideas. They'd walked Pierre through the camp a number of times, hoping the little boy would recognize someone, or at least some of the scenery. The only thing Pierre seemed interested in was going fishing, but George felt guilty at the thought. How could he replace the little boy's father in what had clearly been an important bonding time between them?

Flora and Pierre were singing "Frère Jacques," and George couldn't help but enjoy Flora's melodic voice. Though Flora had spoken disdainfully of her feminine accomplishments earlier, George was impressed with how readily she sang with the little boy, a pastime he seemed to enjoy greatly.

Pierre stopped singing and looked up at him expectantly. *"Chante!"*

"He wants me to sing with you, doesn't he?" George looked over at Flora, who smiled broadly.

"It would appear so." She gave the little boy an affectionate look, and once again George was struck by how readily she opened her heart to a child who needed it. It seemed like the other ladies in the camp hadn't warmed to Flora, and her only friends seemed to be the pastor and Rose. A shame, because from what George could see, Flora had so much to give.

Pierre tugged at his hand. *"J'enseigne!"*

George looked at Flora for translation.

"He said he will teach you." Her words came out with a slight giggle, like she found the prospect delightful.

Delightful, indeed. How could he refuse two such shining faces?

Fortunately, almost every child probably knew the familiar folk song, or at least that's what George thought. "I don't sing as well as you, but I think I can manage."

He began to sing the first few bars, then Flora and Pierre joined in.

Maybe it was wrong of him to think so, but as they strolled through the crowded area of the mine, holding hands with Pierre, who was exuberantly swinging his arms, probably in the hope that they'd pick him up and swing him between them again, this felt like everything he'd always hoped for in a family of his own.

As they rounded the corner toward the mine office, Flora stopped suddenly, cutting off midsong.

"What's wrong?" George asked.

Flora gave him a shaky smile. "Nothing. I just thought I'd seen my father going into that building, that's all. Silly, because he wouldn't be here. Our mines are on the other side of the valley."

Then her face fell as she sighed. "Unless he's checking up on me. I'd hoped I'd earned his trust by now, but he was really disappointed in me when he realized just how badly I'd hurt others with my words."

Flora glanced at him with a look of such remorse, George once again wished he could come clean with her about their past, and how he forgave her for the way she'd treated him when they were children.

"Once everyone got tired of my gossip, it strained my relationship with a lot of people, including friends of my parents. My father had to do a lot of work to repair some of his business interests."

The mournful look George had grown to hate seeing on her face reappeared. "I honestly thought I was being helpful, telling people all those things, and that somehow, it raised my own status of being good. How wrong I was. I'd give anything to take my words and actions back."

George smiled at her, wishing he could take her hand and give it a squeeze to let her know that it was all right. "We all make mistakes," he said. "When I was a child, there was one little girl my friends and I used to tease for having a lot of freckles. We hurt her feelings so badly that her mother came to see my mother, and I got in a lot of trouble for it. Even though I could justify it by saying that she deserved it for teasing me, I should have realized that, as deeply as her words hurt me, mine probably hurt her as well."

It was the closest to admitting their shared past as

George could safely get. But he had to make Flora understand that this was not an unforgiveable sin and that they all made mistakes.

"Children can be cruel," Flora admitted. "I was also teased for my freckles. Mother made me a special lotion I wore every night, and I take care to stay out of the sun. It was awful being made fun of, and I, too, should have remembered that when I tormented others. I suppose I thought that if people were making fun of someone else, no one would dare laugh at me."

She shook her head. "It's good that you learned your lesson early. It took me far too long, and I don't know how to undo the damage. Even when you apologize, it doesn't erase the hurt others feel."

"No, it doesn't. However, just as we are forgiven, we are called to forgive others, as well. You may have hurt people, but the Bible tells them to be forgiving. It's my favorite part of the Lord's Prayer."

Flora smiled softly. "'Forgive us our trespasses, as we forgive them that trespass against us.' I find great comfort in that prayer. I have so much that needs to be forgiven, and therefore I've worked very hard to forgive others. I didn't know what I was doing, so how could they?"

She'd learned. That's what he saw in her words. Did the people who still shunned her take the time to listen? To hear how she'd allowed God's word to transform her life? Though George felt he had a good relationship with the Lord, sometimes being around Flora made him want to grow even closer to Him.

"You make an excellent point," he told her. "I just hope one day you learn to forgive yourself."

Flora groaned. "Now you sound just like Rose and the pastor."

"They're smart people." He grinned at her.

"They are, indeed." Flora glanced again at the mining office. "Would you mind terribly if we crossed over and went to a different area? If I did see my father, I'm not particularly interested in speaking with him. I know he cares about me, and I adore him. But I hate feeling so much like a disappointment when I'm around him."

One more thing George hated seeing in this delightful young woman. Surely her sense of her father's disappointment in her was part of her inability to forgive herself for her past mistakes. But he wouldn't argue this point with her. Though he was reasonably sure Mr. Montgomery wouldn't recognize him, it was better not to take chances.

Still, it seemed interesting and, if George were to speculate, a bit funny that Flora's father would show up at the mine when it was having so many problems. Could George's father's rants about not trusting the Montgomerys have been a foreshadowing of their current troubles?

They turned the corner in the opposite direction and began singing their song again. George noticed that some of the men would briefly stop what they were doing and smile, then go back to work. But no one approached them or even commented on how it was good to hear their native language.

The good thing about being here, in the guise of a miner, was that people talked more freely around him than if he were to have been here as a gentleman. The miners poked fun at the men in suits who frequented the office, and when those men tried talking to the miners, they all clammed up. Since George was a newcomer, and learning the ropes, some of the men had taken him under their wings, telling him details about the mine he'd have never learned otherwise.

The men had told him what they knew of the troubles at the mine, the cave-ins, the practices that seemed shady to them. All of which were helpful to George, in that he now knew that things were far worse than he'd imagined when he'd first learned of the situation here. And, all right, he'd own that Lance Dougherty, the mine manager, likely did not live on whiskey alone, but George found it troubling that the man often smelled of drink.

George intended to use everything he learned to make things better at the mine and prevent future accidents from occurring. George had come because of one cave-in that had nearly cost them several workers' lives. But he'd learned that just before he'd arrived there was another odd explosion, one that none of the miners understood, since no one was supposed to be working in the area. Mr. Dougherty had supposedly investigated it and said that it was an old piece of dynamite that had gone off by itself, and no one was in the area, but George couldn't help wondering if it was true.

The men all said Dougherty was a liar, and though George hadn't let it be known yet, he'd noticed that when Dougherty hired him, he'd verbally told George one rate of pay but written a larger number in his ledger. George had listened to the men talk, grumbling about the lower wages at Pudgy Boy and saying that as soon as they found better jobs at other mines that paid more, they were leaving. George's father had always prided himself on treating his workers fairly, so it seemed odd that now the mine had the reputation of having the lowest-paying jobs in Leadville.

Unless Dougherty's mistake in writing down George's pay wasn't a mistake, and it was part of a larger scheme to embezzle money from the mine.

"Howdy, George!" Peanut McGee, one of the men who worked with him on the mining crew, tipped his hat at him, so George led his merry band over to greet his friend.

"Hello there." George returned the greeting, then indicated Flora and Pierre. "May I present Miss Flora Montgomery? And this is Pierre, the little boy I was telling you about. Flora, this is one of the men I work with…" George paused for a moment, realizing he didn't know Peanut's real name. "Uh, Peanut McGee."

Peanut tipped his hat at Flora. "Right pleased to meet you, ma'am."

"It's my pleasure, Mr. McGee."

She treated him with all the courtesy she would have offered in the finest parlors in the state. Peanut noted it, too, and he blushed.

"None of that, ma'am. It's just Peanut. Can I just say what an honor it is to know such a fine lady willing to take on a child like this? I do feel for the lad, and I've been asking everyone I know if they have any idea where his father might be."

It was Flora's turn to blush, and George liked the way the pink in her cheeks lit up her eyes.

"Anyone would be fortunate to have the opportunity to spend time with such a darling boy." Flora ruffled Pierre's hair and smiled, then bent down to whisper something in his ear.

"Please to meet you," Pierre said haltingly.

George grinned. "Already teaching him his manners, I see."

"A little." Flora smiled. "Just as I am helping you with a few words to communicate with Pierre, I'm also giving him the skills to talk to others. When we find his father, I'm sure he'll be pleased at how much Pierre has learned."

Peanut shifted, looking uncomfortable. "Ma'am, I mean no disrespect, but none of us have heard of anyone who's lost a boy. And we ain't heard no one using them fancy words like what you said to the child. I suppose it might be one of them fellows who keep to themselves, but why wouldn't he also be looking?"

George hated to admit that Peanut was onto something. Why couldn't they find any trace of Pierre's father?

The disappointment on Flora's face was almost too much to bear.

"I'd like to find a way to get into the office and look at Dougherty's ledger. See if there's a record of anyone named Henri working in the mine."

Peanut's eyes widened. "You can read?"

"Of course I can," George said. As the words came out of his mouth, he realized that his confusion about Dougherty's mistake was probably not a mistake at all, and that he'd been on to something in suspecting embezzlement.

Most of these men were illiterate. The ones who could read probably noticed when Dougherty wrote down the wrong number, and were paid accordingly. But men like Peanut…

George shook his head. These men were probably being taken advantage of in other ways, as well, and it made him sick. His father used to say that business ownership carried with it a great deal of responsibility, and first and foremost, that responsibility was to take care of one's workers because without them they would have nothing.

Peanut shook his head slowly. "You are one odd gent. We been thinking a lot about where you come from, why you have fancy manners, and now, come to find, you can even read. What are you doing here?"

George had expected this question. And hated that he had to mislead another person. Peanut was a good man, a hard worker, and it seemed unfair to deceive him. But George still didn't have the answers he needed.

"Like everyone else here. Trying to build a better life for myself. My family hit on some hard times, and I'm doing what I can to make things better."

All true. But at Peanut's sympathetic nod, George couldn't help but feel like a fraud.

"I s'pose we've all been there. You know Reg? He was some fancy lord back in England until his father gambled it all away. He don't talk about it much, but I know he'd give just about anything to strike it rich and restore his family's good name."

George nodded. He'd heard Reg's story before, and at times, he couldn't help but wonder if he'd end up the same way.

Then Peanut looked down at the little boy, smiling as he pulled a piece of candy out of his pocket. "I been saving this for a special occasion, and I think this might be it. A boy, missing his daddy, well, that sounds to me like good use of my treat."

He held it out to Pierre, who looked up at Flora. As she translated Peanut's words, Pierre's eyes lit up.

"Merci, monsieur," he said, smiling. Then Flora bent down and whispered in his ear again.

Pierre nodded, then looked at Peanut. "Thank you, sir."

"Sir…" Peanut waved his hand. "You get on now. Teaching that boy to act like a gent. Miss Montgomery, 'cause of you, this boy just might have a chance at a better life, instead of wasting away in one of these mines."

Flora blushed again, and as George considered the man's words, he realized that they were likely true. Once Pierre got to be a little older, he'd probably be helping in the mine, making pennies a day. At least that seemed to be the way for many of the boys he saw here. That didn't seem to be much of a life for a child. Perhaps, once George got to the bottom of the bad dealings here, he could also find a way to help his miners better themselves.

Working with Pastor Lassiter had opened George's eyes to a lot of things that were wrong at the mine. Not just in terms of the odd explosions and dwindling money, but even the fact that many of these men couldn't read well enough to know whether or not they'd been cheated. Suddenly, what had seemed like a simple issue had grown more complicated.

Peanut turned his attention back on George. "I can't imagine the boy's father not coming forward, not with everyone here knowing you've been looking for him. But I'm friends with the night watchman, Stumpy, and I think he can get you into the office. I'm sure that no-account Dougherty hasn't been any help."

George shook his head. "No, he told me that personnel issues were confidential, and he couldn't give me any information."

Peanut made a disgusting noise. "You'd think a man would do more to help a boy."

One of the reasons George didn't like the mine manager. He could understand the desire to keep certain personnel records private, but Dougherty had literally shut the door in George's face and told him he couldn't give him any information. Had George been in charge, he would have done whatever he could to help. Not just because this was the closest mine to where Pierre had been found, and therefore the most likely place where his father worked, but because it was the right thing to do. All of the other neighboring mines, including ones several miles from here and completely out of the way, had joined in the effort to find Pierre's father.

So what, really, was going on?

George smiled at his friend. "Well, I appreciate you being able to get me into the office so I can take a look. I just don't want to get anyone in trouble."

But if someone did get in trouble, George would find a way to secretly make it right. This was still his mine, after all, and while it seemed like the most expedient thing to do would be to let Dougherty go, George couldn't rightly say that would fix the problem. He didn't have enough information.

Right now, with no real evidence, he wasn't acting on anything. Still, it would be nice to have some answers. Thankfully, Peanut was willing to have his friend help him get them.

Flora was touched by George's discussion with Peanut. Clearly the men cared about what happened to a little boy who'd lost his father. George could have easily left Pierre with her and gone about his business, but when he wasn't working in the mine, he was spending time with them and doing what he could to help Pierre. And, based on this conversation, George spent a good amount of time while he was working trying to find answers about Pierre's father, too.

As they walked back to the camp, the men discussed their plan to get into the office later that night. It amazed Flora how naturally Pierre grabbed both Flora's and George's hands and walked between the two of them. While the men talked, Flora and Pierre sang a few of the songs they both knew. Flora had forgotten how much a simple tune meant to her, and how song lifted people's spirits. She'd sung in many of the finest parlors in Leadville, even sometimes in Denver when they'd go to visit her aunt, but here, in the midst of God's creation, the joy of music made her heart feel even lighter.

As they sang the final verse of "Au clair de la lune," Pierre looked up at her with longing. The poor little boy missed his family dreadfully, and though Flora tried her best to make him comfortable, sometimes it seemed like her heart would break for him. How a man could simply abandon a child like Pierre, she didn't know. But based on what Peanut said, and the responses of others, Flora could only think that something dreadful must have happened to Pierre's father.

She smiled at the boy. Sometimes she wondered if he thought the same. But, of course, she would not discuss her fears with him. Having learned her lesson by openly speculating about everything with everyone, she now worked very hard to keep her opinions to herself. They didn't know what had happened to Pierre's father, and though Flora could not imagine him willingly leaving his son, she wouldn't invite trouble to where it didn't exist.

As they reentered the camp, Pierre let go of George's hand, moving closer to the edge of Flora's skirts. She looked in the direction of the cabin the ministry used and understood why. Sarah Crowley was headed their way, and the expression on her face said that she had a bee in her bonnet.

"Hello, Sarah." Flora greeted her warmly, as though she hadn't done anything wrong. Which was true—as far as Flora knew, she hadn't.

"I wondered when you'd get back from your lollygagging. You're supposed to help get firewood tonight."

"I'm sorry," Flora said calmly. "I thought I was on the schedule for tomorrow. Pastor Lassiter knew we were taking Pierre through the mine area to see if Pierre recognized anyone, or anyone recognized him."

She kept her tone modulated, pleasant, trying not to match Sarah's irritation.

"Maureen got sick. Had you been here, you'd know that. It's about time you pulled your weight."

Rose came around the corner and noticed them speaking. Flora hated that Rose always had to step in and take up for her, especially since it only seemed to make people like Sarah angrier.

"I apologize." Flora gave her a sympathetic look. "Hopefully we'll find Pierre's father soon."

"Was your expedition successful?" Rose asked as she joined them.

"I'm afraid not," Flora said, looking down at Pierre. "But George did run into a gentleman named Peanut who is going to help him look into some things."

"George? Peanut?" Sarah gave her a cold look. "It seems you're becoming all too familiar with these people."

"Who we're here to serve," Rose reminded her. "I'm glad to see you're making friends here, Flora."

Then Rose turned to the gentlemen and smiled. "It's a pleasure to have you here. Peanut, is it? I'm Rose Jones."

"Pleased to meet you, ma'am. I'm honored to be among the likes of you. Some church people brought us some warm blankets over the winter, and I am mighty grateful for the kindness you've all done us."

Rose smiled at him. "I hope you'll join us for dinner tonight. I know Pastor Lassiter would love to meet you."

The bashful look Peanut gave Rose warmed Flora's heart. Until recently, Flora would have been like Sarah, counting men like George and Peanut "those people" and not wanting to associate with them. She would have served them dinner and counted it her Christian duty, and that was that. But there was more to these men than just the label society put on them.

How could Sarah see that, though, when she'd never taken the time to get to know them?

Flora turned to Sarah and smiled. "I know I need to get to collecting the wood, but before I go, I'd like to invite you to sit with us tonight. It occurred to me that perhaps the reason you are so frustrated with me and the situation is that you don't know George and Pierre. I'm sure you'll find them delightful company, and I would so love to catch up with you. It's been forever since we've talked, and I've been rude in not asking you about all of your news."

Sarah looked at her as though she'd rather share her

dinner with a dead rat, but Rose smiled at her encouragingly.

"What a wonderful idea. Uncle Frank was just telling me that he wished the young ladies in our group would make a greater effort to get to know one another and build better relationships. You two used to be best friends. Surely you can put whatever quarrel occurred between you aside to share a meal."

There had been no quarrel. That was the sad part. When Flora's torment of Emma Jane Jackson reached its peak, and the rest of society turned on Flora, Sarah simply stopped receiving her. They hadn't had so much as a conversation until coming to this camp, and even now it was all about what Flora was doing wrong.

Still, Flora remembered Rose's earlier words about how she should offer an olive branch to everyone she'd wronged. Flora had tried with Sarah, but Sarah had never given her an audience. Perhaps this was the opening she needed.

"I believe it's my turn to serve the meal," Sarah said coldly.

"Oh!" Rose smiled. "I'd be pleased to do so in your place. Take the night off. Spend some time visiting with Flora."

Sarah murmured an acceptance, but her eyes flashed fire. For a moment, Flora regretted asking her, but then she remembered that she was called to be a peacemaker, and she was doing her very best.

"Now that we have that settled," Flora said, trying to sound pleasant, "I have some wood to gather."

She bent and told Pierre that they were going to collect some wood, and that he needed to remain close to her.

As Flora turned to go toward the area where they collected wood, George said, "Shall we come help?"

Sarah smirked, like she thought poorly of the idea but knew Flora would accept.

"Yes," Peanut said. "I'd like to contribute somehow. I can carry firewood."

Rose smiled broadly. "Very nice. I love the spirit of everyone coming together. I think I'll join you, as well. Sarah, would you like to come?"

Would it be awful of Flora to say that she'd rather not have Sarah? Yes, she'd done the hard task of inviting Sarah to sit with them during dinner, and she'd be kind and polite to the other woman. But it seemed like more punishment to be continually working with Sarah.

"I need to check on Maureen," Sarah said, a smile on her face but ice in her eyes. "As well as let the others know that I found Flora and she'll be attending to her duties tonight."

"All right then," Rose said. "We'll see you at dinner."

From the murderous look on Sarah's face, she wasn't too happy at the prospect. Knowing Sarah, she'd find a way out of the task, if at all possible.

But at least Flora had tried.

Rose reached forward and squeezed Flora's hand. "You did well. I know it was hard for you to make the overture, but it was the right thing to do."

George nodded. "I was impressed. The friendship is her loss, not yours."

She shouldn't have been so pleased at George's compliment. But the way he looked at her made her want to stand a little taller. He was the most honorable person she knew, and it felt good to have his support.

If only they didn't come from two different worlds.

Chapter Five

Once they'd finished gathering the wood, George left the ladies at the cabin so he and Peanut could talk to Stumpy about getting into the office. As they rounded the corner to the main area of the mine, George saw John Montgomery mounting a horse. Hopefully to go back home. He'd been relieved when Flora hadn't wanted to talk to her father, and knowing that one fewer person was around to recognize him was a good thing.

"That there's John Montgomery," Peanut said, pointing. "Your lady friend's father. I hear talk that he's trying to buy the mine. Would be nice having a gent like him running things instead of those Bellinghams. Just leeching the money from the place, not bothering to grace us with their presence or see how things are being run. Montgomery mines are a nice place to work, that's a fact. I've tried to get hired on, but my back's not as strong as those young bucks."

Peanut grinned. "But if Montgomery buys this place, well, now, I'd be working for him, wouldn't I?"

As if he sensed the men talking about him, Montgomery turned and gazed in their direction, shading his eyes from the glare of the fading sun.

"Flora said she thought she'd seen him earlier, but she wasn't keen on running into him."

Peanut shrugged. "I can't see him being all too happy about her spending time with the likes of us. The man's got more money than a body's got a right to, and that daughter of his is his biggest treasure. He'd be a fool to let anyone without deep pockets himself near her. She's going to marry well, that one."

A fact that made George far more miserable than he would have expected. He'd already made up his mind that he couldn't marry a socialite like Flora. As much as he'd like to, he knew he couldn't give her what she wanted out of life. He'd seen enough of the mine's condition to know that it would take a great deal of capital to improve things, and based on the financial documents his brother-in-law had shown him, the Bellinghams didn't have it.

The best they could hope for was selling to a man like Montgomery, which would at least replenish the Bellingham coffers, but it wouldn't give Flora the life she wanted. Besides, if Montgomery was involved in the mine's sabotage, he couldn't see the man willingly giving his daughter in marriage to the man whose family he'd just destroyed.

They hurried around the building, out of Montgomery's field of view.

Once they were far enough away, George asked, "Do you think Montgomery would be causing the problems here at the mine, trying to make the mine worth less to get a better price when he buys it?"

Peanut looked at him funny. "Him? Nah. Rumor has

it that he's straight as an arrow. Doesn't spend time in the saloons, goes to church and from what I been told, treats everyone fair. Now that Dougherty, on the other hand…"

The other man spat at the ground. "He cheats at just about everything, including cards. If he ever asks you for a game, you say no."

"I don't play cards," George said.

Peanut grinned. "That's right. You're with them church folks. It's a good thing, not being a drinking or gambling man. Ruins a lot of lives up here, that's for sure. You'll do well, avoiding all that."

They approached the guardhouse, a tiny shed in the middle of the activity.

"Heya, Stumpy!" Peanut called the greeting, and a well-muscled man stepped out.

There was no question why Stumpy was the night guard. A man would be a fool to mess with him.

"Peanut. Who've you got there?"

"This is my friend George Baxter. He's the gent trying to find the father of a little boy he found wandering the woods alone."

"I heard about that," Stumpy said. "Sad thing, to lose a child. Can't imagine what it must be like to be on the other end, missing your father. Having any success in your search?"

Peanut looked over at George.

"No, sir." George took a deep breath. "Every mine in the area has been very helpful, but…"

"Dougherty hasn't given him squat," Peanut finished for him. "I heard him yelling at George earlier today for taking too long on his break, when George was just asking the other men if they knew anything about the little boy's father. You haven't met a Frenchy, have you?"

As Stumpy shook his head thoughtfully, George couldn't help but smile. Dougherty had yelled at him, threatening to fire him for disrupting work. George hadn't been late on his break—he'd still had two minutes left. But he'd gotten back to work, anyway. This job was too important to get fired before he had all the information.

"No," Stumpy said. "But there's that trapper, Crazy Eddie. You remember him. Crazy as a loon, but we'd have all died the winter of '79 had it not been for him. I think he has dealings with some French people."

"That's right. Crazy Eddie." Peanut snapped his fingers. "Oh, you'd like him. If you like tales of the Wild West before it was settled, you've got to hear him sometime. He once fought a bear with his bare hands and won."

Stumpy groaned. "That's just a tall tale, and you know it. But you're missing the point. Crazy Eddie is the only man I know who speaks French."

Sighing, Peanut shook his head.

George couldn't help but like the grizzled old man who'd somehow taken up for him. "Thanks. I appreciate the information. But what I'd really appreciate is that Peanut says you might have a way for me to get into the office to look at the records. Dougherty refused to even tell me if the boy's father ever worked here, or was contracted to come."

"He can read and everything," Peanut exclaimed.

Stumpy looked at George suspiciously. "You think he's on the up-and-up? Seems an awful lot like a gent to me."

"Same story as Reg," Peanut said. "Just hasn't gotten beat up like us yet. He's just trying to help an innocent boy. Surely we can do our part."

"We could all lose our jobs." Stumpy held up a hand, and for the first time, George noticed he was missing a couple fingers. "This is all I have, the only way I got to send money back to Ellie and the girls."

George closed his eyes. He knew mining was dangerous business. Had been warned that many a man was injured in the work, losing limbs and sometimes even his life. But what did they do for someone like Stumpy when he was injured at George's mine? What happened to the men who'd been injured in the explosion that had set George on this course? One more thing George needed to investigate and make right.

The trouble with being born into wealth, and having a business that gave a family everything it ever wanted, was that you never asked what that wealth cost. What others had given up so that you could have all the luxuries in life.

"Is that your wife and kids?" George asked.

Stumpy nodded and reached into his pocket for a miniature. "That's them. The boy died last winter. I can't imagine what the little boy you found's family is going through."

Then Stumpy sighed. "Something terrible must've happened to his father, because when you have a boy of your own, you don't leave 'im willingly, you know what I'm saying?"

George nodded slowly. He'd considered that thought dozens of times since finding Pierre. He was a good kid, and based on the way the little boy chattered, and things had Flora told him he'd said, there was no way his father had abandoned him.

Peanut also nodded. "That's what I been thinking. If everything was on the up-and-up, why wouldn't Dougherty let George have the information? What if Dougherty killed him?"

"Dougherty's not a murderer," Stumpy said. "A cheat, a drunkard and stupid as all get-out, but I don't think he'd kill anyone. But something's not right."

Then Stumpy let out a long sigh. "He's still in there working, probably going to work late, on account of Montgomery's visit. You come back around ten o'clock. If Dougherty's gone, I'll have two lights in the window. If you only see one, we'll try again tomorrow."

"Thank you." George reached out to shake the man's hand, then realized it was probably the wrong thing to do.

Stumpy grinned. "I can still shake on a bargain."

The two men shook hands, then George and Peanut returned to the camp for dinner. They could smell the meal before they even got to the cabin, and George's stomach rumbled. As they got closer, George's appetite left him. The horse he'd seen Montgomery get on a short while ago was tied up nearby.

George rubbed the stubble on his face. Though he wasn't shaving as often as he once did, he doubted that the light growth would do anything to conceal his identity. Fortunately, Montgomery hadn't seen him since he was a boy and wouldn't recognize him. George was a common name, and few knew his mother's maiden name. Why would they? It was of little import since she'd come from a working-class family.

When they arrived at the fire, Flora was already

seated with Pierre, talking animatedly with her father. Though she'd said she dreaded seeing him, it was clear that their reunion was a happy one.

"George!" Pierre spotted him and jumped up, running to him. George wrapped his arms around the boy and swung him up, making Pierre laugh.

When he finished swinging Pierre and set him on the ground, Pierre began speaking in rapid French. Though Flora had taught him a few words, the only thing George could pick out was *mange*. Eat.

"*Allons.* Let's go." That was one phrase George remembered. And, as Flora instructed him, when using simple sentences, he used both English and French.

Pierre grabbed his hand and dragged him over to where Flora and her father were seated. They immediately stood, and Flora greeted him with a hesitant smile.

"Father, this is the gentleman I was telling you about. George Baxter. He's working in the mine, and he's the one who found Pierre."

She spoke rapidly, like she was nervous at having to introduce the two men. George didn't blame her. If his sister had brought home a miner, their father likely wouldn't have appreciated it.

Then Flora indicated Peanut. "And this is Peanut. He's a friend of George's, er, that is, Mr. Baxter's, and he's helping, as well."

Looking apologetic, she said to her father, "I'm sorry, I know my lack of formality is out of the ordinary, but I'm learning that things are done differently here."

"It's all right, my dear." Mr. Montgomery gestured to the logs they used as benches. "Please join us. I'd like to hear about your efforts to find the boy's father."

"Let them get their food first," Flora said. Then she craned her head. "I thought Sarah Crowley would be joining us, but I haven't seen her yet."

George frowned. He knew the other girl hadn't looked pleased at the prospect of sharing her meal with them, but he'd thought she'd at least try.

"We'll be right back," George said smoothly. "Is there anything I can get either of you while we're up?"

"No, thank you," Flora said as her father shook his head. "Pierre?" Flora pointed to the spot beside her and patted it.

The little boy looked longingly at him as he took his seat.

"I'll be back," George said, and Flora said something to the little boy in French.

Pierre nodded, but still looked disappointed. Was he afraid that George wouldn't come back, like his father?

Once again, George found himself praying that they would find something good to share with the little boy about his missing father.

As they joined the line for the food, Peanut said, "You're not going to tell Montgomery about our plan for tonight, are you?"

"No. If he is going to buy the mine, I don't want him to have any reason to let Stumpy go. I appreciate what he's doing for us, and I'll do my best to keep him out of it."

"You are a good man, George Baxter," Peanut said, patting him on the back.

The man's praise only served to make George feel guilty once more. Yes, he was trying to do the right thing, and he'd never outright lied to anyone. But it felt wrong to keep misleading everyone. However, with as poorly as they all seemed to think of the Bellingham family, George was convinced that keeping his true identity a secret was still the right thing to do.

When it was all over, George hoped they'd understand. And, hopefully, they would all forgive him. He would make things right at the mine—for all of them.

Flora half listened to her father as she watched George in line, getting his food. Her father didn't seem angry that she'd befriended miners, but she wondered how he'd feel if she told him that she…liked…George.

Oh, this wasn't love. She barely knew the man, and after her many romantic foibles, she could say with absolute certainty that the butterflies in her stomach when she was with George meant nothing.

Her father seemed to notice where her attention was. "That George fellow, he looks familiar, does he not?"

"I can't say that I've seen him before," Flora said. "Perhaps you ran into him in town, at the mercantile or somewhere."

"Perhaps." Her father nodded. "But he doesn't seem like a miner to me. He carries himself and speaks too well."

"Indeed, he does. I don't know his whole story, of course, because we don't get too personal in our conversations. However, it is my understanding that George's family was once fairly well-off, but they hit on hard times, so he's taken up mining to try to restore their fortunes."

Her father looked thoughtful, as though he was still trying to puzzle out where he knew George from. "Do we know any Baxters?"

"I do not," Flora said. "Perhaps you could ask

Mother. She might have come across the family in one of her Ladies' Aid meetings."

George and Peanut returned and sat on a nearby log.

"George, I was asking Flora if we knew any Baxters. Who are your people? It's going to bother me until I figure it out. I pride myself on never forgetting a name or a face."

Flora felt bad for George as he hesitated. Though he appeared to be getting situated on the log, she could tell that he was trying to figure out what to tell her father. When she'd first met him, she'd thought he paused too long before sharing his name, making her think he had something to hide. Now she was certain of it.

"I'm from Denver. There are dozens of Baxters, and you could have come across any number of them, some related to me, some not. My father recently passed away, and I'm just trying to earn enough money to send back for my mother's care. My family is of no importance. I can't imagine the likes of you paying them much mind."

Flora noticed how George never mentioned anything specific, dodging her father's questions. Had her father? She glanced at him and noticed he was staring at George.

"You make us sound like quite the snobs. I don't pay any mind to a person's social station. If you're embarrassed to admit that your family is working class, you shouldn't be. I come from working stock myself. Raised myself up, I did, and I fully believe that every man can do the same."

Had Flora been wrong to think that her father would oppose a match between her and someone of a lower class? He'd always talked about how he wanted to see her marry well, but perhaps…

Flora shook her head. Even if he was willing to countenance such a thing, she wasn't sure if she could spend the rest of her life living in a place like this. The cabin was luxurious compared to the tents everyone else occupied, and Flora hated the dirt floors, the way mice seemed to constantly find their way inside and the fact that it seemed so dark and depressing. But perhaps it would be less depressing with a man she loved by her side.

"Thank you, sir. I apologize for any offense."

Her father looked like he was about to question George further, but Sarah walked up, carrying a plate and wearing what looked like the world's most disgruntled expression.

"I hope I'm not intruding," she said, looking like she'd love to have an excuse to not join them.

"Not at all." Flora smiled. "I'm so glad you decided to come."

Pastor Lassiter came up behind Sarah. "Oh, good. You've found them. I was so glad to hear that the two of you are going to mend fences at last."

"Sarah!" Flora's father said, his face lighting up. "It is good to see you. We've missed having you at the house, with you and Flora conspiring about all things."

"We didn't conspire about nice things, Father." Flora looked up at Sarah. "And I sincerely apologize for encouraging you to join me in my unkindness. It was not well done of me. I was not a good friend to you, but I hope that you'll allow me to begin again."

Though Sarah looked stunned, Flora felt so much lighter having finally gotten the words out. As the confusion washed across Sarah's face, Flora realized that she'd never given the other girl any reason to believe that she was sincere in her efforts.

"Truly, Sarah. I know that you've told the other girls that you think my repentance is all an act, but I am sorry for the pain I've caused, especially to you. If I have hurt you in any specific way, please tell me so I can make amends."

It was easy to apologize in general, as Flora had done. But other than being such a disgrace that people didn't want to associate with her, Flora had no idea if she'd done anything specifically to hurt Sarah.

Her father patted her leg. "Flora, my dear, I am quite proud of you. The pastor has been telling me of how well you've been doing, but until now, I hadn't truly experienced it for myself. I apologize if I've been too hard on you."

"Not at all." Flora smiled at him. "It's just taken me a long time to realize how wrong I'd been, and now I am doing my best to live out that change of heart."

Pierre tugged at her skirt and asked for more dinner. Flora looked at the line of people still waiting to eat, and then down at her own full plate. She scraped some of her food onto his dish.

"So that's what this is about," Sarah said. "Proving to your father that you've changed enough to come home. Well, good for you. Can I go back to my friends now?"

Flora's heart sank at her former friend's words. "I deserved that," she said slowly. "I know in the past, I didn't always mean my apologies. But I am sincere in everything I've said tonight, especially to you. You were a good friend to me, and I hope someday I can have the opportunity to be a friend to you."

The disdain on Sarah's face made it clear that she didn't believe Flora one bit. Flora sighed.

"I would like to have you join us, but I don't want you here against your will. If you want to be with your friends, you're welcome to do so."

Sarah looked hesitant, but Flora smiled at her. "Truly, Sarah. As much as I would like to renew our friendship, it wouldn't be a real friendship if I forced you. Enjoy your evening. But I do hope that at some point, you're willing to share a meal with me."

Though Sarah dipped her head respectfully, the hardness in her eyes told Flora that she had no intention of ever doing so. Of course, there were many things Flora had promised herself she'd never do, like spend time in a place like this. But as she looked around the fire and felt Pierre's soft hand on her leg, Flora was grateful for the way the Lord had worked in her heart. Perhaps the Lord would find a way into Sarah's heart, as well.

As Sarah walked away, George leaned in to her. "You may think your previous conversations with her were not well done, but this one was. I'm proud to know you, Flora Montgomery, and I'm proud to call you my friend."

His words were meant to be comfort, she was sure, but they served only to make the ache in her heart worse. Her entire life, she'd been taught that every group in society had its place. Her mother made sure that she only played with the suitable children, associated with suitable families, and as she grew, she was taught to pursue only suitable bachelors.

But here she was, clearly rejected by a suitable

friend, and the one person she'd begun to count on as a new friend was most unsuitable, indeed.

Flora looked up, trying to escape thoughts of a man she was beginning to lean on a bit too much, and noticed Rose watching them. She gave Rose a tiny smile and wave, ashamed that she'd so quickly forgotten her new friend. No, it wasn't that she'd forgotten Rose. Rose was a good friend. But Flora didn't feel the same camaraderie she once had with Sarah. Despite the mischief the women had gotten into, they'd also had a genuine connection. One that Flora dearly missed.

Who else would she stay up with until all hours, giggling over their silly dreams and wishes?

Flora shook her head. They had been silly, and she supposed that there wasn't time for such things these days.

"Is everything all right, my dear?" Her father's voice broke through her thoughts.

"Of course." She smiled up at him. "Just woolgathering. Entertaining silly thoughts that should best be put aside."

Her father patted her knee. "It isn't silly to wish for circumstances to be different. I'm sure it hurts greatly to have Sarah reject you out of hand. But time will heal the wounds, you'll see."

She murmured noncommittally, as she often did, but when she looked up, she found George's eyes on her. Like he could see inside her and understood the torment she faced. And thought he could make it better. Hadn't he already tried?

What George didn't realize was that he was the one creating so much turmoil in her head. His friendship felt so good, and the more she came to rely on him, the more she wasn't sure how she was going to do without once they found Pierre's father.

Chapter Six

The evening had ended up being a drawn-out affair, in part due to the presence of Flora's father. John Montgomery surprised George, mostly because he hadn't expected the warm smiles and quick wit that reminded him so much of Flora. How had this man come into conflict with his father, so much so that it had destroyed the relationship?

Pierre had fallen asleep in Flora's lap, and George couldn't help but admire her beauty as the firelight flickered across her face. The scent of pine mixed with smoke made it easy to forget they were so close to the mine. Instead, the evening reminded him of going into the woods with his father for an overnight trip. His father had liked taking him on such outings, saying that it was good for George to rough it once in a while, lest he forget that not everyone lived in a mansion in one of the finest neighborhoods in Denver.

As the breeze picked up, he saw Flora shiver slightly.

"Can I get you a wrap?" George asked.

Flora shook her head. "That's kind of you, but I need to put Pierre to bed. I should have done so some time ago, but the company has been so pleasant that I couldn't bear to leave."

George stood and held out his arms. "Let me take him. He's too heavy for you. If you like, I can put him to bed so you can continue visiting with your father."

Not waiting for Flora's answer, George took the little boy from Flora's arms. He'd done so dozens of times before, and it always felt good to help her with Pierre's care. The child had grown very dear to George, and he could only hope that Pierre's father was the sort of man who would allow George and Flora to continue visiting once the family was settled.

Pierre murmured in his sleep and stirred slightly as his weight was shifted from Flora to George.

"You don't have to do this," Flora said quietly, her cheeks faintly pink as she quickly glanced at her father.

"It's my pleasure," he said, smiling at her. But once he turned his gaze toward her father, he understood her hesitation.

Mr. Montgomery didn't look angry, but the older man did have a deeply thoughtful expression on his face. Like he wondered exactly what was passing between his daughter and this strange man in her life.

Sometimes George wanted to know that answer, too. There was no doubt he was growing to care for her, and indeed, would be disappointed when he no longer had Pierre as a reason to spend time with her. But what was he to do? She wouldn't be allowed to be openly courted by a miner, and George couldn't reveal his true identity. How could he, when it was clear the miners had no warm feelings for the Bellingham family? Besides, based on what he'd been hearing about the condition of the mine, he wasn't sure the Bellingham family would have a respectable name in society much longer. Could he do that to Flora, when it was clear that status and reputation meant everything to her?

Despite the fact that they'd had a lovely evening together, he'd caught the longing glances she sent in the direction of Sarah and her friends. Flora had always been the belle of the ball, so to speak. As a child, she'd always been surrounded by others who respected and admired her. He couldn't imagine the pain of losing all that, and as hard as she seemed to be working to regain her status, how could he ask her to give it up once more?

George bade everyone good-night and carried the little boy into the cabin. He supposed it was inappropriate by society's standards that he was so familiar with the sleeping arrangements here at the camp. But things were done differently so far from civilization.

He tucked the sleeping child into Flora's bed. According to Flora, Pierre often had nightmares, and the first night he was with them they'd given up having him sleep on a pallet in favor of being in Flora's bed. It was hard to imagine what it must be like for Pierre, in a strange place, missing all of his friends and family, with only Flora who spoke his language.

"Ah, George." Pastor Lassiter came into the cabin, carrying a lantern. "So good of you to take Pierre so Flora could have more time with her father."

"It's the least I can do," George said. "I know everyone thinks Flora is shirking her duties here in the camp, but she works hard to take care of Pierre, so I'm glad to give her the chance to enjoy herself."

The pastor looked thoughtfully at him. "You seem to care a great deal for Flora."

Most of the time what George liked the best about

the pastor was the fact that he didn't beat around the bush. But here, now, with this, he wished the man wasn't so direct.

"I admire her greatly," George said slowly. "I know there is some tension here with her and the other girls, but I hope that I can learn to handle myself with as much grace and dignity as she does if I were ever to be in a similar situation."

Pastor Lassiter nodded. "She is a great example of how the Lord works if you let Him. But I'm more concerned with the more personal connection you might feel for her."

George took a deep breath as he finished smoothing the blankets over Pierre. "I understand what you're saying, sir, and I'm doing my best to guard my heart, as well as refrain from saying or doing anything that would cause Flora to believe that there is any hope for us. She's an honorable young lady. I will not do anything that might compromise that honor."

He stood and smiled at the older man. "Now, if you'll excuse me, I made some arrangements to meet with some of the other miners to do more investigating into Pierre's father's whereabouts."

Before George reached the door, the pastor stopped him. "You seem like a very educated man, especially for a miner. Flora's family—"

"I've made no secret of the fact that I come from a good family that's hit on hard times. But if you're implying that I'd use Flora as a means of regaining our standing, please remove that notion from your mind right now. She is a good woman, and I am not the sort of man who would raise myself up at her expense. If I cannot restore my family's fortunes by honorable means, then I have no wish to do so."

Pastor Lassiter wasn't given the opportunity to reply, as Flora and Rose entered the cabin, followed by Flora's father. The ladies were giggling, giving George a sense of relief at knowing Flora hadn't overheard the conversation. But the wary look her father gave him made George pause.

John Montgomery loved his daughter, and he wouldn't allow any man to trifle with her. At some point, George would have to have a similar conversation with him. He didn't relish the prospect, since the man's already probing questions made it nearly impossible to hide the truth without lying.

Nodding at the ladies and Mr. Montgomery, George said, "Good night again. I'll see you all tomorrow."

He left the cabin without further conversation, and for that, George was glad. Not just because he was weary of having to explain himself without revealing everything, but also because he couldn't bear to have to keep facing the reality that his time with Flora would soon be over. A necessary parting because he couldn't see them having a future together. He hurried off, hoping his expedition to the mine office would provide him with the answers he needed.

When George arrived at the guardhouse, he saw the lights were on to indicate that the office was empty. The area was silent, still, a welcome respite from all the activity at the mining camp.

The record books were easy enough to find, laid out across the desk for anyone to see. Dougherty was either stupid or truly believed that none of the miners were smart enough to figure out what was going on.

He opened the first book and came across the employee list. The manager's handwriting was terrible and hard to decipher. Ink blots were everywhere, and it was no wonder the business was in disarray. Surely George's father hadn't known how incompetent this man was.

George scanned the list, noting that men were added as they were hired, and a line drawn through the names as they were let go. He found the entry for his name, and the salary listed next to it was more than he was being paid. So George hadn't been mistaken. And based on what others had told him, Dougherty was paying many of the men less than was on the books, and then what? Pocketing the difference? The man might not be able to keep a clean set of books, but clearly he was smart enough to come up with a scheme that was likely robbing the mine of thousands of dollars.

He ran his finger down the list and found the time frame during which Pierre's father would have been hired, based on when Pierre said they'd arrived. Pierre had said his father's name was Henri Martin. Nothing.

The only possibility was a large spot of ink covering up one of the crossed-out names. Carefully scraping away at the ink, George uncovered the first letter. *O.*

Not Henri.

He closed his eyes and took a deep breath. What now? According to the employee records, Henri Martin had never worked in the mine. Then he realized... to an American not familiar with French, Henri could sound like it started with an *O.*

George scraped away more of the ink blotch. Onree Mar...and the rest was undecipherable. But, yes, this could be Henri Martin. Not definite proof, but enough to know that Pierre's father most likely had been working here.

According to the ledger, Onree was still receiving his pay. So why was his name scratched out?

George closed the book, wondering if any of the others would give him a clue as to what happened to Pierre's father. At least George knew one thing: there was definitely something shady going on in the mine. If all the salaries had been inflated, it was no wonder they were losing money. Obviously someone, probably Dougherty, was skimming money from the mine.

The second ledger appeared to be a supply inventory. The prices seemed high, but George didn't know if it was because of the higher prices in Leadville, or if these numbers were also being inflated.

As George was reaching for a third ledger, the door opened and Dougherty walked in.

"What are you doing in my office?"

George froze. What reasonable excuse could he give? Now that he knew Dougherty was most likely lying about Pierre's father, and he knew that there was something funny going on with the payroll at least, it seemed like all he had was more questions. For a moment, he debated about giving his real identity, but at this point, without knowing everything that was going on, did he have enough to fix the problems at the mine? All he knew was that Dougherty was skimming money, not how or why the mysterious explosions were happening.

"I invited him," a voice said from behind Dougherty. When Dougherty stepped into the room, the man walked in behind him. John Montgomery.

Dougherty spun. "What do you mean, you invited him?"

"My daughter, Flora, is caring for the child of a miner who's gone missing. When George told me that the other mines had allowed him to look at their personnel records to see if the father had given any information that might be helpful in his search, I told George to come here tonight and take a look."

Then Montgomery turned his attention to George. "I apologize for being held up. Flora wanted to share a cup of tea before she went to bed."

"You don't have the authority to come in here and go through the records," Dougherty said, his face reddening. "The Bellinghams might be entertaining the idea of a sale, but that doesn't give you the right to come in here as you please."

"It's customary for a prospective buyer to review the books of any business," Montgomery said smoothly.

George took a deep breath. For whatever reason, Montgomery had decided to help George. Probably for Flora's sake, or maybe for Pierre's, to get George out of Flora's life as quickly as possible. But whatever it was, George was grateful.

"I'm sorry, sir, I didn't mean to start without you." George pointed at the books. "I don't really know where to begin."

"You can begin by getting out of my office!"

The door opened, and Stumpy entered the room.

"What's going on in here?"

"Where have you been?" Dougherty demanded. "How did this man get into my office?"

Montgomery stepped forward. "I told him I'd been given access and to let Mr. Baxter in. Again, the fault is mine. I apologize."

"He doesn't take orders from you!" Dougherty's face got even redder. "I'm still the boss here."

"Earlier today, you told me that all the resources I needed would be at my disposal," Montgomery said. "Apparently, I misunderstood."

"All of you, get out!"

They exited the office, and even in the dim light, George could tell Stumpy was worried. He'd promised not to get the other man in trouble, and clearly, by Dougherty's reaction, no one in this situation was safe.

Montgomery motioned for George to follow him, but George held up a hand. "Sir, I appreciate what you did in there. But if I could be so bold as to ask another favor, Stumpy is a good man. Doing the best he can to provide for his family, and if he loses his job, well, that hardly seems fair, now, does it?"

George's words didn't seem to erase the worry on Stumpy's face, but Montgomery nodded.

"I'll see what I can do. If Dougherty lets you go because of this, come see me. I'll find a place for you at one of my mines."

"Thank you, sir," Stumpy said. "Now, you'd all best be going. If Dougherty sees you here when he comes back out, he's liable to…it won't be good."

"Understood." George nodded at him. "And thank you. I know you put yourself out for us, and I appreciate it. I won't forget this."

Stumpy winked. "If you ever strike the big one, you'd best find me."

"I will." George smiled at him as he followed Montgomery down the path toward the camp.

They stopped at a ramshackle cabin some distance from the glowing lights and sea of tents.

"Thank you again, sir," George began. "I don't know how to thank you."

Montgomery stared at him. "You can begin by telling me what you're really doing here, George Baxter Bellingham."

Flora spent the next morning doing chores around the cabin, teaching Pierre the words for the things they were doing, and for simple objects they interacted with. He wouldn't remember it all, of course, but hopefully the more she helped him engage with the English language, the less isolated he'd feel.

"Let's go to the creek for some more water," Flora told him, holding up a bucket. "Do you remember what this is called?"

"Bu-kit."

The little boy grinned at her nod.

"Very good." She held out her hand and Pierre took it.

As they walked toward the creek, Flora spied Sarah and her friends sitting around, talking. For all the accusations the other girl levied at Flora for not working, it seemed like every time Flora saw Sarah, she was idle. She shouldn't judge, she knew, since Sarah probably worked very hard at other times, and just as Sarah never noticed Flora working, it didn't mean the girls didn't work.

"Allo, ladeez!" Pierre waved at the group of women. The little boy was friendly and gregarious, and though he'd gotten off on the wrong foot with many of the ladies at camp, he still liked to greet them.

As long as he didn't notice Sarah. He still liked to

hide from her, and generally didn't say much when she was around.

"What a little darling," Ellen Fitzgerald, one of the women, exclaimed, coming toward them. "Why aren't you with the other children?"

"He doesn't speak much English, but we're trying," Flora explained.

"Well, he is becoming quite the charmer, isn't he?" Ellen turned to Sarah. "He's really not so terrible."

"My name is Pierre," Pierre said proudly in his halting English. "I help Flora."

Ellen bent down in front of him. "My name is Ellen."

"El-len," Pierre repeated. He pointed to the bucket. "I help water Flora. You like water?"

"Oh, he is precious," Ellen said, standing. "Flora, would you like to join us while Pierre gets the water?"

Flora looked at the other girls, who seemed hesitant. Sarah glowered.

Oh, it would be nice to finally be able to socialize in a group like this. Maybe even to have Sarah thaw a bit.

But the little boy swinging the bucket beside her reminded her that she had other duties to attend to.

"I would love that, but Pierre isn't old enough to get water on his own. Some other time?" She smiled at Ellen, hoping the other girl could see she was being sincere.

Ellen nodded. "Of course. Some other time."

The relief Flora saw written on the other girls' faces told her it would be a long time coming, but Flora was grateful Ellen had made the effort. Perhaps everyone didn't hate her, after all.

Flora and Pierre continued their journey to the creek,

noticing that George and her father were standing by the rock where George had found Pierre.

"Hello," Flora said, waving at them. "What are you two doing here?"

George trotted over to see them, immediately picking up Pierre and swinging him around.

"Your father wanted to see where I'd found Pierre," he said, setting the little boy down. "He's decided to help me search for Pierre's father."

Looking over at her father, Flora tried to see if his expression betrayed anything about what he might be up to. Though her father was a good man, she couldn't see him ignoring work and his other responsibilities to help with this project. When she caught his eye, she knew. He was uncomfortable with the amount of time she was spending with a miner and wanted to act as a chaperone as much as possible.

"How kind of you," Flora said, trying not to betray her disappointment that her father felt the need to supervise her so closely. "I'm sure Pierre will be grateful to know that so many people care about finding his father."

Her father nodded. "A man just doesn't disappear like that with no trace, not with a child waiting for him to return."

Once again, Flora tried to force the unthinkable out of her head. Though it seemed unlikely that a man would have willingly abandoned Pierre, she also couldn't fathom something happening to him.

But if something had, all she could think was, what then? What about little Pierre?

She brought her attention back to George. "Why aren't you at work? I'm not used to seeing you so early."

"I had a disagreement with the mine manager," George said. "He told me to take a few days off without pay to see if having less money would make me more willing to listen to him."

"And I will pay you for that time," her father said. "It's wrong of him to punish you for following my directions."

"I'm just grateful he didn't fire me," George said, smiling. "And I don't mind. It gives me more time with Pierre."

Something in the exchange made Flora think there was something else going on between the men. But it didn't seem right to question it, not when she already suspected her father was helping because he thought there was more between Flora and George than there ought to be.

George picked up Pierre again and tickled him, the little boy's giggles ringing through the area. Such a happy sound. It was good for Pierre to have something to smile about.

Flora filled the bucket with water and set it on the ground. "All right, you two. George may not have to work today, but we have plenty to do. I'm sure Rose is wondering where we're at."

Pierre looked up at George. "I help Flora," he said proudly.

"You're learning. Nice job!" George ruffled the little boy's hair, then smiled at Flora. "You're doing splendidly with him. Have you thought about becoming a teacher?"

Of course it would be on George's mind to suggest a job to Flora. Her parents would never permit it, of course, especially since her one attempt at becoming a nanny had failed so miserably.

Still, what Flora loved most about being around George was that he always saw her for the possibilities in her life. He believed in her in a way that no one else had. George saw her for the woman she wanted to be, not the woman she once was.

"I'm sure that would be lovely," Flora said, glancing at her father. "But I can't see my parents permitting such a thing."

"No, we wouldn't," he said, putting his arm around Flora. "You deserve a family of your own, not having to put up with all that other nonsense."

Then he looked over at Pierre. "Present company excluded, of course. I agree that you're doing a fine job with Pierre, and that just proves how you were meant to be a mother. Some fine young man will scoop you up, and you'll have a very nice life, I'm sure."

Her father's words were meant for George, there was no doubt. Basically, keep away from my daughter, because I have a brilliant match planned for her.

The trouble was, none of those men seemed to like Flora very much. George, on the other hand, was constantly reminding her of how much he liked her.

So what was a girl to do?

"Thank you, Father." She smiled at him. "But we must get back to the camp now."

"Let me take that for you." George picked up the bucket. "I think we were done here, anyway."

"Thank you."

Though Flora smiled at him, part of her wanted to ask him what he was thinking. The nicer he was to her, the more likely her father was to keep interfering. And it wasn't that she didn't love her father, but it was hard enough being in this situation without his reminding her constantly of her duty.

It wasn't that she held out any romantic hope for George, but no one understood how good it felt to be with someone who accepted her for who she was without judgment.

George liked her, and she didn't have to earn it.

When they arrived back at camp, the other ladies were gathering up supplies to go to the mine. Pastor Lassiter had taken to going up at the noon break to provide refreshment.

"Ah, Flora!" The pastor greeted her warmly. "Rose needed to return to town today, so I was hoping you'd be willing to join us. Just to serve water, nothing too taxing. People might find little Pierre charming as he helps."

"Of course." Flora gave him another smile, realizing that her cheeks were beginning to hurt from being so agreeable. It wasn't that she didn't want to go help, but she could already feel Sarah's eyes on her, burning into her back in disapproval.

They loaded up a wagon, and Flora walked behind with Pierre and the other ladies on the way to the mine. Though the ladies chattered amiably amongst themselves, they didn't include Flora. In the past, she would have found a way to jump in, but now, she felt insecure about speaking up where she may not be wanted.

Sarah's giggle sounded louder than normal, and it pained Flora's heart every time she heard it. George stepped in beside her.

"I'm so glad to see you joining in with everyone. I think much of the problem has been that you and Pierre have been so isolated. Now that you're working with them, the other ladies are sure to see what a wonderful woman you are."

"Thank you," she said softly, feeling eyes upon her. "I know you're trying to help, but the more the others see you talking to me in a personal way, the more they will think you're a suitor, and we know that's not possible. Besides, it will only make things worse. So please, don't try to help."

"I beg your pardon," George said, walking away.

Part of her wanted to call him back, to beg his forgiveness, to tell him that she was grateful for his friendship. That she appreciated everything he'd done for her.

But that would be most telling of all. And she'd never convince the others that there was nothing going on between herself and George.

The trouble with having spent her whole life trying to enforce society's rules was that she knew what would be going too far. And to lose her heart to someone outside their social circle would make her an outcast forever. Wasn't that what had happened with Cecilia Dean, who'd married the family's groom? Mrs. Dean no longer spoke of her daughter, and most people acted like the poor girl had died or something. Flora might be brave, but she was not that brave.

Chapter Seven

George knew better than to take offense at Flora's words. Were it his sister being courted by a miner, he'd have called the man out. Not that he was courting Flora, of course. They were just friends. But even George knew enough about the rules of polite society to know that there was a fine line between being just friends with a young lady and encouraging an inappropriate attachment.

He sighed as he looked around to find a place to walk so he wouldn't be in the way, but where he could still observe Flora and Pierre. After he left, he heard giggles from some of the women, and Flora had turned a shade of red that wasn't at all flattering to her delicate features. He'd have liked to say something in her defense, but Flora was right, it would only serve to make others think there was something going on between the two of them.

John, as Mr. Montgomery had asked George to call him, had gone ahead with Pastor Lassiter to discuss their plan, and George noticed the other man waving at him. He ran to catch up.

"So," Pastor Lassiter said with a smile, "I thought there was more to you than meets the eye."

"Say no more," George said, looking around. "I don't want anyone to know who I am. There are still things I don't know yet. The more I think about it, the more I have a hard time believing that Dougherty is in on this alone. The man is often too drunk to put two sentences together, let alone come up with such an elaborate plan to steal all that money. Plus, we still don't know what's really going on with the mysterious sabotage that's been happening at the mine."

"It's like I said. He's an honorable man. George's father would be proud of him." John patted him on the back and smiled broadly.

Pastor Lassiter nodded. "What I don't understand, though, is how Elias could have allowed things to get so bad."

George stared at the pastor. "You knew my father?"

"Only by reputation. He was a good man. I was sorry to hear of his passing. Such a tragedy. I believe your mother was injured in the carriage accident, as well."

"She was. Unfortunately, she has a long recovery ahead of her." George hated the image that immediately came to mind of her in bed, still unable to walk, even three months later. The doctors said she might be an invalid for the rest of her life, although that might not last long. Some days, George wondered if she'd simply lost the will to live without her husband.

"It's a terrible shame," Pastor Lassiter said. "From what I saw in the papers, she was the light of society." With a grin, he looked at John. "And based on what you tell me, she led you on quite the merry chase."

George stared at the pastor. "I don't understand. What are you talking about?"

The men chuckled, then John finally said, "Years ago, before I meet my wife, Elias and I were both interested in Honoria. Honoria Baxter she was back then, and that is how I knew who you were right away. Her father was George Baxter, and you were named for him."

John grinned. "Plus you look so much like Elias did at your age, it was almost like looking my old friend in the eye."

"You courted my mother?"

"I did. But once she met Elias, she only had eyes for him. And I'm glad for it. I can't imagine life without my Anna. Or Flora." A warm smile lit up the man's face, and George couldn't help but be grateful Flora had a father who loved her so deeply.

"Is that why you and my father had a falling-out? You never said."

George looked at the other man. Though John had told him he had every intention of helping him, and that he was on his side, he still didn't know if he could trust him.

"In part." Then John shook his head. "No. We both married, and were happy in our marriages. Then Elias was befriended by a man named Ross Eldridge. He seemed like a swindler, and I thought the investments he wanted your father to make were ill-advised. Ross didn't like my interference, so he started a rumor that I was still in love with Honoria. I met with her to tell her that it wasn't true. Elias was out of town, but my wife was with me. Everything in the open, nothing untoward. But Ross saw us. He lied and told your father he saw us embrace. A few of his friends confirmed his words, and nothing any of us said made Elias believe that there was nothing going on."

Granted, his mother wasn't a young woman anymore, but George couldn't imagine her involved in some kind of love triangle. Especially because his parents always seemed to have such a deep affection for each other. How could his father have believed his mother would do something like that?

And for Uncle Ross to have been involved with it, as well? George shook his head. No wonder he knew nothing about any of this.

John sighed, looking out at the scenery like it was transporting him back to that time. "The investments I thought were schemes turned out to make a great deal of money, which, to Elias, was proof that I was just jealous. Originally, Elias had planned on coming to Leadville with me, to oversee his mine as I was overseeing my own. But Ross convinced him it wasn't necessary, so he stayed behind when I moved here."

Turning his attention back to George, John continued. "Elias and I never spoke again, and there hasn't been a day since that I haven't mourned the loss of that friendship. Anna and Honoria tried to keep in touch for a while, but I believe it just became easier over time to let it go. From what I hear, Elias wouldn't even tolerate the name Montgomery to be spoken in his presence."

George nodded. "It's true. He often spoke of you as though you were the worst kind of criminal. He said we weren't to trust you."

"I can imagine." John looked thoughtful for a moment.

George nodded slowly, trying to process the other

man's words. "Why would my father believe it? Why would Uncle Ross say such a thing?"

"Uncle Ross, huh?" John chuckled. "I really thought your father would have seen through his act and sent him packing."

Even with the time that had passed since Uncle Ross's demise, it was still hard to hear of the man's misdeeds. John wasn't too far off the mark in his assessment of Uncle Ross, but it was still hard to fathom the man being so devious.

"He died several years ago in a duel. I know my father was disappointed with some of his choices, but he was still like family to us. We took in his son, who even married my sister."

John frowned. "I didn't realize Ross had a son."

"Arthur. He's a good man. He's been helping me sort through my father's estate. I don't think he realized how bad things were at the mine. He tried getting me to go back to school, but I felt it was my duty to do what I could here while Arthur sorted out the rest of Father's businesses. Arthur doesn't know I'm here. He was so set on me fulfilling Father's dream of sending his son to college. Poor Father, I think he put money in just about every investment he thought had a chance. He truly wanted to help people make something of themselves."

For the first time since coming up to Leadville, George felt slightly melancholy over his father's death. Perhaps Uncle Ross had advised him poorly on a few things, since many of his father's investments had been suggested by him. But George knew that if a man had a good idea and seemed to be a good sort, his father would always invest in his ideas. Which was why the family's disappointment in Uncle Ross had had more to do with his drinking and other profligate activities. His father used to say that Uncle Ross was a good man until the drink got hold of him. That was the thing George had loved best about his father. He always saw the good in people. Except, apparently, for John.

"That's what we all admired about him, son." John patted him on the shoulder and Pastor Lassiter nodded. "I always hoped I'd be able to keep him from being taken advantage of, but from what you've told me, and what I've seen, his mine managers have been robbing him blind for years."

George had been afraid of that. He only hoped that they'd be able to find a way to turn things around before it was too late. All of his father's recent investments had been losing money, and while Arthur was desperately trying to keep them from bleeding the family dry, George feared that the only way to keep his family from going under was to save the mine.

"Is there any hope?" George asked.

"There's always hope," Pastor Lassiter said cheerfully. "But I believe we're coming upon the mine now, so we'd best keep our confidential discussion to a minimum."

"Thank you," John said. "One last thing before we are among others. When are you going to tell my daughter the truth about who you are and make your intentions clear?"

George should have expected this question. It had been hanging in John's watchful glances ever since he learned George's true identity. But what was George supposed to say? Sometimes he wasn't even sure of what any of this was. And yet, he knew with a high degree of certainty, all his reasons for not courting Flora remained the same.

"With all due respect," George said slowly, "I can't tell her who I am until this situation with the mine is resolved. Right now, she keeps me at arm's length because I am a miner, not a gentleman. Back when we departed camp, she cautioned me against being too good of a friend because the others wouldn't approve of her friendship with a miner."

Both John and the pastor nodded. "If I tell her now who I am, she won't be as guarded near me, and people might guess who I really am, or at least be able to tell that I am not who I appear, especially if you seem to approve. I'm already uncomfortable with the two of you knowing my secret. I can't risk anyone else knowing, not until I can resolve the situation."

George took a deep breath and looked at the mine spread out before him. "Working here, getting to know the men, I owe it to them to figure out what's really going on and to make it better. Technically, they're my employees and under my care. I can't jeopardize their well-being, even though it pains me to be less than completely honest."

But there was one thing George needed to be completely honest about. At least in dealing with the father of a young lady. "All that said, I have no intention of courting Flora. I'd like to be her friend, yes, but only as far as propriety allows. My family's financial situation is bleak, and I don't see a way out. Flora is used to a life I can't guarantee I can give her, and it's not fair to ask her to live otherwise."

John looked like he was about to say something, but George shook his head. "I will not marry a woman for her money. And I will not marry a woman who has the expectation of a lifestyle that I may or may not be able to provide for."

Taking a deep breath, George thought about Shannon and the gift she'd unwittingly given him in breaking off their engagement. "I was engaged before my father died. She was a lovely young woman, and when rumors of our financial troubles hit, she called off the wedding. I realized that anything can happen to a person—money is a thing that can be gained or lost in an instant. I want a wife who will love me for richer or for poorer. Flora is a lovely woman, and I like her very much. But I can't see her being happy about accepting a marriage for poorer."

Pastor Lassiter clapped him on the back. "You are a wise man. Far wiser than most of the men who come into my church to be married. But I hope you don't give up on love because you've underestimated a woman's ability to cope with changing circumstances."

John wore a thoughtful expression. "I'd like to agree with the pastor, but he's never had to pay Flora's shopping bills. She's already asked me to take her into town to buy a few things for Pierre."

"She is determined to spoil that boy," Pastor Lassiter said, chuckling.

"And so she should," George said. "That's who Flora is, and it's part of why we all have affection for her. I can't ask her to be someone she's not. It might start off as a fun adventure, but ultimately, she'd grow resentful of not having the finer things in life. Of not having the social standing. I see how she tries to act like she's all right with living a good life but not having the regard of her old friends, but when she thinks no one is watching, she looks miserable."

George took a deep breath as he looked at John. "Sir, I have too much respect for your daughter to encourage her down a path that will only lead to her misery. Let some other man tempt her with the treasures of this life. I cannot."

"I understand." John held out a hand and George took it. "I agree that my daughter is too fond of her worldly goods, which is partially why I wanted her to come on this expedition. It's good for her to know that not everyone has a fine feather mattress and people waiting on her constantly. Our family comes from a humble background, and I suppose we spoiled her, giving her everything she wanted, making sure she never went without."

He looked like he had more to say, but Pierre came running up to them. "George!"

As he always did, George picked up the little boy and swung him around. Pierre's laugh rang out, filling the air with so much joy, it was hard to remember they were here for far more serious matters.

Flora joined their merry group. "Pierre," she said with a smile, then spoke in rapid French to the boy. She looked up at them. "I asked him not to run away like that. Even though he saw you, I did not, and for a moment I was quite frightened, wondering where he'd gone off to."

The worry in her voice touched George in a way he hadn't thought possible. He knew Flora cared for the little boy, but this spoke of something deeper, more powerful. Once again, he found himself wishing others could look past the prejudice they felt toward her and see the love in her heart. If only he could have something like that for himself.

* * *

Flora wrapped her arms around the squirming boy, knowing that he didn't understand that moment of terror when she didn't see him. But she couldn't help pressing a kiss to the top of his head.

"Time to go work," she said, letting go of him and holding out her hand.

Pierre looked longingly at George, but George made motions with his hands that Pierre should go with Flora.

They made a good team, Flora and George, and she was grateful for his assistance. If only their stations in society weren't so different. Hopefully, like all the other passing fancies in life, this would soon be replaced by something else. What, she didn't know, since she hadn't met a more honorable man than George Baxter.

As they rejoined the women, Flora caught Sarah looking askance at her. It was tempting to ask her what was going on, but having endured the whispers on the walk, Flora wasn't sure she could stand another round of criticism.

Out of the corner of her eye, she noticed her father walking with George over to an angry-looking man. Whatever their conversation, it looked heated and unpleasant. Surely not something having to do with Pierre's father?

The man made a motion with his arms, and they followed him into a nearby building that held the mine's office. *Please let it not be bad news for Pierre*, she prayed.

"You can't take your eyes off him, can you?" Sarah's voice sounded behind her, and Flora jumped.

Flora turned to face the other woman, who wore a nasty smirk on her face.

"I'm curious to know what he and my father have found about Pierre's father. In case you didn't notice, my father was with him."

"Interesting that your father is allowing you to have such a suitor." Sarah gave a tiny laugh. "But, of course, no one else will have you, now, will they?"

Her former friend's words stung, especially because Flora could remember all the times she'd confessed to Sarah about wanting to marry well and how she'd feared never finding a suitable husband.

"I suppose we all have our difficulties in finding suitors," Flora said. "Who would have thought we'd both still be unmarried at our age?"

Yes, the kinder, gentler Flora wasn't supposed to make digs anymore. But she was growing weary of turning the other cheek, especially because no one seemed to care that Sarah was being so unkind.

Sarah blanched and Flora knew she'd hit her mark. But it didn't give her the same satisfaction as it would have in the past.

"I'm sorry, Sarah. That was uncalled for. I knew as soon as it came out of my mouth that I shouldn't have said it." Flora took a deep breath. "It's hard, being reminded of a state that neither of us thought we'd be in. But I'm learning that God has a plan for me, just as I know He has a plan for you. Perhaps it's still possible for us to have that double wedding we used to dream about."

"You wish." Sarah spun and stomped away.

Pastor Lassiter approached, and Flora sighed. He'd seen their interaction, and he probably wasn't pleased with the outcome.

"It was my fault," Flora said, not waiting for him to

ask. "She provoked me, and I responded in kind. I realized what I did, and I apologized, but the damage was done. I keep praying for better control of my tongue, but sometimes, people's words are so hurtful that my mouth takes over."

The pastor nodded. "It is hard to resist hurting someone who's hurt you. But I wonder, have you thought about the hurt Sarah must be feeling? How hard it must be to see one's best friend turning her back on the life they used to lead together?"

Flora thought for a moment. "But it was wrong for us to go on as we did."

"But she hasn't changed from who she was back then. Even though you haven't condemned her behavior, perhaps it feels to her as though you are, given that you are continually apologizing for that behavior and trying to live differently."

"But only for my behavior," Flora said. "I'm not fit to judge Sarah."

He looked thoughtful as he nodded, then inclined his head to where the other girls were talking among themselves. "But could it appear to her that your rejection of that lifestyle is also a rejection of her? Could she feel judged by you?"

It seemed a particularly cruel form of irony that in attempting to be less judgmental of others, people would view it as a judgment against them.

Flora sighed. "I hadn't thought of it that way." She looked over at the other women, who were now busying themselves with preparing what was needed for the miners. "I only meant to condemn my ways, but I can see where it would appear as a condemnation of her."

Then she turned her attention back to the pastor. "So

what do I do? The more I apologize for my behavior, the more it points out to her that her behavior is less than exemplary. But I can't join in on the kind of meanness I was once party to."

He nodded slowly. "It is a difficult situation, that's for sure. Perhaps, rather than continuing to apologize, you let the apologies you've made stand on their own. Move forward living life as you know is best and stop focusing on the past."

With a fatherly expression, he smiled at her. "I can imagine that you miss the camaraderie of your friends very much. But I also think that if you were accepted in their midst again, you wouldn't have as much fun if they aren't living the same as you."

Gesturing to the path leading to where they would be working, he continued. "I've had the opportunity to minister to men who had problems with the drink. The hardest part for them is learning to live life in a new group of friends, people who don't frequent saloons or other places where they might be tempted. Some of their friends support this and are willing to accept this change. Others end up going by the wayside because they don't want to miss out on what they think is the right way to live. I believe that's what it will be like for you. In time, you'll find a way to interact with your old friends that is comfortable for everyone. But some of them will be beyond your reach, and you have to accept that as being within the Lord's timing."

Flora nodded as they reached the serving tables. "Thank you. I think I understand."

"Good." He smiled broadly, then pointed at a barrel of water and a dipper. "You'll be serving water to the men."

She murmured her agreement and looked down at Pierre, who'd calmly walked beside her as she and the pastor spoke. "Thank you for being so good and patient," she told him in French. "You're a very good boy."

Pierre smiled and puffed up his chest. "I good for Flora," he said loudly in English.

"You certainly are," she said, giving him a squeeze.

Then Pierre turned and pointed. "Is George! Pierre say hi to George?"

The trouble with trying to get a certain man out of your mind was that when that certain man was so connected to the little boy you were caring for, seeing him was inevitable.

"Yes. Thank you for asking." She smiled at him, and he bounded off.

Flora watched as Pierre leaped into George's arms and George swung him around. The little boy giggled, and Flora couldn't help the way her heart did a small leap of its own at the sight.

"He is very good with him, isn't he?"

Flora turned to look at Ellen, who'd come to stand beside her.

"Yes, he is."

Ellen gave her a warm smile. "I wanted to apologize for earlier today. I meant no harm. I thought that if I invited you to join us, we could all get to know each other better, as the pastor asked. I know Sarah is the ringleader, but I think that many of the ladies, including myself, are favorably inclined to giving you a chance."

"Really?" Flora stared at her. "Why?"

"Someone who could care for a little boy who must be missing his father dreadfully, yet give that child so many reasons to smile, can't be all bad." Ellen gave

her a sheepish look. "We've been judging you based
on your past actions, and we should have been looking
at the present." She sighed. "No. Not we. I can't speak
for anyone else. But I can speak for myself when I say
that I'm sorry for any insult that I may have given you."

"Thank you." Flora smiled at her. "And I apologize
for any insult I have given you."

Pierre came toward them, dragging a laughing
George with him. Flora shook her head and glanced
over at what she hoped would be a new friend.

"Those two. I don't know what to do with them."

"Guard your heart," Ellen said softly. "It's easy to
get caught up in the romance of an exciting situation.
But Pierre will go back to his father when he's found,
and George…" Ellen let out a long sigh. "He is handsome, but without the recommendation of a good family, who will receive him?"

For a moment, the silence was thick between them,
sticky and oppressive, because Flora knew what was
coming and dreaded it.

"I know I sound just like Sarah," Ellen continued.
"But the man is a miner. None of the good families
would allow their daughters to be courted by one, so
they wouldn't be able to condone it in someone else.
I'm not saying this to be unkind, but because it's clear
you like him, and I can't see it ending well."

Flora couldn't argue. After all, wasn't that her own
thought process in not wanting to pursue George?

Then Ellen leaned in to her. "I know you must be
thinking I'm being a busybody, but I understand what
you're going through. No one knows this, but last summer, when I was in Boston visiting relatives, I formed
an inappropriate attachment to one of the delivery

boys. My family was horrified, and fortunately, Mother brought me home before things got out of hand. It's hard, when you think you love someone. But what good is love, when it will ruin your life?"

Turning her attention back to George playing with Pierre, Flora honestly couldn't give an answer. But when she caught her father's watchful gaze on them, she knew. It wasn't just Flora's life she was hurting by pursuing a man so completely outside their social class. She could still remember the way her mother had sobbed at not being invited to an event at the Jackson Mansion because Flora had made a snide comment about Emma Jane Jackson. Her mother loved her, but Flora had seen how her mother had suffered with each one of Flora's misdeeds. At the time, Flora hadn't realized the significance, but now, as she looked back on how her actions affected others, it seemed unreasonable to let herself get caught up in a romance that would be frowned upon in their social circle.

"I have no interest in George romantically," Flora said. "It's, as you say, impossible."

Though Ellen nodded, it was clear the other woman was still concerned for Flora. And Flora didn't blame her. As many times as she'd tried telling herself that she wasn't interested in George, she kept finding her eyes and thoughts drawn back to him. But as Flora was learning, her actions weren't just about her own happiness, but about doing what was right for everyone else.

Chapter Eight

The day at the mine had been a bust, as far as George was concerned. Though Dougherty claimed he wanted to help them, it was also clear that the man was doing everything in his power to thwart them. He let them examine the books, or so he'd said, but they weren't the books George had seen the night before.

John approached, carrying a plate. "Did you get any dinner?"

George nodded. "Flora and I ate with Pierre earlier. She said he'd been staying up too late and wanted to get him settled in to a better bedtime routine."

"For someone not interested in my daughter, you seem to be spending a lot of time with her."

"I know." George looked over at the cabin, where Flora was tucking in the little boy. "But I don't know how to separate spending time with her from spending time with Pierre. I had every intention of dining without them tonight, but Pierre insisted. How do I say no to a little boy who's already missing his father?"

The older man followed George's gaze, and of

course, Flora picked that moment to exit the cabin and head in their direction.

"I don't suppose you can," John said, taking a bite of his beans. "What do you make of the books Dougherty let us examine?"

"They're completely different. The records aren't the same. My pay is correct in that ledger. And the writing is different."

John nodded. "I thought so, as well. I didn't get as good of a look as you yesterday, but what you had in your hand last night seemed much sloppier."

Exactly what George had been thinking. And unfortunately, he had a good idea about the records they'd seen today. "The clean books are in Robert Cooper's handwriting. He's been my father's closest advisor since Uncle Ross's death."

"That's who approached me about buying the mine. Said the family was struggling and they needed an investor."

George looked over at him. "Why you?"

"Why not me?" John shrugged. "I started just like your father, with one mine. But as various outfits needed investors, I bought in. I now have an ownership stake in over a dozen mines here. People know that when they need to raise quick capital, I'm the one to talk to."

Quick capital. As in, John had already known the family was in trouble. "How bad is it?"

"The mine?" John looked over at him. "Honestly? The equipment is in dire need of repair, the place is run inefficiently and your best veins of silver are played out. I'm surprised they didn't try to seed the mine the way some folks have, but I suppose they knew it would be useless, given the state of things."

With a long sigh, John shook his head. "To be honest, were it not for the fondness I feel for your family, I'd have passed. But rumor has it that your father had a lot of debt tied to his various companies, and you need this sale to satisfy the creditors."

"Wouldn't it make sense to sell the mine at a higher price, then? It seems like everything happening is devaluing the mine, not making it worth more."

In the waning light, it was hard to read the other man's expression. But from the way his shoulders rose and fell, he was thinking deeply about the same thing.

"There's something else going on, and I don't know what," John finally said. "But you can be sure that I will get to the bottom of it, even if it means buying the mine myself."

The crunch of gravel made George turn. Flora. They'd been too indiscreet in their talk, but it was good to hear John confirm his suspicions. Well, not good. But at least George knew he was on the right track.

"What are you getting to the bottom of?" Flora smiled at them. "And don't you dare buy another mine. Mother will have a fit."

John grinned. "I'll just buy her that diamond necklace she wants, and she'll forget all about it."

"Well, you'll have to buy me a matching one so I don't tell her how you were preying on her weakness."

"Done."

Flora bent and kissed her father on the cheek. Though it was a minor exchange, such conversations were probably common in the Montgomery household. And, as George saw the twinkle in Flora's eyes, one of the reasons he couldn't marry her. Now, more than ever, he was convinced that he'd never be able to support Flora in any kind of decent lifestyle, let alone be able to bribe her with a new diamond necklace.

"Now, really, what were you discussing? What did you find out in the mining office?" Flora sat on the log beside her father, opposite George. Still a little too close for comfort, but at least she wasn't sitting directly next to him, as she'd done on several other occasions.

"Well, sweetheart," John said in a syrupy tone, "it's complicated. Why don't we talk about something else, like the new dress catalog I brought up with me?"

Flora groaned. "Do not make me get a whole new wardrobe out of you. Honestly, Father, you could buy all of Paris and not distract me from the task at hand. What news do you have of Pierre's father?"

John hesitated, and though George understood the man's reticence, he also knew it wasn't fair to keep Flora even more in the dark than she already was.

"There are discrepancies in the records," George said. "Last night, I clearly saw a notation for an employee named Onree. May not be Pierre's father, but it seems reasonable to assume. Today, when we examined the books, they were different, and the man's name did not appear."

One more piece of the puzzle that didn't make sense. Why hide the fact that Pierre's father worked there?

"You would buy the mine just to find out the truth about Pierre's father?" Flora wrapped her arms around her father's neck. "That is the sweetest thing you've ever wanted to buy me."

"Now, sweetheart, I didn't say I was going to, just that it's tempting."

Flora released her hold on her father, then returned to where she'd been seated. "But why would they lie about Pierre's father?"

"That's exactly what we were discussing," George said. "Clearly Mr. Dougherty is hiding something, but we're having a hard time finding out what it is."

"If it's something he wants hidden, then he's not going to give you an easy time of finding it," Flora said, looking thoughtful. "And if he's making it difficult, then that tells me it must be something pretty terrible."

A haunted expression crossed her face, making her look older and wiser than her years. "Poor Pierre. It can't look good for finding his father, can it?"

George shook his head, wanting to do more to comfort Flora, but with her father sitting there, in light of their conversation about keeping his distance from her, it seemed like the worst thing to do. But what was he supposed to do when there were tears in her eyes?

"Sweetheart, don't trouble yourself with all this nonsense. Leave it to George and me. You just keep taking care of that sweet child."

"But I care about Pierre, too," Flora said, tears in her voice.

Lord, I know what it looks like to everyone, me taking up for Flora. But I can't just let her sit here, crying, because her heart is breaking for an innocent boy.

George took a deep breath after sending his silent prayer upward, then leaned forward and took her hand. "If something happened to Pierre's father, and people are going to such great lengths to hide it, which is what I think we're all thinking, then we're dealing with some dangerous people. You're a smart, capable woman, and I have no doubt that you would be an asset to our investigation. But if these people are so dangerous as to have done harm to Pierre's father, how much more dangerous would they be to an innocent woman and child? Will you trust your father and me to handle this and keep you and Pierre safe? Please?"

Flora nodded slowly. Though her eyes were still filled with tears, she looked stronger, more confident.

"You think I'm smart?"

Feeling John's gaze upon him, George gave Flora's hand a final squeeze, then pulled away, straightening. "I do. I've had a number of very intelligent conversations with you, and I respect your opinion greatly. Which is why I know you'll see the wisdom in focusing your attention on Pierre's care and letting us handle the investigation."

Flora looked at the ground. "No one's ever called me wise before." She sighed softly. "Usually they think I'm silly, and say that I have nothing in my head but fashion and nonsense."

"There's nothing silly about fashion," George told her. "My sister is constantly talking about the latest fashions, and I teased her about it once. Let me tell you, she set me straight. I couldn't believe how smart a person needed to be to be so knowledgeable about fashion."

As John cleared his throat, George realized his mistake. Being knowledgeable about fashion meant being well-off. At least there was one way to salvage things.

"I just hope I can someday buy her one of those dresses in that magazine she likes so well."

Flora leaned forward. "Ooh, which one does she read?"

"I can't rightly say," George told her. "Whatever the ladies pass around after church. But that's exactly what

I mean about you. You take an interest in others, and you like to read. That's smart in my book."

In the dim firelight, he thought he saw her cheeks turn pink. He supposed a beautiful woman like Flora didn't hear too often about how smart she was. People probably spent so much time thinking of her beauty that they missed her other admirable qualities.

Which, of course, he had no business thinking about. Especially now. John had confirmed that George's family was in even more dire financial straits than George had originally suspected. And, based on the conversation they'd all had just now, George couldn't give Flora the life she was accustomed to, the life she deserved. There would be no pretty baubles to make up for his transgressions, and Flora would be relegated to the same misery his sister, Julia, was living.

He took a deep breath as he thought about the dress he'd like to be able to buy his sister. Yes, he knew it was Arthur's job to take care of his wife, but he didn't think Arthur understood how miserable Julia was, having to wear the same fashions, or remake them, when she loved nothing more than something new and pretty to admire.

Unfortunately, recognizing what a good woman Flora was meant that George cared too much for her to ask her to make the kind of reductions in living Julia was enduring. Serving at the mine was a temporary endeavor, but everyone knew that at the end of the summer, Flora would be back in her fine house, cared for by staff and surrounded by all the comforts George could no longer give her. Sitting here with her, without the excuse of Pierre, it just wasn't right.

George finished his cup of coffee, then stood. "I

think I'll go to bed now. Dougherty wants me back to work in the morning, says it's a worse distraction having me not working than it is to have me on the job."

"Morning does come awful early up here," John said, nodding at him. "We can meet tomorrow night to compare notes."

"Sounds good." George looked over at Flora. "Good night, Flora."

She smiled at him, and he didn't like the sparkle he saw in her eyes. No, he liked it. But that was the problem. He was a fool if he didn't see how she was starting to become fond of him, as well.

Fools, both of them. Wanting something they couldn't have.

Flora watched as George disappeared into the night. Why did this man affect her so? Why couldn't a man of means, a respectable man, say the kind of things George said to her? She'd been flattered countless times; it seemed all men could do when near her. But George... his words made her feel something she couldn't quite express.

"Father," Flora said quietly. "What do you make of George?"

He looked at her, his typical indulgent expression missing from his face. "I think he's a good man."

Then he shook his head. "But it's a shame, the way things are. I know what you're asking, and I think you have to ask yourself if pursuing that line of thinking is worth giving up everything that's ever been important to you. The dances, the parties, the dresses."

Her father made her seem so shallow. If she truly loved George, wouldn't she be willing to give all that up? Isn't that what the ladies did in the serialized stories she and her friends used to pass around? But the women in those stories also didn't live in the real world.

Her friends. Flora sighed. Would she ever have friends like that again?

"It seems I don't have most of that, anyway," she said quietly, hating that the life she wanted wasn't hers anymore. Not really.

Though she'd been encouraged by her newfound friendship with Ellen, Flora couldn't help but remember the way Ellen had warned her off George. That seemed to be what everyone was doing these days. Reminding her that even though she was living in reduced circumstances, it was by choice, and the reality of her station was that once she returned home, propriety dictated that...

Flora looked at him. "Why do you suppose it is that, despite you saying George is a good man, he wouldn't be welcome in our parlor?"

Her father made a choking sound. Flora turned and patted him on the back.

"I'm fine, I'm fine." He waved her away. "What do you mean, George wouldn't be welcome in our parlor?"

"I can't see you inviting him to dine with us." Flora sighed. "The only employees of yours that I've met have all been, well, not the laborers. Why is that? Why such a division?"

He looked thoughtfully at her, nodding slowly. "You have grown a lot since coming up here. I'm sorry it took George pointing it out to recognize how much wisdom you have. But, you know, if this is about George—"

"No." Flora shook her head. "I mean, yes, but..." Flora sighed. "Last night, when Peanut joined us for supper, I enjoyed his company. His stories are so colorful, and I'm finding as I get to know more of the miners, that, despite our differences in social status, they're good people. I like them."

Shaking her head again, she said, "But I can't see Agnes being happy about any of them walking on our carpets with their dirty boots."

Flora chuckled softly as she thought about how persnickety their housekeeper could be. "Do you remember that time when there was trouble at one of your mines, and the foreman came into the house to tell you? I thought for sure Agnes was going to beat the man to death with her broom."

Her father also chuckled. "She does run a tight ship. Even I don't dare go in the front door if I've been at one of the mines."

In the past, Flora had always privately agreed with Agnes's horror at the wanton disregard for propriety. After all, it's what had always led Flora to judge people with such swiftness and cruelty. But living here, in the mining camp, even for a few short weeks, had taught her that many of the things she'd once disdained in others were not their fault, and that she should have looked deeper.

For example, a miner often only owned one pair of boots, and they lived in such dirt and mud out of necessity. How could she turn up her nose at that? How could she consider someone less than herself because of dirty hands and face, when that person likely didn't have the same access to clean water for washing? She knew nothing about the people she'd once judged, and she felt ashamed for not being able to see that underneath all the things she'd thought were important existed decent people she was now proud to know.

So what did that mean for her relationship with someone like George?

Her father patted her on the knee. "I can see this experience has changed you. And if you wish to invite some of your new friends for dinner, I can smooth things over with Agnes and your mother."

Flora took a deep breath. "Would you consider…" She closed her eyes. No, she couldn't ask that question. George had never asked if he could court her, and as much as she liked him, she still wasn't sure she could live in a place like this camp forever. Even now, she dreaded going in to sleep on the lumpy mattress that was considered extravagant here.

Could she do that for the rest of her life?

Flora shook her head.

"Never mind. It's—I'm being silly, I suppose."

Her father put his arm around her and gave her a squeeze. "It's not silly to think about other people and how you interact with them. In truth, I'm learning a great deal myself. Your questions are prompting me to look deeper at my own values and motivations. I used to be just like the men at this camp, until I found riches and began making more. But it's been a long time since I've spent time with my workers, looking at them as people, thinking about their needs and values. We get so caught up in life that we often forget those who support the life we live."

Then he looked at her sympathetically. "I would be a fool not to notice that you're developing feelings for George. I would just caution you that everything is not as it seems, and you should guard your heart for the time being. Once things are in the open, and you have all the information, we can talk."

He gave her another squeeze. "I know it's difficult, but keep in mind that you're dealing with a lot of emotions right now—living up here, the changes in your friendships, caring for Pierre, even the difference in how you view things. God is still working in you, so it's best not to make life-altering decisions in the midst of it."

Flora swallowed. "I know George has secrets. There are times I feel like he's hiding something, but then it's gone, and I don't know what to think."

Taking a deep breath, Flora looked up at him. "Are his secrets so very bad?"

"He hasn't killed a man, if that's what you're asking. But he has taken me into his confidence, and while I am choosing to keep his secrets, you must know that…" Her father let out a long sigh. "I can only say that it's not going to be an easy road for him, and until you have all the facts, don't start making up romantic dreams that may never be."

Which told her nothing, except that her father was doing his best to dissuade her without explicitly telling her not to pursue George.

"Does he know you feel this way?"

"I have asked him not to encourage you. He understands the situation and why. I believe he and I are in agreement."

What made the twist in her heart even more particularly painful, she couldn't say. Was it that George had been open with her father and not her, or was it more that George actually agreed with him? It shouldn't matter. She'd already known that anything between herself and George was bound to be an impossibility.

Ellen approached, a reminder that all of this turmoil should be dismissed. There was no point to putting herself through all this angst. Not when everyone around her had made it perfectly clear that Flora had no future with George.

Sometimes she felt like a child, gorging herself on her mother's chocolates, rather than taking just one, because they were so delicious. Even though she'd been warned she'd get sick, she'd gone headlong into disaster, then spent the next day in bed because of it.

"Hello, Flora."

"Have you met my father?" Flora gestured at him.

"I haven't had the pleasure. It's nice to meet you, Mr. Montgomery."

"Father, this is Ellen Fitzgerald, one of my new friends."

He stood and took her hand. "It's a pleasure, Miss Fitzgerald. Am I correct in thinking you're Seamus's daughter?"

"I'm the eldest." She smiled at him.

"He's said many fine things about you. I'm glad to know my daughter counts you as a friend. Will you join us?"

He gestured to one of the nearby logs as though it was the finest chair in the parlor. Flora had often forgotten that her father's roots were not in wealth, but in the same humble beginnings as many of these miners. And whether it be here in the woods or in the finest ballroom, he always managed to put people at ease. She should have paid more attention to him and recognized how he treated others. Now that she thought about it, she'd never seen him act with the same disdain for people in lower classes that she'd once had. Not that Ellen was of a lower station, but he'd treated Peanut with equal consideration.

"I'd be delighted, thank you."

Funny how, even in these primitive circumstances, everyone still managed to have impeccable manners.

Ellen sat across from Flora, in the spot George had vacated, and Flora mentally kicked herself for immediately making the connection. It wasn't as if George owned the log. Why couldn't she get him off her mind?

"I hate to impose," Ellen said, looking truly regretful that she was asking. "But I was wondering if tomorrow we could switch jobs at the mine? My dear friend, Diana Jeffries, is coming up for the day, but only the day because she has to get back to her husband and children, and it would be so much more pleasant for her to help serve water than it would be to wash dishes."

"Think nothing of it," Flora said. "Pierre loves to splash his hands in the water and play with the bubbles. It would be my pleasure to help you."

"Oh, good," Ellen said, letting out a sigh of relief. "The other girls were so beastly about trading jobs, I'd begun to despair that I'd find a solution. Everyone hates washing dishes, so I appreciate your assistance."

Flora smiled. "That's what friends are for."

Ellen leaned forward and squeezed her hand. "I will be sure to let people know how amiable and considerate you've been in helping me. I think Sarah is being unfair in her treatment of you, and you're so busy with Pierre that the others haven't had a chance to make up their minds."

Giving her a smile, Ellen continued. "Tomorrow,

FREE Merchandise is 'in the Cards' for you!

Dear Reader,

We're giving away FREE MERCHANDISE!

Seriously, we'd like to reward you for reading this novel by giving you **FREE MERCHANDISE** worth over **$20** retail. And no purchase is necessary!

You see the Jack of Hearts sticker above? Paste that sticker in the box on the Free Merchandise Voucher inside. Return the Voucher today... and we'll send you Free Merchandise!

Thanks again for reading one of our novels—and enjoy your Free Merchandise with our compliments!

Pam Powers

Pam Powers

P.S. Look inside to see what Free Merchandise is **"in the cards"** for you!

▲ If offer card is missing write to: Reader Service, P.O. Box 1341, Buffalo, NY 14240-8531 or visit www.ReaderService.com ▲

BUSINESS REPLY MAIL
FIRST-CLASS MAIL   PERMIT NO. 717   BUFFALO, NY

POSTAGE WILL BE PAID BY ADDRESSEE

READER SERVICE
PO BOX 1341
BUFFALO NY 14240-8571

NO POSTAGE
NECESSARY
IF MAILED
IN THE
UNITED STATES

when I invite you to dine with us, you will say yes, won't you? I know Diana will enjoy your company, especially if you tell her how you make those lovely hats. She's been quite envious."

"Of course. In fact, when we get back to town, I'd be honored to have you both over to learn how I do it. People think it's a silly hobby, but I quite enjoy arranging all of the elements to make a perfect hat."

With a twinge, Flora recalled George's words of admiration about her intelligence and that fashion wasn't silly at all. Oh, to be able to dismiss him as readily as everyone else wanted her to.

"Oh, it's not silly at all. We've all long thought you had a talent, but well, in the past, it was too intimidating to approach you, and then…"

Ellen looked ashamed of where her thoughts were leading, and Flora understood. When Flora became persona non grata in their circles, it would have been social suicide to ask. What Ellen offered her was the opportunity to find her way back into her former friends' good graces in a way that would be less intimidating to everyone. She'd be doing them a favor, and they'd be thinking they were getting the better end of the bargain. But hopefully, in that space, the other ladies would realize just how much Flora had changed.

"It's all right," Flora said. "I understand perfectly. Not only would it be an honor to share what I know with everyone else, but it might be a less threatening way for us all to get to know one another again."

"Exactly." Ellen smiled warmly at her. "I'll admit, I never took the time to know you before. I was always too daunted by your status. It seems silly, but I'm grateful that your circumstances changed enough that I could find the courage to speak to you. I daresay many of the other women in our circle feel the same way."

"I would agree with that," Flora's father said, joining the conversation. Flora had nearly forgotten he was there. "It seems to me that so many people would spend more time watching and admiring you from afar that I don't believe any of them truly knew you."

Flora nodded. "I was also never very warm and inviting, certainly not in the way Ellen has been to me. I should have done more to make others feel welcome and included."

"It's an honor," Ellen said. "I know you'll do just fine in the future."

"Indeed she will," Flora's father said, standing. "Now, if you ladies will excuse me, it's time for me to turn in for the night."

"We should do the same." Ellen stood and held out her hand to Flora.

Flora joined her new friend and her father, feeling more hope in her heart than she had in a long time. It seemed almost too good to be true, finding a friend in Ellen. And yet, it also felt like the most right thing she'd done in a long time. For years Flora had sought out the women with the most standing and worked to keep them in her inner circle, priding herself on surrounding herself with the best of the best.

She'd never paid much attention to Ellen, because while Ellen was from a good family, it wasn't an important one. Her father owned a successful hotel in Leadville, but it wasn't the best. Yet of all the friendships Flora regretted losing, she couldn't rightly say that any of those friends had the same depth of compassion as Ellen.

One more perception Flora was finding had changed. Perhaps her father was right. Until she'd sorted out all of the things in her life that were in flux, it was best not to put her heart on the line for something she knew little about.

Chapter Nine

Despite his plan to go to bed early, George found himself tossing and turning most of the night. Which left him exhausted the next morning as he worked in the deepest part of the mine. Punishment for getting on Dougherty's bad side, he was sure. Was there a way he could turn his family's business around and make a proper offer for Flora?

But even if there was, what happened if things fell apart again? His father used to say that the market was volatile, and it was important to keep business interests diversified in case one was doing poorly. Except it seemed like everything was in trouble right now, confirming George's opinion that there was nothing certain in life or in business. Which meant he couldn't guarantee Flora the kind of life she wanted.

He shook his head as he turned his attention back to the pile of rock he'd been moving. Running through these ideas for the thousandth time wasn't going to solve anything. Flora was the least of his worries. How could he think to add to his burdens when he still had his mother to consider? And then there was Julia, Sam and the coming baby. Yes, he knew they were Arthur's concerns, but sometimes he felt like Arthur was so consumed with business that he didn't really look at what Julia needed. Personally, George had always thought that Julia could do better than Arthur, but she loved him, and he'd do what he could to support his sister.

All that to say, why was he wasting so much mental energy on trying to find a way to make a relationship with Flora work? If that wasn't enough to consume him, he still had Pierre's father to find.

"George! You're back!" Peanut, his face so grimy that George only recognized him by his voice, joined him. "I thought Dougherty wanted you off for a week."

"Apparently I was more annoying poking around in his business."

George reached for a pick. "But if you notice, he's got me in the depths of the mine, doing the worst work. I suppose I can't get into as much trouble here."

Peanut grinned, looking more sinister than nice in the dim light. "Just as long as you steer clear of where they're blasting. It's amazing how many times people who get on Dougherty's bad side end up on the wrong end of an accident."

Looking around, Peanut continued. "Not that anyone can prove anything. But if he's mad at you, you've got to know that there's been a lot of trouble here. Folks don't talk about it, and I shouldn't be saying anything, but there's some of us that believe that the accidents that have been happening lately aren't accidents."

"I was afraid of such." George also looked around, noting that they were alone, but lowering his voice anyway. "Pierre's father was listed on the employee roll when I snuck into Dougherty's office. But when he gave us access to examine the books, it was a different set of books, and the boy's father didn't appear. Could he have met with one of those accidents, and Dougherty's afraid we'll discover it?"

Peanut looked somber. "It's possible. When did you say the man disappeared?"

"As best as we can tell, based on what Pierre has told Flora, sometime around May 17 is most likely. That's the last time he saw his father."

"Two weeks ago." Peanut sighed. "I think there was a strange explosion around that time. I can't be certain of the date, but I'll ask Billy if he can look at the log. We all thought it odd, since it came from a part of the mine that's not being worked right now. Dougherty said it was probably from some old dynamite that never went off properly and said it was too dangerous for anyone to go look at. Common story up here, and no one's stupid enough to go in if that's what's going on."

"But if someone was killed and Dougherty wanted to cover it up?"

"Wouldn't be the first person we thought Dougherty had killed. But why this man? No one here's ever heard of him."

Good question. One that no one seemed to have an answer to. Hopefully John would find something to help. He was supposed to be going in to the office later today to do some more investigating, in the guise of being more serious about purchasing the mine.

"Based on what we learned from Pierre about their arrival, they were only here a couple of days before his father disappeared. He probably didn't have time to make friends."

Peanut made a noise. "Plenty of time to make an enemy of Dougherty."

That was what George was afraid of. "Is it possible to get to the area where the explosion happened?"

Peanut frowned. "Yes, but I wouldn't recommend it. I was being straight with you when I said it was stupid. Not unless you got a death wish. That man wouldn't be the first to disappear down here. Probably won't be the last."

Considering they didn't know for sure that's what happened to Pierre's father, or even that he'd been there, George was inclined to agree. Ever since he was young, his father had told him how dangerous dynamite was and how easy it would be to get hurt or killed when using it improperly.

One more reason to hope that John would be able to get better information than George.

Light in the tunnel indicated someone was coming toward them. George picked up the pick.

"Thanks for your help, Peanut."

The other man grinned as he started pushing the ore cart the other way. They'd been talking long enough that they could get in trouble for shirking their duty, and since that was one of the reasons Dougherty was upset with George, he didn't want to give him more fuel for the fire. Or tempt the manager to turn his rage on Peanut.

As Peanut disappeared down the tunnel, the light stopped. Whoever it was most likely wanted Peanut, not George. The other men hadn't been as talkative as usual with George, probably because they were afraid of risking Dougherty's wrath. He didn't blame them. These men needed jobs, and many of the other mines weren't hiring. Plus, the mine bosses tended to talk to one another. If a man were fired for poor work habits, it would be hard to get on at another place.

One more reason to hurry and make things right here at the mine. It wasn't right that everyone here had to work in fear.

Peanut came running back to him. "Come quick. There's been an explosion up top. Them church people got hurt."

Dropping his pick, George followed, and the two men ran out of the mine. It appeared that everyone else had already exited, and the area outside the mine was in utter chaos.

The ministry had set up their operations to serve food and water to the miners near an unexcavated rock formation, but from the way debris and rubble was strewn about, it was hard to tell the rocks had ever existed.

George passed a wheel lying on the ground. From the looks of it, it had belonged to the ministry's wagon.

He ran toward where the wagon was supposed to be. Yesterday, that's where Flora and Pierre had been working.

"Flora! Pierre!"

In the din of people wailing and crying for their friends, he doubted they could hear his voice.

The air was thick with dust, making George cough. He pulled his handkerchief out of his pocket, covering his mouth and nose. An injured miner passed him, holding his arm.

Men were lying on the ground, some moaning, but others eerily silent.

Two women were huddled together, sobbing.

"Have you seen Flora and Pierre?" he asked them.

They shook their heads.

George continued closer to where the wagon was supposed to have been. He passed a piece of broken board with the partial lettering of the church's name. A sour taste filled his mouth.

Please, God.

George didn't even know what to ask for. Even through his handkerchief, the scent of blood assaulted his nostrils. More injured men lay around him, their bodies in unnatural positions.

A pile of rocks blocked his path, and a woman's foot stuck out from underneath.

"Flora!" George clawed at the rocks.

"I'll help," Peanut said, coming behind him.

The men worked together, moving rocks. He could tell others had joined in the effort, but he wasn't taking the time to check it out. With each rock he moved, he called out her name, but there was no answer.

As they cleared out more rocks, George realized the woman buried in the rubble wasn't Flora. And though he might have been relieved at the sight, it was obvious the woman was dead.

"Diana!" A woman's wail pierced his ears. "Diana is dead!"

More wails and sobs sounded behind him as he lifted the last rock from the woman's body. He turned and saw several women from the church group huddled together, sobbing.

Flora wasn't among them. Nor was Pierre.

He spied John running toward him. "Have you seen Flora?"

George shook his head. "I can't find her. Pierre is missing, as well."

As George started closer to the area where Flora would have been, John stopped him.

"Where are you going?"

"To see if…" George shook his head. He didn't want to say he needed to find her body, but at this point things looked so bleak, it seemed to be the only possibility.

"She switched jobs today. She's supposed to be by the creek, washing dishes."

George turned and ran for the creek, leaving the other man behind.

As he left the scene, he passed more injured people. More sobbing women. Then he stopped. Froze.

Flora was coming toward him, carrying Pierre. Her face was a mixture of terror and confusion.

"What happened?"

"Are you all right?"

He put his arms around her, not caring about propriety or anything else. Flora was alive. Pierre was safe.

"There was an explosion at the mine," George said, holding her close. Pierre squirmed between them, so he loosened his grip.

"I'm so glad you're all right." He gave her a final squeeze, then let her go.

Looking at her, he took in every detail of her perfect face. He thanked God she'd been at the creek, away from the danger.

Flora started to head in the direction of the mine, but George stopped her. "Don't. You shouldn't have to see that."

She stared at him as she set Pierre down. "But…the ministry. Pastor Lassiter."

John joined them, out of breath from running. "Is fine. I just ran into him. He's asked us to gather the ladies and escort them back to camp. They're headed in our direction."

Stepping away as John pulled his daughter into his arms, George watched the man's tears fall.

"Come here, Pierre," George said. The little boy didn't have to be told twice. Though he hadn't seen the devastation at the mine, the child seemed to understand that something was terribly wrong.

George held the little boy, repeating the only French he could remember that seemed to fit the situation. *"Ça va bien,"* he said over and over.

But as he turned to survey the site of the explosion, George wasn't sure he could say for certain that anything would be all right ever again.

An innocent woman had died. Many others were injured and possibly also dead. The very thing George had come to the mine to prevent had happened. Only it was more unthinkable than he could have ever imagined.

Flora tried to hold back the flow of tears as her father told her what had happened at the mine.

"I thank God you let that other woman switch jobs with you," he said, embracing her again. "I don't know what I would have done had it been you."

"What do you mean?" She pulled away and stared at him.

"Ellen's friend is dead," he said quietly. "And they haven't found Ellen yet."

It should have been her. Tears rolled down Flora's cheeks. Her one attempt at a new friendship, and because Flora had chosen to help her friend out, a woman was dead and her friend missing.

"You're safe. It's all right." Her father reached for her, but Flora resisted.

"It's not all right," Flora said. "Diana is dead, and Ellen...they died in my place."

"That's right, they did." Sarah's voice came from over Flora's shoulder.

She turned to face her former friend.

"You killed them, Flora Montgomery. Because of you, two of our friends are dead. I knew we shouldn't have listened to Ellen in giving you a chance. This is all your fault."

"That's not fair," her father said, glaring at Sarah. "And I'm ashamed of you for saying so. Your parents would be disappointed in you. Flora didn't cause that explosion. For reasons only God knows, Flora was spared, and we should all be grateful."

"Ellen and Diana were worth a thousand of Flora," Sarah said, her glare burning Flora. "I will never forgive you for being so selfish as to make them take your place today."

"But I didn't." Tears streamed down Flora's face. "Ellen asked me last night, saying she wanted a more pleasant job for Diana."

"And now you're blaming her? You're a horrible person, Flora Montgomery."

Sarah stomped away, leaving Flora staring after her.

"Sweetheart, you can't blame yourself." Her father tried to put his arms around her, but Flora resisted his embrace.

"She's right. I was supposed to be working there today. It should have been me."

More tears streamed down her face as she watched Sarah speak to the other women, occasionally looking back at Flora with such hatred in her glances that Flora couldn't imagine anything worse in the world. No, there was something worse. Dying a horrible death the way Diana apparently had, all because of a change in plans that had her taking Flora's place.

Then she saw Pastor Lassiter, leading a horse that was pulling something behind it.

As they got closer, Flora could see that it was some kind of sled and a woman lay on it, moaning.

Ellen.

Flora ran toward them. Her friend was alive. Though Flora could see blood seeping through bandages on Ellen's head, the other woman was still alive.

"John, I need you to get your horse and run for a doctor. One's already been sent for, but your horse is faster, and you're the best horseman I know. We don't have much time."

Her father dashed into action. "I brought the buggy up. Let's get Ellen loaded in there and I can drive her down. It'll be quicker than waiting for the doctor."

She followed her father, noting that George had joined them, Pierre still clinging to him. "I should take Pierre. You're probably better at hitching a horse to a buggy than I am."

George nodded, and Flora took the little boy out of his arms. Pierre looked terrified, and she realized that since he didn't understand English, all the little boy knew was that something terrible had happened. Even being fluent in French, Flora had no words to explain the tragedy that had befallen them all. She wasn't sure she could even do it in English.

Slowly, she put together as simple an explanation as she could for the child. Her voice cracked as she spoke, trying to convey things in a way he would understand.

Pierre placed his hands on her cheek. *"Ça va être bien."*

Flora closed her eyes. It was going to be all right. George. She'd seen them talking, and though they knew little of each other's language, Flora knew George had given this little boy the quiet strength to comfort her.

She watched as George helped her father hitch his horses to the buggy, the men focused on getting the job done as quickly as possible.

George had held her so tight when he'd come upon them. Clearly he'd thought that she was serving water, as well, and had feared the worst. He hadn't wanted to lose her.

And in the light of all this death and destruction, Flora wasn't sure she wanted to lose him, either.

"Flora!" Pastor Lassiter waved her over. "I need you to go with them. Sit in the back of the buggy, keeping pressure here, on the wound."

He gestured to the blood-soaked cloth on Ellen's head. "I'll have George hold her as still as possible while your father drives. I need to remain and bring order to everything, as well as see to the injured miners, but Ellen's injuries are more serious and she needs a doctor right away. Someone is coming with more bandages. The ones you have are soaked through."

"What about Pierre?" She looked down at the little boy in her arms. She wasn't willing to let him too far out of her sight. Not now, not knowing how precious life was and how easily it could all be taken from a person.

"You can bring him with you. He's small enough that there should be room. Once we get Ellen settled with the doctor, your father can meet up with me and we'll figure things out. But Ellen is our primary concern right now."

Flora nodded as she set Pierre down and took over applying pressure to Ellen's wound. The men worked together to lift Ellen into the carriage, keeping her steady while allowing Flora to continue caring for her friend.

Pastor Lassiter laid his hand on Ellen's head. "Help her, Father." Then he looked at the rest of them. "God be with you all."

As they got themselves situated, Flora found the best way to tend Ellen meant being pressed against George. Pierre was nestled against her father as he drove, and it warmed her heart to see how tenderly her father had put his arm around Pierre, keeping him close as he held the reins.

Pastor Lassiter leaned in to Flora. "I heard what Sarah said. This is not your fault. You did not cause the explosion, and you did not make Ellen trade with you. I know as well as you that she asked for the switch. This is not Ellen's fault, either. I have no answer as to the whys and wherefores of today's tragedy. But you must hold on to the belief that God is good, and He surrounds us with His love, even though we have no explanation."

Tears filled Flora's eyes, and she wished she could believe him. Yes, she knew God was good, and in a very intangible way she knew He loved them, but it seemed horribly unfair that people as good as Diana and Ellen had taken her place.

"He's right," George said, giving her a tender look. "You can't blame yourself. Other forces are at work here, and they have nothing to do with you or any one of us." A dark expression crossed his face. "Someone set that explosion, and that person will be brought to justice."

"We've already sent for the sheriff," Pastor Lassiter said. "Please don't make this about revenge, but let the law handle this."

George nodded.

One of the women arrived at the carriage, breathless from running. "Here are the extra bandages."

Flora took the new bandages, switching out the old ones, her stomach recoiling at the sight of Ellen's wound.

Please, God, don't let her die. More tears filled Flora's eyes, but she willed them back. She would stay strong for her friend.

Her father looked back at her. "Do you have Ellen settled?"

"Yes." Flora tried not to despair at the grim expression on her father's face.

He gave a quick nod, then urged the horses forward.

Flora had never seen her father drive so fast. It took every ounce of strength she had to continue applying pressure to Ellen's wound, and she was grateful for the way George's body pinned them both to the seat. Pierre was secure by her father's side.

With every thunder of the horses' hoofbeats, Flora

prayed. It almost became a sort of rhythm. *Please, Lord. Lord, have mercy.* And it was only those words that gave her the strength to carry on.

Chapter Ten

When they arrived at the hospital, people ran out to meet them. News of the tragedy had already spread through town, and the hospital was ready for the victims. From the brief snatches of conversation, Flora learned that the other injured parties, all miners, had been loaded into wagons and were being brought down.

Though she heard disdain in some of the voices that they were only miners who'd been hurt, Flora sent the same fervent prayer she'd prayed for Ellen regarding those men. They were people, too, who had families and loved ones, hopes and dreams. They hadn't deserved this, either.

Once Ellen had been whisked away, Flora turned to her father. "Please. I know this isn't your responsibility. But I've heard that the current mine owner isn't one to concern himself with the well-being of the miners. Could you please tell the hospital that you'll pay to care for the men who were hurt? And to spare no expense?"

Her father looked at her, a serious expression filling his face. "Father, please. If it's about the money, I promise I won't ask for any more dresses. Use that. But don't let these men suffer."

Tears filled his eyes as he took her into his arms. "My dear child. Of course I will help them. Thank you for revealing your heart."

Then he turned to George, who was standing nearby with Pierre. "It's too dark to return to the mine tonight, and I know Anna is probably beside herself with worry. Let's go home, get cleaned up and have a good night's sleep."

Flora looked down at her dress and realized for the first time it was filthy with dust, grime and Ellen's blood. A bath would be most welcome, but she wasn't sure it would be enough to wash away the pain of today's tragedy.

They'd barely pulled up in front of the house when Flora's mother came running out.

"John! Flora! You're safe!"

Flora hadn't had a chance to alight before her mother had put her arms around her.

"My sweet girl. You're home. I don't care what anyone says about you. I'll not have you go back to that terrible place. I want you close to me where I can keep you safe."

Her mother covered her with kisses, an ordinarily embarrassing display of affection. But Flora didn't care. Until now, she hadn't realized how good and safe it felt to be in her mother's arms.

"Now, Anna, let's get everyone inside," Flora's father said gently.

She seemed to realize where they were, and given her mother's high regard for public decorum, she nodded. "Yes, of course."

Then her mother noticed the other two passengers in the buggy. "And who might these two be?"

As Flora's father explained the situation, the expression on her mother's face darkened. Like the last thing she wanted under her roof were a miner and a child of unknown origin. But she nodded meekly when Flora's father ended his explanation with a firm, "And they'll be staying with us tonight."

Something in Flora's heart lightened when she heard her father take up for their friends. They still didn't know what had become of Pierre's father, and in all the turmoil of the day, it looked even less likely that they'd find answers soon.

They entered the house, and Agnes looked ready to pounce. But before Flora's father could tell her to back down, Agnes rushed at Flora and put her arms around her.

"Dear child, you're safe." Then Agnes pulled away. "And wearing filthy rags. I'll have a bath prepared for you straightaway."

After one last squeeze, Agnes dashed off to the kitchen.

Her mother ushered them into the parlor. "Sit, sit. It will take some time to heat the water, and I'm sure in the meantime Agnes is preparing something for you all to eat."

Then she turned to Flora's father. "John…" The tender expression in her mother's eyes surprised Flora. Though she knew her parents cared for each other, she hadn't realized that they shared such a deep love.

"Everyone's safe, Anna." He looked back at his wife with an equally loving expression.

It was foolish to think such things so soon after a

tragedy, but Flora hoped that someday she would have a love like that.

Pierre climbed into Flora's lap as soon as she was seated. She held him close to her, murmuring words of comfort in French.

He cuddled up against her, and before Flora knew it, the little boy was asleep.

Her parents were speaking in a low tone, and Flora couldn't make out their words. She looked over at George, who was uncomfortably perched on one of the chairs. Though he'd said he came from a good family, he probably wasn't used to being surrounded by such finery.

"Please, make yourself comfortable," Flora told him, trying to smile and be a good hostess, but she found herself too exhausted to make more effort than that.

Before George could answer, Agnes bustled in, carrying a tray filled with sandwiches and a pot of tea.

"Eat up, everyone. Miss Flora's bath is almost ready, then we'll get the rest of you cleaned up."

Agnes gave George a disapproving glance. Had it been up to her, she probably wouldn't have let him sit on the furniture, but with everyone else as filthy as he, it would have been hard to make the argument. Despite the fatigue that seemed to make even the slightest movement impossible, a tiny smile twitched at the corners of Flora's mouth at the thought of Agnes's dilemma.

"Let me take the boy," Agnes said gently. "I'll put him to bed."

Flora let her pick up the sleeping child. "Put him in my bed, please. He sleeps with me because, otherwise, he has terrible nightmares."

With the same frustrated set to her lips as she'd had at the idea of George ruining the furniture, Agnes nodded. The one good thing in this terrible situation, if there was one to be found, was that neither Agnes nor Flora's mother were likely to go against Flora's wishes for the time being.

They ate quickly and in silence. Though Flora would have initially argued that she was too tired to eat a bite, she devoured everything put in front of her. After her bath, she sat by the fire in the kitchen, trying to stay awake long enough for her mother and Agnes to dry her hair.

The few times Flora allowed her eyes to flutter open, she caught sight of tears rolling down her mother's cheeks.

Had her mother known just how close Flora had come to being the one dead or in the hospital, those tears would have been worse. For the first time, Flora was grateful it hadn't been her. Her poor mother had already suffered so much because of Flora.

But as Flora turned to say something to her mother, her mother patted her on the cheek and said gently, "Rest. I'm going to help Agnes put more bricks in your bed." After her mother left, Flora closed her eyes and could hear the faint sound of George and her father arguing.

"You've got to put an end to this farce, George. You're a Bellingham, with the power to make things right."

Flora stilled. George, a Bellingham? As in the Bellinghams who owned the Pudgy Boy Mine?

But that meant George was… Flora closed her eyes. Pudgy Bellingham. The little boy everyone in their circle in Denver had teased for being so fat. She'd forgotten his real name had been George. She supposed people didn't call him Pudgy anymore; after all, it had been more than ten years, fifteen at least, since Flora had seen him.

Why had he lied to her?

A sour taste filled Flora's mouth as her stomach rolled around. She'd been so cruel to him when they were children. The other kids called him Pudgy because Flora had given him that nickname. He'd called her Big Mouth Flora, the brat who couldn't keep a secret.

Despite all the wonderful and encouraging things George had said to her, he must still think her that same brat. He had to have known that the reason she was spending time working in the mission was as punishment for her gossiping ways.

"Flora, dear, are you all right?"

She could feel her mother's gaze on her, and when she opened her eyes, she saw the concern filling her mother's face.

Had she heard what Flora's father had told George?

Would it even signify to her that the man who'd been introduced to her as a miner was, in fact, the child of an old family friend?

Flora shook her head slowly. "I'm just tired, that's all."

"Yes," Agnes said, wrapping a shawl tightly around Flora. "We must get you to bed. I sponged that boy down as best as I could. Him sharing a bed with you—it's not right, I say, but I won't be going against your wishes."

Flora tried to smile, knowing she'd been right about

Agnes's feelings, but the pain in her heart dragged the corners of her lips down.

Despite everything between Flora and George, he hadn't trusted her. Of all the people in the world, he should have been able to trust her. What must he have thought, as they discussed the impossibility of a romance between them? He must have known that her family would heartily approve of such a match.

But he'd dissuaded her. Just as her father had. Knowing exactly who George was.

The backs of her eyes stung with tears. After all the crying she'd done today, surely there wasn't anything left. It was as though the last ounce of everything she had in her had to be wrung out.

A woman had died. Her friend might still very well do so. And countless others were injured. And now, the one person who'd given her the courage to believe that she might be more worthy than she ever thought possible had betrayed her in the worst way.

If her father and George had known all along that all the reasons for Flora not to be with George didn't exist, and they'd kept that from her, reminding her not to let her heart get involved, clearly it meant that George didn't share her regard—or wasn't available. Or, worse, knowing who she was, didn't trust her. But they'd given all those warnings too late. Her heart had already become irrevocably entwined with his, and now…

Flora shook her head as her mother and Agnes led her into the hall. They passed her father's study, where she saw George talking with her father and Will Lawson, one of the town's deputies. George glanced her way briefly, and her heart ached.

"You scoundrel," she whispered.

* * *

George thought he was hearing things when Flora went by, guarded by her mother and the housekeeper. The two older women seemed more concerned with keeping George from catching a glimpse of Flora in her nightclothes. But as his eyes met hers, he knew he'd heard correctly.

Despite her body looking completely broken with fatigue, Flora's eyes flashed fire and anger.

"Flora?" He took a step toward her, but Agnes glared at him.

"You stay where you are. And that's Miss Montgomery to you. I'll have no improprieties in my household. Our girl been through enough without the likes of you to make it worse. Avert your eyes like a gentleman. If you know what one is."

George forced his gaze back to John. "I'm sorry, sir. I meant no disrespect toward your daughter."

"Everyone's just tired, George. Pay Agnes no mind. It's been a difficult day for everyone."

John suddenly looked even more weary than he had a few short moments ago. The women continued down the hall, and as footsteps sounded on the stairs, George knew they'd taken Flora to bed.

"We don't know who's behind all of this," George said, continuing the conversation where they'd left off before Flora had come into the hall. "The culprits think they're safe, because George Bellingham is off studying at Harvard, living it up and unaware of what's going on. If I reveal my true identity, they're going to be more cautious, and we'll lose the element of surprise."

Will Lawson, one of the deputies assigned to investigate the case, nodded. "True. The question is, why would they take such a risk in harming innocent people?"

George had spent the entire ride to town alternating between praying for the injured, particularly Ellen, and asking himself that same question.

"I don't know. Unless it really was an accident."

"No." John shook his head. "There's no way an accidental explosion could have happened in that spot. But..." The older man sank into his chair. "Flora." He ran his hand over his face. "She's been working there. What if she was the intended victim?"

"I won't believe it," George said. "Who would want to kill Flora? People are upset with her, yes, but no one would go to such lengths as to do such a thing."

Looking as though he'd aged forty years in the past few hours, John turned his gaze back to George. "But they would hurt her to get to me."

"What enemies do you have?" Will asked, opening his notebook.

"Plenty." John's expression didn't waver. "But I think the answer is not so much about my enemies as it is about the fact that I've been looking into the mine. I've been pushing too hard to be merely an interested buyer. What if the accident was designed to harm Flora to distract me from asking questions? They had to have known that if Flora had been injured or killed, I'd be too consumed with that to pursue my interest in the mine."

George shook his head. "Why not kill you, then? Or me, for that matter? We're the ones stirring up trouble, not Flora."

Anguish filled John's face, like he knew the answer, and it wasn't one any of them wanted to hear. "It's how Ross used to operate. A man isn't afraid for himself so much as his family. What if the explosion was an accident in the sense that it wasn't meant to kill Flora, but to send a message to me that if I pursued this purchase, she'd be hurt?"

Will crossed the room to stand next to John. "Who is Ross?"

"Ross Eldridge," John said, turning to George. "I know you said he was dead, but what about his son? Could he be working the same angle his father did?"

Despite the sick feeling in the pit of his stomach, George shook his head. "I can't even imagine it. Arthur was young when his father died, so how would he know how his father operated? Besides, Arthur loves Julia. He dotes on her. Why would he force her to live in such reduced circumstances as she is now?"

Recalling the differences in the record books he'd seen, George frowned. "It doesn't make sense for Arthur to be involved. Based on the discrepancies in the payroll I saw, whoever's behind this has to be pocketing a small fortune, probably more, given that I only had a brief glance."

He looked back at the other men, feeling slightly relieved that his sister's husband couldn't be involved. "Arthur never refuses Julia a thing, but in her last letter, she talked about how she was upset that she was going to have to remake some of her gowns because they couldn't afford new this year. If he was stealing that kind of money, he'd be able to buy her new gowns."

"Could your sister be involved?" Will asked, his voice gentle, but full of enough accusation to sting.

"Julia knows nothing about the family business. Our father used to joke that the only thing she knew of finance was how to spend money."

George smiled as he remembered how defensive Julia used to get when their father teased her. Though she was younger than Flora, and the girls had never known each other, he'd always thought Flora and Julia could be friends. They had many of the same interests, and like Flora, people often underestimated Julia's compassion and intelligence.

The other men chuckled, and for a moment, the air didn't seem so heavy with death and destruction.

A quick glance out the window was all George needed to remember. From the Montgomerys' study, George had a clear view of the mountain where the mine sat.

"It's going to be extremely expensive to repair the damage," George said, turning back to Will and John. "Wouldn't it be foolhardy to cause such destruction when there's no way we can pay for it?"

George hadn't thought much about what it would all cost, not until now. The memory of the rocks and debris that would have to be cleared filled his head, making it ache. The loss, in terms of lives and people injured, was bad enough. Fortunately, as far as he knew, only one woman had been killed, but several more people were injured, and it all seemed to be too much.

To have to put a price on top of it...

"We're ruined," George told the other two men. "I honestly see no way out of this. Even with what we know of the money being stolen, it's not enough to make it worthwhile for Arthur to be involved."

He looked around the room, admiring the gleaming bookcases and fine furniture that had most likely been imported. Their home in Denver featured similar decor. All expensive, and it now seemed like a waste of money with what they were facing. "I can't see us being able to keep anything. Arthur told me that the mine was the only thing keeping us solvent. That's why I felt compelled to come here, even though he told me not to. I thought that if I could fix the things that were going wrong at the mine, that would ease the other problems."

George sat on the high-backed chair that reminded him of the one in his father's study. If only his father was here to give him wisdom about how to handle the situation.

"Your father had one just like it," John said, coming around and sitting in a nearby chair. "We thought they symbolized the success we hoped to achieve."

"It still sits in his study." George shook his head. "What once was his study, I suppose. Arthur has taken it over now."

"I understand your father recently passed away," Will said, joining them. "What happened?"

With a sigh, George turned to the other man. "It was a carriage accident a few months ago. Apparently, they were going too fast and the carriage overturned. My father was killed instantly, and my mother is still recovering from her injuries. They aren't sure if she'll ever walk again."

One more worry to add to George's plate. The doctors were so expensive. He'd already been concerned about how they were going to continue providing for her care, but now it seemed all the more impossible.

If there was any blessing to be had for his not becoming involved with Flora, it was knowing that at least she would not have to sort through the damage to his family. To suffer as they all would. Still, he couldn't forget the way she'd looked at him, as though she despised him more completely than any human being was capable of.

He shook his head. One more thing he had no ability to make right.

"Your father was going too fast with your mother in the carriage?" John asked.

George turned his head. "Yes. Why?"

"Has Honoria changed that much? She was terrified of high speeds. I can't see her allowing your father to go so fast as to make a carriage overturn."

The sick feeling in George's stomach returned. John was right. It hadn't made sense when George had been told of the accident, but then, nothing about the accident had made sense. How could it, when his father was dead?

"I was at school," George said, trying to shake the suspicion that John had planted in his head. A suspicion he didn't like at all. "All I know is what I was told."

"Who told you?" Will asked.

"I got a telegram from Arthur. He said not to come home. But how could I stay at school when my father had died? I came on the next train. Arthur met me and told me of the details."

Will made a noise in the back of his throat, and George looked at him.

"Why didn't they want you there?"

George took a deep breath as he thought about his father. "My father was so proud that he'd had the ability to send his son to a place like Harvard. No one in his family had gone to college, let alone somewhere as wonderful as that. Everyone thought it important that I continue with my father's wishes.

"They don't know I didn't go back," George said.

"I have a friend there covering for me, just in case, but so far, they seem to think I'm still there. I know they want me to honor my father's legacy, but to me, it honors him more if I do what I can to save it. Otherwise, what's the point of a degree I can't use?"

John put his hand on George's shoulder. "I know your father and I had a falling-out years ago, but for what it's worth, I believe you did the right thing, and he would be very proud of you."

George would have liked to say that he thought so, too, but at this point, he didn't even care about making his father proud. An innocent woman had died, and others had been injured. His family stood to lose everything. And though all the things they had were nice, honestly, what George cared about the most was making sure his mother would be taken care of and that Julia and her family had what they needed. Yes, Arthur could provide for them, but Julia was his baby sister, and George felt responsible for her.

Will stood and looked at George with sympathy. "I can't imagine how difficult this is for you. You've faced a great deal of loss lately."

"I don't care about that." George took a deep breath. "I'd be lying if I said I didn't miss my father. But that woman, the one who died today, she had a family, and I'm sure they will miss her every day for the rest of their lives, just like I will always miss my father. I know I didn't cause her death, but it happened at my mine, and I feel responsible for bringing whoever caused the explosion to justice. I don't care how difficult it is, whatever must be done, I'm willing to do it."

George stood, straightening his back. "So, what now? If telling the truth about my identity is what needs to be done, then so be it. But those men, they hate the Bellinghams, because they blame them for poor management and low wages. I'm willing to be hated, but I think they'll talk more to George Baxter than George Bellingham."

"I agree," Will said. "Which is why I want you to keep up the charade. We're going to put more pressure on the culprits to draw them out."

The lawman looked over at John. "I realize this potentially puts your family at risk, and I promise I will have my best men here at the house to protect them. But if you're willing, I'd like you to make it known that the accident has strengthened your resolve to buy the mine. You realize that it could have been your daughter who died, and you are going to buy the mine to prevent such a tragedy from ever happening again."

"I already intended to do so. Not just in word, but in deed. And for exactly the reason you stated. I will not be bullied or cowed in or out of a business deal. Whatever assistance I can give, you can count me in."

Will nodded. "Good. I'd like to also let it be known that George Bellingham himself will be coming to stay with you to work out the details. You'll tell people that George here is your new right-hand man to oversee the mining parts. That way, people aren't suspicious of having him around."

He turned to George. "I want you to talk to your friend at school who's covering for you and have him aware of what's going on in case people ask questions. I'll find someone to pose as George Bellingham when it's time for him to come to town."

"What about my family?" George asked.

"For now, I want them in the dark. The fewer people who know what's going on, the better."

The plan made sense. Especially because he didn't want to worry his mother or Julia. Knowing Arthur, he wouldn't be able to help himself from telling his wife. The couple had always been close, which was one of the other reasons George couldn't see Arthur knowingly being involved.

Will gave George a solemn look. "I know you say that you trust your father's advisor, Robert Cooper, but I'd like you to write down everything you know about him and all of his associates, particularly anyone who might connect him to this Ross fellow. Ross's son might be innocent, but if this is how Ross would operate, my guess is that there's someone close to the family with the same way of operating. Who better than the advisor who took over after Ross's death?"

"Of course." George nodded. "I truly believe that no one we know could be involved in something so dastardly, but I have been away at school for a couple of years now, so there could be something I'm missing. I'll do anything I can to help."

Though he tried sounding confident in his belief in his father's friends, he couldn't shake the feeling that he might be wrong. He had been gone a long time, and before college, he'd spent time traveling, because it was something his father wanted him to do. Before that, he'd been in boarding school. If George was being honest, he didn't really know anyone at all.

"Good," Will said. "A friend of mine, Owen Hamilton, will be calling on you. He used to be a deputy in Denver, but he recently bought a ranch and moved here with his family. I'm going to have him investigate your family and their connections, see if there's anything that turns up."

Will had been gently prodding him in this direction, but George finally accepted that, despite all his faith in his loved ones, he could be terribly wrong. That was the difficulty in the situation. The piece that seemed almost unfathomable. But until today, George would have said that an innocent woman dying at his mine was equally so.

Anymore, he didn't know what to believe. All he could do was hope and pray that no other innocent lives were lost in this dangerous game.

Chapter Eleven

Waking up in her own bed was a pleasure Flora hadn't thought she'd find so absolutely delectable. Who knew that one could enjoy a bed so much?

Flora stretched and smiled, then realized that Pierre was still curled up next to her.

And then she remembered everything that had happened the day before. Suddenly, it didn't feel right to enjoy having such comfort, knowing that today children would be waking up without a mother.

It should have been her.

Though everyone had been telling her differently, it didn't ease the pain in her heart that a woman had died doing a job that was supposed to have been Flora's.

Pierre stirred and looked up at her, his dark eyes full of confusion.

"Good morning," she told him gently in French as she gathered him into her arms and hugged him. If there was a positive in yesterday's horrible situation, it was that she needed to count her blessings and be sure her loved ones knew how very dear they were to her.

"Où est George?" Pierre asked, looking up at her.

Where is George? Flora sighed. The last thing she wanted was to talk about him. In the past, Flora would have made a snide comment, letting Pierre know what a horrible person George was. The liar. But not only did George's lie have no bearing on Pierre, but it hardly seemed fair to tear down one of the few people Pierre had left these days.

The old Flora wouldn't have hesitated. Would have only thought of her own rage at being deceived.

"I don't know," she told him gently. "But let me get dressed and we'll go find him."

Flora put on her robe and opened the door, peering out to see who was around.

"Miss Flora!" One of the maids was coming down the hall. "You're awake."

"I am," she told the girl, smiling. "Could you please take my young friend to the kitchen and help him find some breakfast?"

Flora turned and gave Pierre instructions in French. Then she brought her attention back to the maid. "Please be kind to him. He doesn't speak English, so if he does something wrong, do not shout. He doesn't understand, and it will only make things worse. Come get me, and I'll deal with the situation."

"Yes, miss." Then the maid bent and spoke to Flora's charge in perfect French.

"Wait," Flora said as the maid started to leave with Pierre. "You speak French?"

"My family comes from France," she said. "My mother and sisters all work for the dressmaker, producing the finest fashions from Paris. But I have no skill with the needle, so here I am."

The maid ruffled Pierre's hair. "He is adorable.

Where did he come from? Our family knows everyone from France, and I do not know anyone who has a little boy."

Flora explained the situation to the maid, who looked puzzled. "That is simply not possible. No one from my country would abandon their child like that."

"I don't think he was abandoned. Who could abandon a child like Pierre?" She took a deep breath, hating to give voice to her concern, but after yesterday's events was better able to face tragedy. "I fear something terrible happened to his father, but he seems to have disappeared without a trace. There's some mix-up at the mine as to whether or not he worked there. Could you ask among your people if they knew Pierre's father?"

"Of course! Perhaps my father knows something I don't."

"Thank you." Flora smiled at her as she took Pierre's hand. The maid turned to guide him downstairs, but Flora stopped them.

"Wait. I realize this sounds incredibly rude of me, but I don't know your name. I'm so sorry. I should know our staff, but I don't. Until recently, it didn't occur to me that you were a human being, just like me. I hope to behave differently in the future."

The young woman smiled, pretty dimples in her cheeks that Flora would not have noticed in the past. "It's Marie, Miss. And I will take good care of Pierre."

Though people in Flora's social circle had always called it unseemly to be too familiar with the help, Flora realized, as Marie left with her charge, that it seemed even more wrong not to know who was in your home, caring for your children. How could she have let someone whose name she didn't even know take care of Pierre?

Flora reentered her bedroom and looked through the dresses in her wardrobe. Though her father had teased her about buying her more, the number of dresses she owned seemed almost overwhelming. Worse, as she looked at each garment, she realized how unsuitable they were for caring for a small child.

Pierre liked to run and play, and though Flora had not yet acquired his affinity for mud, she also knew that staying neat and tidy when he was around was nearly impossible.

"Miss Flora, you're awake." Agnes bustled into the room, carrying a tray. "The maid brought the little boy down, and they are chattering up a storm. How fortunate to have someone to take that child off our hands."

"Her name is Marie," Flora said, turning her attention back to the dresses. "And she's not taking Pierre off anyone's hands. I accept full responsibility for him until we can find his father."

"Yes, of course it's Marie," Agnes said. "They're all called Marie. As for the child, I'm sure your parents will have something to say about that. Wear the pink, it brings out the color in your cheeks."

Flora glanced at the dress in her hand, and while the pink did, in fact, show off her color quite nicely, the lace along the edges was white and would get soiled too easily.

She turned and looked at Agnes. "I thought only the wealthy were supposed to be snobs. Marie is a very nice young lady, and I'm grateful for her help. My father knows how I feel about Pierre. He will be staying with us. Say nothing further on the subject."

With a sigh, Flora turned to the tray. "Things are going to be different around here now, Agnes. I have to think more about what's best for Pierre. And I have to do more to show my concern for those around me, not in looking down on them in judgment, but in seeing them as my fellow human beings."

After pouring herself a cup of tea, Flora sat in one of her chairs. "I shouldn't have called you a snob. I'm sorry."

She watched as the older lady looked through Flora's wardrobe.

Agnes turned, holding up a green dress. "I suppose I am a snob, miss. I'm a firm believer that everybody has their place and they should keep to it. I think it's good that you wish to be kind to this maid. More mistresses should. But that doesn't mean they're your equal. Wear this one. Folks have been calling, and you won't want to be an embarrassment to your family. I'll get the boy bathed. Your father purchased some clothes for him."

Agnes's gruff tone betrayed her frustration in being thwarted by Flora and her father. It felt good to know that at least Flora's father was on her side.

And, as Flora examined the dress, she was pleased to notice that Agnes had chosen something suitable.

"I'd forgotten about this one. It's perfect," Flora said.

"I saw the way you turned your nose up at the lighter-colored dresses. On account of the child, I imagine. Not that I blame you. Boys are filthy creatures, and I am so grateful that your parents weren't blessed with one. I know every man wants an heir, but some things are not worth the sacrifice."

Agnes kept muttering to herself about what a burden it was to deal with small boys, and Flora had to stifle a laugh. She'd had her own moments of horror caring for Pierre, particularly when he'd found insects and other equally disgusting items to show her. But oddly enough, those moments were part of what made her love the little boy so dearly.

Once Flora finished dressing, she went down to the parlor, where her mother was sitting with Rose Jones.

"Rose! I'm so glad you came. It wasn't the same at the camp without you."

With a pang, Flora remembered the one other friend she'd made up there. "Is there any word of Ellen? She and I became friends after you left, and I've been worried about her."

"No change," Rose said as she gestured to the chair beside her. "But the doctors think that she'll recover."

Flora took the seat beside her friend. "I hope so. I feel terrible about what happened to Ellen, and I wish I could do something."

"That's why I'm here." Rose gave her a gentle smile. "I know you blame yourself for what happened, but you need to remember that you didn't cause Ellen's accident. You have to let this go."

"All right." It wasn't an agreement Flora wanted to make, but from the expression on Rose's face, she wasn't going to accept anything else.

The door opened, and Milly, Rose's stepdaughter, came running in. "Miss Flora! I bringed you a fwower! Pierre helped me. Not Ma-few. Him's still too little."

Milly ran into her arms and handed her a rose from the garden. Flora sniffed it and smiled.

"It's beautiful. You've met Pierre?"

George entered the room, holding Pierre's hand, followed by Silas, Rose's husband, holding Rose's infant son, Matthew.

"Flora!" Pierre ran to her, telling her about the flower he'd found for her. The boy chattered about meeting Milly, who, despite being just a little girl, was very nice. He also talked about Marie and how welcome she'd made him feel.

"Now that everyone's had a chance to say hi, I'll take the children back outside to play," Silas said. "I know you all have a lot to discuss."

"Thank you," George told him. "It's good to see Pierre playing with other children."

"I'm happy to do so. Especially since you're working with Will to bring whoever caused this horrible tragedy to justice. It might have happened at the Pudgy Boy, but those of us at other mines, like the Mary May, we're nervous. If it can happen there, it can happen anywhere, and we all want to keep our loved ones safe."

Silas managed the Mary May mine, owned by Rose's family, so Flora could understand his concern. Flora gave Milly and Pierre one last hug each, and they followed Silas out while George sat in a nearby chair.

For the first time since he'd entered the room, Flora looked at George. Though still dressed like a worker, in clean clothes, with his hair washed and slicked back, he was quite handsome, indeed. Not that Flora cared about such things. George could be the handsomest man in the world, and she wouldn't care. Not even when his eyes looked at her with such…

She turned her head away, focusing her gaze back on Rose. It didn't matter what George was thinking, or how he looked at her. The pain of his lie ate at the pit of her stomach. Of all the terrible things Flora had said or done, she'd never befriended someone, toyed with their feelings and completely lied about who she was.

Why couldn't he have believed in her enough to trust her with his secret?

George hated the way Flora looked at him—so much disdain and disgust. What had changed between them since coming down the mountain? It was like Flora had turned into a completely different person.

No, that wasn't true. She was still loving and kind to Pierre, and even Milly. But she acted like George was waste stuck to the bottom of her shoe.

Then again, they were back in civilization. In Flora's parlor, where a miner would never dare set foot. Even the housekeeper had looked down her nose at him, acting as though he didn't deserve to be in such a fine house as this. He'd have had to have been deaf to not hear her arguing with John about allowing the likes of George to sleep in their guest room. Not wanting to cause trouble in the household, George had chosen to sleep in the barn.

At least it would continue to help sell the ruse that he was a mere miner, and that George Bellingham would be on his way soon. After all, most good families wouldn't allow someone of such low status to grace their halls. George just wished it hadn't meant being right about Flora. There was no way she'd be able to accept the kind of life he had to offer.

The sheriff had closed the Pudgy Boy Mine, pending an investigation. John was at the sheriff's office with the sheriff, Will and Dougherty, discussing how the investigation should proceed. Dougherty was refusing to allow John access to any of the records, even though they had approval from George Bellingham.

George sighed and focused his attention on the ladies. He'd have preferred to be in with the men, but Dougherty said George had no business in there.

"George, what do you intend to do for work, now that the mine is closed?" Rose asked, smiling at him.

"For now, Mr. Montgomery has asked me to work with him, sorting out the status of the mine." Then he looked at Flora and smiled. "Plus, I promised a little boy I'd help find his father. Now that the law is involved with the mine, Will has said that they'll also look into Pierre's father's disappearance."

Flora gave him a frosty look and turned her head away, then focused her gaze on her cup of tea.

"I don't understand why the law hasn't been involved before now," Flora's mother said. "It's disgraceful that a child would be left on his own like that."

"Mother, I told you, we think something bad happened to Pierre's father, preventing him from being able to return for him."

"Yes, but you are a young lady, not a lawman." The fierce gaze Flora's mother gave her brought a smile to George's lips. There was no doubt where Flora got her iron will.

"Ma'am, I believe a missing person report was filed with the law. I understand that they get many such reports, and since there was no evidence of a crime, it wasn't a priority."

"Disgraceful," Flora's mother said again, frowning. Then she turned to her daughter. "I just can't understand how you came to be involved in this mess."

Flora let out a long sigh, and in the time George had

gotten to know her, he'd come to find that sound endearing. She was trying so hard to be patient and get her mother to understand the changes in her life, just as she was trying to convince everyone else, but no one seemed to be able to see through their image of who she'd once been. Sometimes it made George glad he hadn't known the old Flora—the grown-up one at least. His vision wasn't clouded by the times she seemed to regret so much.

"I told you, I was the only person who could communicate with him. And now…" Flora looked out the window, presumably to where the children were playing. "I love him. Pierre is a darling child, and he deserves someone who cares for him. Until we find his father, I'm going to be there for him."

"And what if you don't find his father?" her mother asked.

Flora shrugged, her gaze still focused out the window. "I'll keep him for as long as he needs me."

"That's so kind of you," Rose said, smiling. "Anyone can see that you have a special connection with Pierre. I hope, when his father is found, that he'll allow you to still spend time with Pierre."

"I hope so, too," said Flora. "It breaks my heart to think of never seeing Pierre again."

The expression on Mrs. Montgomery's face softened. "You do care about this child, don't you?"

Flora nodded, and the gleam in her eyes once again made George wish things could be different between them. Only a fool would miss the tenderness and longing, the depth of emotion in a woman who had no reason to care, except that she chose to open her heart to a boy who needed it.

"Well, I suppose we must do our best to make him feel at home." Mrs. Montgomery sounded like she was steeling herself for an unpleasant task, but her words made Flora smile.

That, at least, was reason to give George hope.

"I agree," Rose said. "And with that, I'm going to check on Silas and the children. He tries, but sometimes I do wonder what he's thinking in what he allows them to get away with. Mrs. Montgomery, won't you join me? I understand you speak passable French and can help with Pierre."

At first the older woman looked like she might refuse. But Flora shot her a meaningful glance, and George realized what was going on. Flora must have asked Rose to get her some time alone with him. Perhaps he'd misheard Flora's words last night.

Mrs. Montgomery gave Flora a hard look, then turned her attention on George. "We'll be right outside and will return shortly."

What was she expecting, that he'd ravish Flora as soon as they were out of the room? George tried not to groan. But, he supposed, Mrs. Montgomery was only looking out for her daughter.

As soon as Rose and Mrs. Montgomery were out of the room, Flora turned to him.

"I know who you are," she said.

Before George could respond, she continued. "My father did not break your confidence. I overheard last night."

It *did* make him feel better to know that John hadn't betrayed him, but it was a good reminder of why they had to be so cautious in their endeavors. Who else had overheard them? Mrs. Montgomery? No. She'd be less hostile if she knew he came from a good family, as would Agnes.

"Flora, I need you to—"

"Not gossip about you?" She stood, looking at him with such venom in her eyes that he almost didn't recognize her. "I don't do that anymore. I can't believe that after all the time we've spent together, you would still have questions about my character, that you wouldn't trust me."

Her eyes were filled with pain, and George took a step toward her. "That isn't what I was trying to say. I never meant to hurt you. You have to believe me."

"I don't have to do anything," Flora said, tears in her eyes. "Why couldn't you trust me?"

"Because…" George took a deep breath, trying to find the right words. "I didn't know who to trust. And when I realized I could trust you, there were too many reasons I couldn't reveal the truth."

"Like what?" She stepped into his space, her face turned up to his, inches away.

The pain, the anguish, the rejection he'd inadvertently placed in her heart stared at him, making him feel like an even bigger heel than he'd thought he'd been in keeping this information from her.

All he wanted was to fix it, to make it better.

So George did the only thing he could think of. He closed the gap between them, and he kissed her.

A full-on, deep kiss, projecting all the emotion he'd been trying to hide. Things he had no business feeling, except that Flora was hurting, and he had to let her know how desperately he cared for her.

For a moment, Flora kissed him back, then somewhere in the house, a door slammed, and she jumped away.

She stared at him with an expression of absolute bewilderment.

"That's why," George told her. "There's something between us, and I've done my very best to fight it. But Flora Montgomery can't be courted by a miner. And George Bellingham isn't here."

"But…you could have told me."

"No." He shook his head. "Even if you kept my identity a secret, you would have treated me differently. People would know something was amiss because of the affection you were bestowing upon a miner."

"Even if?" Flora shook her head as she stepped away, wiping her mouth. "No, you don't trust me. You're like all the others, thinking I'm a pretty face, willing to amuse yourself with me. But when it comes to sharing the deep parts of your heart, you let my reputation get in the way."

George's stomach fell. "I didn't mean it that way. You're twisting my words. All I meant was that while I knew you would keep my secret, it wouldn't stay a secret, not because of anything you would say, but of how you would act. Every time things started to look like we might be getting close or having an affection for one another, you would pull away, and it was obvious you were fighting your feelings for me because they could never be. If you knew who I was, you would have had hope that we could someday be together, and you wouldn't have pulled away."

"You pulled away, too!" Her eyes were red with unshed tears, and George hated himself for putting them there.

"I did," he said gently. "Because I knew the truth, and the truth is, you are right to think of me with the same status as a mere miner. The situation at the mine will be the ruination of my family, though it was well on its way prior to the accident. I cannot support a wife. I cannot offer for your hand in any honorable fashion."

Watching the emotions play across her face was like watching himself being slowly tortured by a villain of his own making.

"Then why did you kiss me?" Her voice was soft, hesitant and spoke of a deep betrayal that made him feel even worse.

"I know I shouldn't have," he said. "I apologize. I should not have taken such liberties. Sometimes when I'm with you, I can't think straight, and I forget myself."

The way she looked at him made it even worse. Not that he'd expected her forgiveness or even understanding. But she looked at him like he'd crushed something in her.

"Flora, I didn't mean to hurt you."

"Well, you have," she said, looking forlorn. "I suppose I should be more understanding. After all, I've done my share of hurting people, but I can't understand…"

Flora shook her head. "I shared things with you that I've never shared with another human being. I trusted you. But you didn't trust me. You don't know how I would have acted. Maybe I wouldn't have acted any differently. Especially since you're telling me that there's no way we can be together."

If there was anything that would make him feel

worse, it was how she pointed out the difference in the way she'd treated him. She'd been open with him, trying to be a better person and prove her worth. He hadn't done the same for her.

He'd been too worried about keeping his secrets to think about how they affected her.

"I'm sorry," he said again. "But hopefully we can start again."

The look she gave him tore his heart in two. "And what would be the point of that? It is, as you say, impossible for us to be together. Since you don't want me treating you any differently, I see no point in changing things."

She straightened, looking in the direction of the door. "However, I do think that in light of the fact that we're back in town, and I am trying to reestablish my reputation, that you keep your distance from me. I have no problem with keeping your secret."

The front door opened, and the sound of children laughing greeted his ears. Only a few seconds left with Flora, and then it would be back to the cold shoulder.

"Flora, I just…"

She shook her head. "I understand that you'll want to spend time with Pierre, but please keep your attempts at personal conversation with me to a minimum."

Before he could answer, Pierre ran into the room, a wide smile filling his face. "George!"

He leaped into George's arms, and George held the little boy tight.

The other ladies entered the room, and over the little boy's head, he caught a look passing between Flora and her mother. He should have known that this was what the other woman wanted and that she was guiding Flora in her decisions.

However, this wasn't just Flora's mother speaking for her daughter. No, the hurt in Flora's eyes was real, and George hated that he was the man responsible. Hopefully someday he'd find a way to make it right.

Chapter Twelve

Flora's mother bustled around the house, preparing for guests like she hadn't done since before Flora's fall from grace. On one hand, it made Flora happy to see her mother in such a good mood. Her father had asked her to invite all the important ladies of Leadville to tea to share the news about George Bellingham's impending arrival. It had been far too long since her mother had had the joy of entertaining like this. Yet Flora knew she was the one responsible for the lack of entertaining in their home these past few months.

"Flora, find me that lace tablecloth Mrs. Crowley admires so much. Agnes can't remember which one it was, and I know you do, so please go and get it."

Then her mother turned and looked at little Pierre. "And do change his tie. I know you like the blue, but I've been told the green is all the rage. Marie is going to take him after we've made all the introductions, yes? It's not proper, including the child like he's one of the family, but everyone's heard about him, and has been praising you for doing your Christian duty by the boy, so I think he ought to be introduced."

Before Flora could respond to any of her mother's requests, her mother continued. "And please change your dress. I didn't have that silk brought in just so it could gather dust in the closet and you go around wearing rags. You have one of the finest wardrobes in all of Leadville, and I'm quite disappointed that you haven't been showing it off since you've been back. I know it wasn't right to dress so fine at the mining camp, but here, we have an obligation as pillars of society."

Only a few short months ago, Flora would have been inclined to agree with her mother. After all, she'd spent much of her time just like her mother, fussing over details that she thought would most impress everyone else. But she hadn't once given thought to what was the most important example to those around her—the kind of character she showed to others.

But that wasn't something to discuss now, not with her mother frantically preparing for what would appear to be an effortlessly flawless tea with many of the leading matrons of society. The ladies were all coming to discuss the situation at the mine now that word was out that Flora's father was going to purchase it and that George Bellingham himself was coming to stay with them to finalize the deal.

Though rumor had it that the Bellingham fortune was in trouble, rumor also had it that Mr. Montgomery was prepared to pay a great deal of money for the mine, making the Bellinghams very wealthy, indeed.

Gossip. The very thing that had gotten Flora into trouble, and yet both George and her father were doing their best to spread all kinds of false information. She'd have liked to discuss this with George, to understand why they felt the need for this course of action, because he always had a way of explaining things to her that made her feel a part of everything going on around them.

Flora shook her head. She wasn't part of anything. He'd made that clear when he'd failed to take her into his confidence.

She grabbed the tablecloth her mother wanted and set it where her mother would easily see it, then took Pierre by the hand.

"Let's get you ready for the tea," she told him in French. As they climbed the stairs, they passed Marie, who greeted them warmly in her own language.

It was such a difference to see how friendly things could be with the staff once you took the time to get to know them. She'd always thought Marie standoffish, and Flora supposed she hadn't been nice to the girl, either. Why should she? Marie had just been the help to her. But now Flora saw her as a human being, in need of compassion just like anyone else.

"Are you still going to watch Pierre during the tea?" Flora asked, giving the other woman a smile.

"*Oui.* I was hoping you wouldn't mind if I brought Pierre with me to my cousin's. They are having a small party for his son's birthday, and it would be good for Pierre to have a chance to speak with children in his language. And I will have a chance to ask my father if he knows Pierre's family. He has been so busy with work, I have not seen him."

Though Flora agreed it would be good for Pierre, she wished she could be there to see the sweet boy getting to play with others and finally be around his own people. Not that there was anything wrong with the people Pierre had been spending time with, but she recognized a longing in him that she couldn't fill. The poor child had lost so much, and Flora wished she could somehow give it back to him.

"I think that would be good for him," Flora said, ruffling Pierre's hair. "Mother wants to introduce him to her friends, and then he'll be free to go."

Marie made a noise. "Like a trained monkey. You rich people, showing off your children but not letting them be children. Pierre will have more fun with me."

In the past, Flora would have been insulted by Marie's words and chastised her for not knowing her place. But now, she could recognize the truth in the other woman's words. At least in part.

"I agree that children need to play. But it's also good for them to know how to act according to society. Whether we like it or not, there are rules of deportment, and you must follow them to live in our world."

"I do not like your world," Marie said, switching to French. "You might have the fine houses and beautiful gowns, but you lose sight of the important things in trying to maintain them. It is an illusion, and you are foolish to think it is anything but temporary."

Sometimes, Flora thought the other woman didn't realize how good Flora's French was, because the woman spoke rapidly in her own language, like she needed to say it, but was afraid Flora wouldn't like what she had to say.

"I agree," Flora said in French, smiling. "You are right that much of what we hold dear is an illusion, though you are wrong that I have lost sight of that. I believe for the first time in my life, I am learning what is important, which is why I have devoted myself to Pierre's care."

Marie gave a nod. "Perhaps. But I remember what a spoiled girl you were. Only time will tell if you have changed, or if this is merely another of your whims."

Then, in English, Marie said, "Just remember that you are playing with a little boy's fragile heart. Do not abandon him when he becomes inconvenient."

Flora stared at Marie, then looked at the child standing between them. Though Pierre understood most of their conversation, at least in terms of the words, they were adult concepts he would know nothing about.

With a smile, Flora answered in English. "I will forgive you the insult because I know you care about him, as well. Rest assured that I am fully committed to being there for Pierre, whatever it takes."

"Flora!" her mother called from downstairs.

"Come, Pierre," Flora said, giving the little boy a warm look.

She helped Pierre with his tie, then got him settled playing with a toy train her father had brought home for him. Her mother might still not be sure about Pierre's place in their home, but Flora's father had already taken to spoiling the boy.

Once Flora had changed into something more suitable, she heard voices in the corridor.

"I'd like to accompany you to your cousin's," George was saying.

George. Flora tried not to sigh at the thought of him. She couldn't hear Marie's response, so she leaned in closer to the door to try to hear the conversation. She'd once excelled at listening on the other side of doors to overhear other people's conversations.

"Flora." Pierre tugged at her skirt. "Open door? See George?"

He looked at her with his big, brown eyes, and the way he spoke, in faltering English—could he be any more lovable?

And he was right. She shouldn't be listening at doors. If she wanted to know what George's plans were, she should just ask. But that meant talking to him. They hadn't spoken since Flora had asked him to maintain his distance. Which he had.

Was it wrong to miss their easy conversations? To have someone with whom she could discuss the tumultuous feelings at the changes in her circumstances? People who hadn't deigned to look her way in months were now coming to tea, and she owed it all to the impending arrival of the Bellingham heir. Him. Only not.

Flora opened the door and they entered the hallway. She tried pasting a smile on her face, but she knew George would see right through it.

"George!" Pierre brushed past her to greet the man who spent way too much time occupying her thoughts.

"Pierre!" George wrapped the little boy in his arms as he always did.

"George play wiv Pierre?" The little boy looked up hopefully at George, and Flora found her heart breaking just a little bit more.

Of course George would play with Pierre. It wasn't in his nature to refuse the child anything, and the open love between the two created a longing in Flora that made it almost impossible to breathe.

Why couldn't George have trusted her? Flora shook her head. For as many times as this thought went round and round in her mind, she was no closer to answers than she'd been when she'd asked him that question. Besides, the more she thought about it, the more she realized that, at the very core, it wasn't so much about trust as it was about the depth of their feelings for each other. Flora had cared for George enough to share all of her secrets, but George…

Taking a deep breath, Flora willed herself not to let the tears form.

"George will play with Pierre," George said slowly, making his words clear for the boy to understand. Then he turned to Marie. "How do you let him know that I'll be joining you two today?"

As Marie bent and spoke to Pierre, Flora tried not to resent the way George had come to rely on her instead of Flora. After all, that's what she wanted, wasn't it? She'd asked to communicate only when it was absolutely necessary in regard to Pierre. And now that Marie could help him translate, Flora wasn't necessary.

Shifting awkwardly as he stared at his feet, George looked just as uncomfortable in Flora's presence as she was in his. But it was his own fault, considering it was his misrepresentation of the truth that had gotten them there.

Pierre turned to George. "You…" Looking as though he was trying to find the right word, he glanced at Flora. *"Viens?"*

"Come," Flora said.

With a smile, Pierre said the entire phrase. "You come? George come?"

"George come," George confirmed, picking the little boy up and tickling him.

Pierre giggled, and Flora couldn't help but admire the way George connected with the child. Though Pierre could never be difficult to love, it was hard to have her heart torn every time Flora saw him with George.

"And now we must finish preparing for our tea. Then you can go with George and Marie, all right, Pierre?"

As if her mother understood the pull on Flora's heart, Flora heard her mother call her name.

"We must go," she told Pierre in French, taking his hand. "You'll be back with them again soon."

She felt George's eyes on her as they turned to go back downstairs. Part of her wanted to hear him call to her, to offer some kind of pleasantry or at least give an indication that he was just as miserable as she. But, she supposed, that was foolish thinking, considering none of it was possible.

The distance between them became even more excruciating the longer George and Flora didn't talk.

Every time George summoned the courage to say something to Flora, her mother found a way to interrupt. Either Mrs. Montgomery hadn't been let in on George's secret, or she thought that a Bellingham in reduced circumstances wasn't a good fit for her daughter. Rightly so, considering George didn't know how all this was going to end or how he could offer for Flora in an honorable way.

But there was the other reason he hesitated in pursuing Flora. From his vantage point in the kitchen, he could see her smile as she warmly greeted each of her guests. This was Flora Montgomery in her element. She'd seemed happy enough at the camp, spending time with Pierre, caring for him, but George had also seen the longing in her eyes. Flora wanted more. And here, wearing a silk gown, the likes of which he'd likely never be able to afford, she sparkled and shone brighter than the jewels adorning all the women in the room.

Flora's melodic laugh filled George's ears, and though it made him happy to hear the sound, he could only feel dismay that he'd never hear it directed at him again.

The trouble with wanting to offer for a woman in an honorable way was that there was nothing honorable about taking a woman from a life she loved and forcing her to live a life that didn't suit her. Sometimes he asked God why He'd put a woman like Flora in his life when He knew it wasn't meant to be. But God never answered, and George just had to trust that God had a plan in all of this, somehow. He couldn't imagine meeting someone better than Flora, but he also didn't have the imagination God had. To find someone with the gentility, kindness and earnest desire to be a more Godly woman that Flora had, but who would also be willing to live the adventure of a life that had no certain provision, would be one incredible task, indeed.

"It is not good to moon over what you cannot have," Marie said, coming up behind him. "She is like the beautiful flowers of my country. The cherry blossoms, the peonies, the lilies. But they cannot live here in the mountains. The weather, it is too harsh, too difficult. They will die. Even if your flower would be permitted to marry beneath her, you would pluck her from a delicate garden and throw her out in the harsh elements."

George turned and looked at her. Though Marie didn't have all the facts in the situation, she was right. Flora was a flower who belonged in the garden of society, a place where she thrived. He couldn't ask her to come to the mine with him and wither.

When George was a child, his mother used to tell him that even though he loved the flowers he found on their walks, the best way to show his love was to leave them growing in their places so that everyone could enjoy their beauty.

Flora laughed again, and as the other ladies joined in, it only served to confirm George's resolve to keep his distance. Yes, she hated him, and as much as he'd like to make things right with her, it was better this way. Better to keep the longing hidden and under wraps where no one knew how much his heart was breaking.

He smiled at Marie. "Do you think we can take Pierre now? I hate to interrupt if they're having fun, but I haven't had much time to spend with him lately."

Marie looked at him as though she didn't believe him at all. "I do not understand you people and your fascination with this child. Someday, you will have a boy of your own, and you will not need Pierre. And then what? Will you toss him in the streets like the fine dresses Miss Flora considers rags because they are no longer fashionable?"

"We're talking about a boy, not a dress." George glared at the woman. "I'm surprised at you for thinking so little of her. She's a good woman and does not deserve your criticism."

With a shrug, Marie said, "Maybe not. But you do not know her like I do. You have not spent time catering to her whims that change faster than the weather. What will happen to this poor boy when she tires of him?"

"You have obviously not spent time talking to her, seeing how she's grown as a person. Her dedication to Pierre is inspiring. She truly loves him. As for me, if I am to be so blessed with a boy of my own, he will be no more dear to me than Pierre, and I hope that they will be friends."

"You would take him from his father?"

George shook his head. "I would hope that his father and I could become friends, and that he would allow me to always remain a part of his life."

Then George took a deep breath and looked at Marie with what he hoped to be sincerity. It was hard to say, considering the woman was constantly questioning him and his motives.

"Which is why I wanted to come with you today. Though I always hope to be part of Pierre's life, the boy needs his father. I hope your father can help me find him. I want what's best for Pierre."

"Even if it means returning him to his father?" Marie looked doubtful.

"I recently lost my father," George said. "I know the pain of not having a father you dearly love to confide in and share your life with."

Though the pangs of loss were coming less frequently now, particularly with how busy George was in looking into the explosion at the mine and looking for Pierre's father, there were moments when he ached at the loss of the man he'd so admired and looked up to. His father could always be counted on for his sage advice, and George would have loved to have been able to sit down with him and go over all of these troubling situations to find wisdom.

"And I know the pain of having someone take you in because they have no children and you have no parents, but to then be discarded when their own children come along," Marie said. "My mother still speaks of the hurt she suffered when it happened to her. You mean well, I know this. But do not toy with a child's heart. What happens if you do not find Pierre's father? Will you care for him forever?"

The pain written in the woman's eyes made her arguments against Flora make sense. They were less about Flora and her character and more about the heartache Marie's mother had suffered.

"I will do whatever is necessary for Pierre. Return him to his father, or adopt him as my own son. There is nothing I won't do for him."

George gave the woman a gentle smile. "I am sorry for the way your mother was treated. I can't imagine how much it must hurt to have been abandoned by someone you thought loved you. But I am not those people, and neither is Flora."

With a sigh, George realized just how little credit he'd given her by not confiding in her. He hadn't examined the true depth of her character and the strength of her heart. Though he had no idea how he would have done things differently, he wished he'd found a way to more carefully consider Flora and her feelings.

"Thank you for that," Flora said quietly, entering the kitchen with Pierre in tow. "I appreciate that you do not find me completely lacking in human decency."

"I don't find you lacking at all," George said, turning to her. "In fact, Marie's concerns over our intentions toward Pierre only serve to remind me just how greatly I wronged you by keeping the truth from you. We think we know a person, what they would say, what they would do, but we often make decisions for them based on what we think will happen rather than letting that person choose. I chose for you, Flora, and I apologize."

As the words came out of his mouth, he knew that

her ability to keep his secret wasn't the only decision he'd made for her. Could he say for certain how she'd react to the only kind of life he could give her?

"I accept your apology," she said. Then she turned to Pierre and bent to speak to him in French. Once she was finished, she brought her attention back to George again.

"He's all yours. I hope you both have a wonderful time."

Flora turned to walk back into the parlor.

"Please wait," George said, hoping they weren't going back to her cold treatment of him.

"Is there something else you needed?"

"Do you think we could talk about…things…later?"

She stared at him like he'd just spoken in fluent French. "What do we have to talk about? Pierre seems to be doing just fine, and if it doesn't have anything to do with his care, I believe I've made myself quite clear that I have nothing further to say to you."

Giving him one of the fake pleasant smiles he'd come to despise, Flora turned and walked away. When she re-entered the parlor, George heard the murmur of voices, then Flora's sweet twitter of laughter. Only now it didn't seem so sweet.

Chapter Thirteen

"Flora, I declare that miner hanging about is a disgrace," Sarah said, fanning herself to hide what was probably a smirk. The other girl was only here because she wanted to hear the gossip about George Bellingham's coming visit. But having a miner around was probably just as juicy of a tidbit for Sarah.

"Not at all," Flora said with a forced smile as she poured another cup of tea. "Father quite depends on him, and he's rather good with Pierre. It would be a disgrace to send away a man who is so important to our family."

"I knew it! You do have an understanding with him." Sarah smiled broadly.

"If by *understanding*, you mean that Mr. Baxter knows that there can never be anything romantic between us, then, yes, we do have an understanding."

"Indeed," Flora's mother said, straightening. "Surely you know by now that the Bellinghams are an important family connection, and with George Bellingham coming to stay with us, we have high hopes that the connection will be strengthened."

Flora stared at her mother. Was it possible that she

honestly didn't know who George was? As her mother
went on and on about how the Montgomerys were committed to renewing ties with the Bellinghams after their
friendship had been so tragically lost all those years
ago, Flora could hardly put a coherent thought together.
Why hadn't her father told his wife the truth about the
man they harbored under their roof?

However, as Flora continued listening to her mother
tell the others about how, when their children were in
infancy, she and Mrs. Bellingham would dream about
the day their children might someday form an alliance,
Flora became more convinced that her mother had no
idea who George was.

If her mother knew the truth, she'd have accepted
George and made him feel welcome. She wouldn't have
encouraged Flora to make sure he understood that she
could never marry a man like him. Her mother wouldn't
have gleefully been able to tell everyone about how
George Bellingham was coming to stay with them and
how excited she was to see how the little boy she'd had
such fondness for had grown up.

Flora closed her eyes. Her mother would have had
to lie to all these women. Just as Flora was doing now.
Playing along with a farce because that's what was re-
quired of her.

"Are you all right?" Sarah asked, turning her fan
to Flora.

"Quite," Flora said, pasting on a smile. "I'd forgotten just how close our families once were."

"True, true," her mother said. "Do you know that
Flora is the reason some people called poor George
Pudgy as a child?"

"Mother, I'm certain he wouldn't appreciate that

story. I'm sure he's changed." Flora wished she could run away from all this reminiscing and the reminder of her unkind past.

"Indeed. I heard he's quite handsome now," her mother said with a smile.

One of the other ladies leaned in closer to Flora's mother. "I heard the very same thing. He has quite the reputation for being a ladies' man at Harvard."

The chatter around her all turned to speculation about the kind of man George Bellingham had grown up to be. The old Flora would have told them all. He was handsome, far more than even their wildest imaginings could have come up with. None of them would have understood how his eyes shone in such a way that made a woman want to forget herself. Or how he listened and made her feel like what she had to say was important. Or even how he was willing to give his heart to a little boy who'd lost his father.

George Bellingham was far more man than the ladies in the room gave him credit for, but Flora was powerless to say so. All she could do was murmur noncommittally and pretend she didn't have this secret welling up inside her.

Sarah leaned in to Flora and whispered, "Are you going to let him court you?"

No. She'd already rejected him soundly. Though part of her continued to question whether or not it was the right thing to do. Not because he was George Bellingham, from a proper family, but because, as the women in the room extolled all the virtues of what a man ought to be, Flora couldn't deny George had all those qualities and more. But what did any of those things mean when the man himself didn't believe her worthy of his trust?

"I don't know," Flora said, giving the other girl an honest answer.

"Well, make up your mind quickly. If you don't want him, then I'll have Mother invite him to supper."

Because that's all an eligible bachelor was to any of them. A potential husband. A commodity to be traded like a favorite recipe.

"You're welcome to do so," Flora said with a smile. "I'm sure the gentleman is more than capable of choosing what he wants."

Besides, she was fairly certain the gentleman in question would have nothing to do with Sarah, no matter how many machinations she tried.

Sarah seemed pleased with the answer, because the other girl sat back in her chair, practically preening at her victory. But what was won, exactly? And why did Flora feel so much discontent at a conversation that should have made her wildly happy? After all, this was what her previous friendship with Sarah had been like. Giggling over eligible bachelors and deciding who got to pursue whom.

As much as Flora once thought the idea appealing, suddenly it didn't seem so attractive, after all.

"Has anyone had word of Ellen? Is her condition improving?" Flora asked, interrupting the flow of conversation. But she simply couldn't waste any more of her energy speculating on a gentleman that Flora already knew more about than she should. Surely there were more important things to discuss.

Sarah gave her an odd look. "No, I don't believe we have. I'm surprised. Why would you give that any thought?"

"She and I became friends at the mining camp. It's only natural I'd be concerned for her."

"I don't know why," Sarah said. "Her family really doesn't signify. What happened to her was a tragedy, of course, but they don't have much social standing, do they?"

Flora tried not to sound as discouraged as she'd felt. Sarah had been so harsh with her at the time of the accident, and now that Flora's standing had risen, Sarah's nasty words to Flora seemed to be forgotten. What good was working to regain a friendship when she wasn't sure she wanted that friendship, after all? Worse, as everyone murmured in agreement with Sarah, Flora felt deep shame at the remembrance that once she'd have been right there with them.

"She's a delightful young lady," Flora said slowly. "It's a shame that you haven't developed a deeper friendship with her. As for one's significance, I'm learning that perhaps we are…" Flora shook her head. "It's not a topic for a tea such as this," she said, reaching for the teapot. "May I get more for anyone else?"

Rose smiled at her as she held up her cup. "Do go on, Flora. Mrs. Jasper Jackson and I were just speaking of the very thing a few days ago. I would so love to hear your thoughts."

As Flora looked around the room, she realized that while some, such as Sarah, did look perplexed, others appeared genuinely interested in her words.

"Well," Flora said, after refilling cups that needed it. "One of the things I've come to realize, serving in the mission, is that God doesn't look at our dresses or our names, but at our hearts. I wonder if I'd spent as much time considering the condition of my heart as I did my hairstyle and wardrobe, what my life would be like, instead."

Taking a deep breath, Flora thought for a moment, then turned to Rose. "But I suppose I do know. In the mining camp, where we had no means for improving our outward appearance, I did spend more time thinking about my heart and my character."

Smiling, Flora brought her attention back to her mother. "And I do find it much improved. I was very angry with you for agreeing with Father that I should go. I apologize for anything hurtful or unkind that I might have said regarding that issue. Or any other, for that matter."

With a peace Flora could have only said came from the Lord, she said, "I am truly grateful for the experience, and I can say without hesitation that my life is richer and better for having it."

Her mother dabbed at the edges of her eyes with a handkerchief, an extraordinary public display of emotion for her. Which meant Flora should leave the subject alone. She'd said her piece, or at least part of it, and it was enough for the time being.

Flora looked back at Rose. "I hope that adds to your own discussions. Your friendship is one of the things that helped me see the value in people I would not have ordinarily sought out. I did not deserve your friendship, but you kindly bestowed it upon me anyway. Thank you."

Rose smiled and gave a tiny nod, as if she appreciated Flora's words, but like Flora, knew this wasn't the appropriate setting for such a discussion.

And so Flora brought the subject back to Ellen. "Which is why I am concerned for my new friend.

Ellen showed me measures of kindness and friendship I'll never forget. That signifies to me greatly, and I have been praying for her recovery, and, I hope, a renewal of our friendship."

Mrs. Crowley also dabbed at her eyes with her handkerchief. "What a lovely sentiment. I suddenly feel quite ashamed of myself for not inviting Ellen's mother to tea last week. Nathan has been doing a lot of business with the Fitzgeralds, and he suggested I invite Mrs. Fitzgerald to tea. But..." Mrs. Crowley shook her head. "I suppose I was more concerned with the fact that she always wears those silly hats, and I just couldn't. And now her poor daughter..."

The woman fanned herself, and many of the others murmured their own shame at having not accepted the Fitzgeralds so readily into their fold, keeping them at the fringes of society, being polite, but not completely befriending them.

Lottie Grant leaned forward. "Ellen is my friend," she said slowly. "And I know it would encourage her greatly to know of this conversation. She used to tell me that if people would just get to know each other, they would realize just how much in common they had, and they could be friends."

"She told me the same thing," Flora said, smiling. "Do you have news of her condition?"

Lottie sighed. "Only that she hasn't woken up yet. They say the longer she doesn't wake up, the worse it will be. Fortunately the rest of her injuries appear to be minor."

"Then we will pray for her to wake up soon," Mrs. Crowley said, straightening. "And I will pay a call on her mother. I'm sure she'll be pleased to know how many people care about Ellen's recovery."

Flora's chair had a nice view out the window, and though fine lace curtains covered most of it, she could see silhouettes of people walking past. Specifically, George leaving with Pierre, hand in hand as they followed Marie. Though it was none of her concern, she was pleased to notice that Marie wasn't holding Pierre's hand, and they didn't appear a family unit. Silly, since she knew there was nothing between George and Marie, but her heart had a small pang at the thought that someday George would be part of a family of his own. Sooner, rather than later, if all the matchmaking mamas in the room had their say.

Which, by the way conversation had shifted again, seemed to be what everyone was talking about.

George and Pierre disappeared from view, and Flora wished she could somehow call them back. An afternoon at a child's birthday party, at least with George and Pierre, was infinitely more entertaining than sitting in her mother's stuffy parlor with all these women. Especially since they'd been invited solely for the purpose of spreading the news about George Bellingham's arrival, not because they were all genuine friends. Yet every woman in the room held an important role in Leadville society.

What was wrong with her? Wasn't this exactly what she'd been longing for all this time?

Sarah leaned in to Flora. "You must invite me for tea when you know that Mr. Bellingham will be around. Since you're not interested in him, you might as well give me a leg up. After all, us unmarried women must stick together."

She gave a conspiratorial wink, like she hadn't been offended by Flora's comments about them being unmarried back at the camp. Like they'd never stopped being friends.

Everything seemed to be completely back to normal in Flora's world, and yet the sick feeling that had fluttered in her stomach for all these months of being left out had returned.

George had never been to a French child's birthday party, but it seemed to him that everything was similar to how any other birthday party he'd attended had been. Except that everyone spoke French, and George sat by himself in a corner as he watched Pierre play with all the other little boys.

"George, this is my father, Jean-Paul." Marie gestured to an older man.

"It's a pleasure to meet you." George stood and shook the gentleman's hand. "Thank you for having us."

"You are looking for the boy's father?"

George nodded. "Yes. Henri Martin. Do you know him?"

Marie had laughed when he'd asked her, shaking her head.

With a broad grin that reminded George of Marie, Jean-Paul pointed at a man. "That is Henri Martin."

The man was old, too old to be Pierre's father. Then Jean-Paul pointed again. "And he is Henri Martin."

Another man who could not possibly be Pierre's father. Jean-Paul indicated another man. "And him."

As Jean-Paul pointed out a few more Henri Martins, George understood why Marie had laughed at his question. In the French community, Henri Martin seemed to be as common a name as John Smith.

Which meant that George's mission was going to be a lot more difficult than he'd hoped. No wonder people looked at him like he was crazy when he asked about Pierre's father.

"But if any of them were missing a child, they'd have said so," Marie said. "I've asked everyone. Besides, all the Frenchmen are too smart to work at the Pudgy Boy. It's the worst mine, with the lowest wages. People only go there until they can find something better."

Her father murmured in agreement. "We would never let one of our own work in that terrible place. We stick to the other side of the mountain, where the mines and wages are more abundant."

As many times as George had heard how bad his mine was, it never got easier. Nothing about the mine's working conditions fit with how his father had always taught him to run a business. His father had believed that you should always take care of your people, even if it cut into profit margins temporarily. Long-term, a happy workforce meant a stable workforce, and in the end, it worked out to the benefit of the company's health. He'd always heard that people thought his father too generous in how he treated his employees.

So, how did things get to be so bad at the mine?

George nodded at the man. "I understand. And I appreciate you taking the time to talk to me. But Pierre was found near the Pudgy Boy Mine. That's where his father told him to wait. Something isn't adding up, and I don't understand why."

The older man nodded slowly. "It is a puzzle. I usually meet every Frenchman who comes to town, and I don't recall meeting a man with a young son."

Jean-Paul turned to chat with another man, seeming to have forgotten that George was there. George continued watching Pierre. Too bad Flora couldn't see the little boy playing with the others. She'd tried to get him to play with the children at camp, but they never seemed to get past the language barrier. She would have been so happy to see him finally getting to interact with others.

George sighed. That was the other problem. Trying to figure out what to do about Flora. The trouble with her anger was that he knew he'd been wrong to hide the truth from her. So how did he make it up to her? And how did they move on?

But how could he ask Flora to give up the life she so clearly loved? Even if they were able to work things out, what future did they have?

This party should have been a pleasant diversion, yet all he could think about was Flora. When Shannon had broken things off with him, he'd been able to let go of his thoughts of her quite easily. Perhaps too easily.

"George!" Pierre ran into his arms, and automatically George picked him up.

The little boy chattered at him so fast that despite Flora teaching both of them words to communicate with each other, George couldn't understand any of it.

One more reason he wished Flora was with them. But Flora belonged in her mother's fine parlor, not in this old barn, which had been cleaned out enough to host the party. Based on the number of people present, the child's birthday had merely been an excuse for the gathering.

"He is like your own son," Jean-Paul said.

George turned to the other man. "Yes, but I would never deprive a man of his child. If Pierre's father is out there, then we owe it to him to find him."

"You are a good man," Jean Paul said, patting him on the back. "If this man wants to be found, we will find him. Come, let me introduce you to Crazy Eddie. He is not French, and can only speak enough to get himself in trouble with the ladies. But he knows more people than I do. If Crazy Eddie can't find him, then no one can."

Stumpy had spoken of a man named Crazy Eddie. Finally it felt like they were seeing progress. George tried to put Pierre down, but the little boy remained glued to him. "I come George," he said.

"You can come." George gave him a reassuring squeeze and continued holding him as they walked across the room to meet this Crazy Eddie fellow.

When they approached Crazy Eddie, the grizzled man wearing animal skins and looking like he'd earned his name honestly, grinned broadly. "Pipsqueak!"

Pierre buried his head in George's shoulder.

"Ah, he is still afraid of me. I've told him I'm not so scary, but he does not believe me." Crazy Eddie laughed, a sound that erased any doubt as to how he'd gotten his nickname. And seemed to make little Pierre even more afraid.

But for the first time, they'd made progress.

"You know Pierre?" George asked, rubbing the little boy's back.

"Ah, yes. I helped him and his father come to Leadville. Someone stole all their money. I saw it happen, and we couldn't catch the villain. I was already planning on coming to Leadville as a guide for another man. It seemed the least I could do to help the poor man and his son."

Crazy Eddie looked around, noticing for the first time that Henri was not among them. "But where is this little fellow's father?"

"That's what we're wondering," George said, and filled him in on the circumstances of finding Pierre and the mystery of Pierre's father.

"Of course he went to the Pudgy Boy Mine for work," Crazy Eddie said, smiling broadly and puffing out his chest. "I got him the job. He was nervous that he'd lost some letter he had with his things when he was robbed. Something about a job here. I told him not to worry, I knew people at the Pudgy Boy Mine, and they'd hire him."

"Why didn't you bring him to me?" Jean-Paul said. "You know we take care of our own."

Crazy Eddie shook his head. "I didn't think of it. He was worried that he had lost his opportunity for a job, and once I mentioned this job, everything was fine. I couldn't really talk to him, he didn't speak much English."

Which still didn't give him a lot of information, but at least it confirmed that Dougherty was lying about Pierre's father not working there.

"Who was the other man you brought with Pierre and his father?" George asked.

"Herman Schmidt," Crazy Eddie said, shaking his head. "Terrible tragedy. He also went to work at the Pudgy Boy Mine. They'd brought him in specifically to help with the explosives. I think they were going to try to tap into another vein. Poor man set the charge wrong, got some of his bits blown off, and now he's living in a rattrap by State Street, begging for scraps."

Crazy Eddie shook his head slowly. "I know Onree was pretty torn up about it. He was talking crazy, and I couldn't understand him. I was going to bring Onree to you, Jean-Paul, just so I could understand him, but he threw his hands in the air the way you people do, and stomped off."

At least that solved another mystery. Crazy Eddie also called Pierre's father "Onree," so at least he knew for sure that the scratched out name matched George's assumption tying the men together.

Still, it didn't solve the mystery of what happened to Pierre's father.

Jean-Paul shook his head and clucked his tongue. "If only you'd brought the man to me. We would have gotten him a better place to work than the Pudgy Boy Mine. I heard about what happened to Herman Schmidt. Terrible tragedy."

A terrible tragedy, indeed, especially since it had been one more instance where George's mine had caused devastation in someone else's life.

George turned to Crazy Eddie. "You know where he is?"

"Oh, no," Jean-Paul said. "You can't go to State Street. It's not safe."

"Terrible place." Crazy Eddie nodded. "At least, for a gent like you."

"I'm no gent, just a miner," George said.

"And I'm the King of France," Crazy Eddie said, laughing.

"France has no king!" Jean-Paul crossed his arms and glared at the other man.

Crazy Eddie just laughed.

"Still," George said. "Could you take me to meet him? He might know something about Pierre's father. Surely the man wouldn't have abandoned his son."

"Of course not!" Crazy Eddie shook his head. "That boy was all he had. He would call him his precious. It sounded like precious, anyway."

"Enfant précieux," Jean-Paul said, smiling as he reached out to pinch Pierre's cheek. "He is a precious child."

Pierre smiled, but buried his head further into George's shoulder.

"Enfant précieux," George repeated, nuzzling the little boy. "You are precious, aren't you?"

Eyes full of unshed tears, Pierre said, *"Mon père."*

His father. The words reminded him of his father, and the poor child was missing his father.

"Tout sera bien," George said, hoping he remembered correctly what he'd heard Flora say to the little boy.

"Flora," the little boy said, the dam of tears breaking as they began to fall down his face.

Of course he wanted Flora. Though George loved the little boy and did his best to comfort him, Flora always had the right words.

"Do you want to go home?" George tried remembering the right words but then wondered if it would mean anything to the child. Did Pierre think of Flora's house as his own? Clearly he still missed his father, so what would home be to Pierre?

George turned to Jean-Paul. "Would you mind asking him if he'd like to return to Flora's house? I guess he really doesn't have a home now, does he?"

Sighing as he looked down at the little boy, George could only pray that they were able to find Pierre's father. To give the child some comfort that George could not.

Jean-Paul leaned in and spoke softly to Pierre. The little boy responded with stilted words between sniffles. They spoke at length for what should have been a simple question. But with each response Pierre gave Jean-Paul, the little boy seemed happier and more content.

Then Jean-Paul looked at George. "He does want to go back to Flora. He says that she rocks him and sings to him the way his mother used to, and it always makes him feel better."

George nodded. "Of course."

Giving Pierre a little squeeze, he said, *"D'accord."* Another phrase he'd learned from Flora to let Pierre know that what he wanted was all right. "We go to Flora."

Pierre looked doubtful, but George smiled and squeezed the boy again. *"Je t'aime, Pierre. D'accord."*

Finally smiling as he heard George's reassurance that he loved him and it would be all right to go back to Flora, Pierre snuggled up to him again. *"Je t'aime, George."*

"He loves you," Jean-Paul said. "Pierre is afraid that you are hurt that he still misses his father and wishes for his safe return. He does not understand how it is possible to love both you and his father, and also to love Flora and his late mother."

George took a deep breath. How did you tell a little boy that you felt the same way? That despite everything that told him that giving his heart to both Flora and this child was a bad idea, he simply couldn't help himself?

"Tell Pierre that I understand. And that because I love him, I want the same thing. I am trying to reunite him with his father, and no matter what happens, I will always love him and be there for him. Tell him that the heart…"

George thought about a recent discussion with Pastor Lassiter. Perhaps the concept was too adult for a child, but it was the only thing George knew to say. "The heart has an immeasurable capacity for love, and the more we love, the more we are able to love. It's big enough to love your mother, your father, Flora, me and whoever else comes along, without taking from anyone else."

The older man's eyes filled with tears as he bent to translate for Pierre. As the little boy processed the words, he squeezed George tighter.

Maybe George had conveyed something too hard for most people to understand, but whatever Jean-Paul had told Pierre, it made sense.

"You are a good man, George," Crazy Eddie said, as Jean-Paul spoke softly to Pierre. "I cannot, in good conscience, take you to the terrible place where Herman Schmidt is, but I will bring him to you. Where are you staying?"

George took a deep breath, hating that saying where he was staying would make Crazy Eddie even more suspicious of his identity.

"I'm staying at the Montgomery home. Mr. Montgomery has hired me to help him sort out the situation at the mine, so he likes to keep me close in case he needs me."

Crazy Eddie raised his eyebrows, as if this information did, in fact, diminish George's credibility.

"I sleep in the barn," George said. "But I know both

Mr. Montgomery and Flora will also be interested in what Herman has to say, so bring him to the house."

As Crazy Eddie nodded knowingly, George was glad for the temporary discomfort of sleeping in straw as opposed to a feather mattress. Besides, with the financial disaster they were uncovering as they dug deeper into the mine's paperwork, it was becoming more evident that a straw mattress was likely to be the best George could hope for.

"I will come to the back door. The likes of us are not fit for the Montgomery parlor."

George wanted to argue, but the man was probably right. Given that Agnes still glowered at him every time he was in the house, George couldn't see the housekeeper greeting with open arms a man who probably hadn't bathed in years.

"All right, then. I'll see you soon." George looked down at Pierre, who'd finished his conversation with Jean-Paul. "Are you ready to go?"

Pierre nodded.

As George turned to leave, Jean-Paul touched his free shoulder. "We pride ourselves on taking care of our own. But I have no doubt that Pierre is in the very best care. Please don't be a stranger, and bring him back often."

"I will," George said, smiling at the man. "Thank you for your help."

Jean-Paul nodded, and George quickly said goodbye to Marie. Though he'd meant it when he said that he wanted nothing more than to reunite Pierre with his father, George couldn't help but feel a twinge of sadness that everything was going to change soon. He hoped. Maybe.

Chapter Fourteen

Flora peered through the curtains for the tenth time since their guests had left. Why hadn't George returned yet with Pierre?

"Stop mooning," her mother said, coming into the room and taking a seat in her favorite chair. "You act like you're waiting for a suitor. Come, sit. We've embroidery to do. Mrs. Bellingham always admired the things I made. I understand she's recovering from a terrible accident, and I think it would be a lovely gesture to make her a pillow with a nice Psalm. I don't know if your father told you or not, but Honoria and I used to be close friends."

Flora turned to her mother, who looked wistful. "What happened to divide the families? I only remember them vaguely."

"George? You don't remember George?"

With a pang, Flora thought about what she remembered of George in their childhood. As a boy, he'd been overweight, and she and the other children had teased him mercilessly about it.

"I wasn't very kind to him," Flora said slowly. "I

know you have high hopes, but I can't imagine him having fond memories of me."

"Nonsense. You were children. All children tease each other. George used to pull your curls and make you cry."

"And you want me to marry him?" Flora glanced out the window again.

"I must insist that you sit down," her mother said. "Not only is it unseemly for a young lady to moon about, but you keep watching for that miner. You cannot think that your father and I would condone such a match."

If only her mother knew that the miner she mooned over was her precious George Bellingham. It was on the tip of her tongue to say just so, but a twinge in her heart reminded her that was exactly why George and her father had been hesitant to tell her the truth. Her mother would fawn over the poor man, and there was no way anyone in society would believe that George was a mere miner.

"And what would be so wrong about my marrying a miner?" Flora went over to one of the chairs opposite her mother and sat. A small concession to her mother's wishes. But right now, after having endured an afternoon of society snobbery, Flora wasn't sure this was the life she wanted anymore.

"Please tell me you're not serious!" Her mother dropped the piece she'd been working on and stared at Flora. "I will not tolerate such nonsense from you."

"But why?" Flora stared at her. "Father says *he* came from humble beginnings. What would be wrong with me finding an honorable man like him?"

"Because I did not sacrifice all those early years so

that my daughter would have to do the same. Can you honestly tell me that you enjoyed living in a hovel with a dirt floor and leaky roof?"

Flora shook her head. "No. I hope to never do such a thing again," she said quietly. "But I've been trying to improve my character with everyone's encouragement, and it seems to me we have a double standard. Can you honestly say that everyone in the so-called good families you're encouraging me to associate with has the kind of character you wish me to emulate?"

Her mother stared at her like she'd gone insane.

"What is good character, Mother? Simply because they come from a good family and people show respect to them, that doesn't mean they're good people. And I've learned that, above all, I wish to be a good person, the kind of person God will smile upon instead of shake his head in disappointment at. I am not superior to others simply because of my father's wealth. Even though I have spent most of my life acting like it."

The truth of Flora's words made her heart twist, forcing her to take a deep breath. "I'm sorry, Mother. But I find that I cannot abide society's standards of behavior when they don't always match up with God's. I would rather be known for my kindness and my good heart than to have all the ladies in town emulate my fashions."

Her mother looked as though she'd just been doused with a vat of ice-cold water.

Before either woman could speak, her father entered the room and sat in the chair beside her mother.

"Anna, I hope you're as proud of Flora as I am."

"But, John..." Tears fell down her mother's cheeks.

"No." He shook his head. "We had it all wrong."

"She doesn't know how hard it was." Flora's mother looked at her, her face filled with despair. "I spent my whole life dreaming of being a fine lady, of my daughter being a fine lady, and here we are. And now she wants to throw it all away for a miner?"

"Would you rather she be like Mrs. Fischer—or like Mrs. Cornelius?"

Her mother's face went white. Her father turned his gaze on Flora. "Before your mother and I married, she worked as a lady's maid to a woman named Mrs. Fischer. Mrs. Fischer was a cruel woman with a nasty temper, and she made your mother's life miserable. Then she went to work for a lady named Mrs. Cornelius, who was a kind woman, devoted to caring for others and promoting Christian charity. We used to promise each other that when we became wealthy, we'd be more like the Corneliuses and less like the Fischers."

Then he turned to his wife. "I'm sorry, my darling. But somewhere along the line, we lost sight of our promise."

Her mother began openly sobbing. "I'm going to go rest. I have a headache coming on."

"Can I bring you anything?" Flora asked.

"I think you've done enough." Her mother flounced out of the room.

Flora sighed. "Father, I—"

"Don't apologize. The past few weeks, I've been forced to confront the man I've become and my own snobbery." He let out a long sigh. "The truth is, I should have done more to repair my relationship with Elias. I should not have forgotten the example the Corneliuses gave me. The only reason I had money to stake my first claim is because when Mr. Cornelius died, he divided his estate between all of his employees. Your mother believed in my dreams, and she told me to use the money to pursue them. I did, and we always said that we'd use our money in the same way."

Then he gestured around the room. "And look at us. The finest money can buy and, until recently, the most selfish, spoiled daughter in town because of it."

His description of her stung, but it was true.

He leaned forward and took her hand. "Flora, I'm sorry for not being a better example to you. I'm sorry for indulging all of your whims and making you think that material things were more important than the kind of person you are." Tears filled his eyes as he squeezed her hand. "Can you forgive me?"

Flora came forward and wrapped her arms around him, hugging him tight. "Of course I forgive you. I'm sorry for being so selfish. I hate how I've treated others, and I'm trying desperately to make it right. But I'm finding that people don't want me to make it right. They just want me to be a nicer version of who I used to be, and I simply can't. I'm not that person at all."

"No, you're not," he said, smiling at her. "You are an incredible young lady, and I feel privileged to call you my daughter. In spite of all my mistakes, I am so pleased to see who you've become."

Flora smiled back as she pulled away and returned to her chair. "Oh, I'm fairly certain I made my own share of them."

Then his expression grew serious. "Now, tell me. Do you care for George?"

Flora sighed and looked toward the window again. "Sometimes I think I do, but then I think about how he deceived me, and I get so angry. Why didn't he have the faith in me that I had in him?"

She swallowed the emotions that unexpectedly welled up.

"Can you see that he did what he thought was best? That he meant you no harm?"

"I've tried." She shook her head and then looked at him. "Why haven't you told Mother?"

"The same reason George didn't want to tell you," he said. "Can you imagine her reaction if she knew? She would be fawning all over him, and we would lose our element of surprise. I've got telegrams by the dozen from Bellingham family advisors, telling me things that don't line up with what George says, with what we're finding at the mine. I believe that someone very closely connected to the family is behind all of this, but we don't yet have evidence proving it. George is going to be the key to unlocking it, but we can't reveal that key until the right time. Until we have all the pieces, we need to keep his identity a secret."

All things she'd heard before. Flora took a deep breath. "Perhaps you shouldn't underestimate Mother. After all, I know the truth and I haven't revealed it, not even to Mother, who is horrified that I might have developed a tendre for a miner."

Her father nodded slowly. "And we're back to the topic I most wish to discuss. He's an honorable man. I would have no objection to a match between the two of you. I can't think of any man I would be more pleased to see you marry."

Flora looked out the window again. "It's not that simple. It's hard to say what's between us. None of it has been based on truth. I've spent so much time fighting what I thought was an impossibility. I don't know what to think or believe anymore. I'm not certain I can trust my heart."

"I see," her father said. "I will be praying for you to find clarity. And I hope that, as you seek to prove that you have changed, you are willing to offer the same forgiveness to others that you wish they would give you."

Flora closed her eyes. He had a point. If she couldn't forgive George for his deception, how was she supposed to expect others to forgive her?

He leaned forward and squeezed her hand. "They're not easy, matters of the heart. And I know there is more for you to sort out besides forgiving him. But I hope you know that, in the end, it's worth it."

She opened her eyes and smiled at him.

"And now I have my own matters of the heart to work out," he said. "You're right that I did not give your mother enough credit. She's a good woman, and I love her dearly. Be gentle with her during this time. As hard as the changes in your life have been on you, I believe your mother is in for similar difficulties."

Flora smiled at him. "Then go to her. And I'll be here, supporting her as she has supported me through what I imagine must have been difficult times for her."

They both stood, and her father hugged her tight. "Even in the worst moments, we have always loved you with all of our hearts. No matter how trying you've been, your mother's love has never wavered."

"I know."

As her father released her, Flora spotted George standing in the doorway.

"I'm sorry. I didn't mean to intrude. I can come back."

"No need." Her father waved him off. "Come, sit. Tell us how the party went. Did you meet anyone who knew Pierre's father?"

"I did."

Flora listened as George relayed what he'd found out at the party. It was hard to hold on to her anger at him as she watched the emotions play on his face. How could she not care for a man who loved a little boy like Pierre so deeply?

"Where is Pierre?" Flora asked, as George explained how Pierre was feeling sad over missing his parents.

George made a noise in the back of his throat. "Agnes took one look at him, declared him filthy and is giving him a good scrubbing."

Flora turned to her father. "Sometimes I think Agnes needs to learn a little about what we've been discussing."

He laughed. "She's pretty set in her ways, but if anyone can convince her to see things differently, it's you."

Then her father turned to George. "Let me know when this Crazy Eddie fellow arrives. I'd like to hear what he and Herman Schmidt have to say. I'm going to go talk to my wife. Flora very graciously reminded me that I've been remiss in how I've treated her."

Hesitantly, he added, "I know I said I would keep your confidence. However, I cannot continue deceiving my wife. I hope this doesn't make things difficult for you, but trust is the bedrock of any relationship. Anna deserves better from me."

George was shamed by the older man's words. Though they were not meant as an insult to him, he couldn't help but be reminded of how his relationship with Flora had been harmed by the lack of trust.

"Of course," George said. "It was wrong of me to make you feel as though you needed to keep your wife in the dark, just as it was wrong of me not to tell Flora the truth."

"I was party to that decision," John said, looking at Flora. "George did not choose to keep you, or your mother, in the dark on his own."

The words were meant for the woman who still looked at George like she didn't know what to believe. For whatever reason, John had decided to take up George's cause. And for that, George was grateful. Even though Flora's acquiescent nod was still filled with doubt and mistrust.

"Thank you, sir," George said. "If there's anything I can do to smooth things over with your wife, I will do my best."

John gave a wry smile as he returned his attention to George. "I expect that there will be a large party once your identity is known. Be a sport about it, and if she wishes for you to escort Flora—" John looked back at his daughter, then to George again "—you will both be delighted to entertain her whim."

"Done," George said.

Flora laughed. "I will even let her choose my dress."

John joined in her laughter, and George could see the resemblance between father and daughter.

"I'm sure it will be a great hardship. Try not to suffer too much." John winked, then turned to George. "I pity the man who will eventually pay her dressmaker's bill."

It was supposed to be a joke, but George couldn't help but feel inadequate at the words. At this rate, he wouldn't be able to buy Flora one dress, let alone a whole wardrobe. Perhaps when he got a few moments alone with John, he'd make it clear that his entire financial picture looked as dire as that of the mine.

"Father!" Flora picked up her fan and playfully smacked it at him. "I'm not that bad!"

The look John gave George indicated that Flora was probably even worse. And, from what he'd seen of Flora's wardrobe, George was inclined to agree.

As Flora caught the look passing between the men, she frowned. "I'm being serious. I don't need all those dresses."

She let out a long sigh. "In fact, I've been thinking. The accident that hurt Herman Schmidt—why was it not known in our circles?"

John shook his head. "Accidents happen all the time at the mines. It's part of doing business."

"They happen at our mines?" Flora stared at him, and George felt a great deal of compassion for the woman who was having the same reaction he'd had to being told the same thing.

"I'm afraid so, sweetheart."

"So, men like Herman Schmidt. What happens to them when they're hurt at our mines?"

The question appeared to surprise John, whose brow immediately furrowed. "I…" He let out a long sigh. "I suppose I haven't given it the consideration I should. Thank you, Flora, for making me realize my oversight. I'll discuss it with my mine managers at the earliest opportunity."

In an instant, John looked far more aged than he had when George had walked into the room. "I suppose I'm guilty of a great many oversights. But I need to start with the most important. If you'll both excuse me, I'm going to go see to my wife."

George murmured assent, though his mind was on the woman giving her father another hug. All this talk of misjudging. Was it possible he was misjudging her and her ability to accept his reduced circumstances?

After John left, George turned his attention to Flora. "I just wanted to say—"

She shook her head. "Please don't. I know. We've discussed this. My father and I have spoken at length on this matter. What I need most right now is to sort out my own heart, to seek the Lord and His will for me. Not more of your explanations and apologies."

The pain in his heart was more than he'd expected at hearing the same words she'd been giving him ever since they'd discussed his identity. How was he supposed to convince her of the sincerity of his feelings when she wouldn't let him tell her how he felt?

Her expression softened. "You're a good man, George. I would be lying, both to you and myself, if I said I didn't care for you. But so much is changing in my world right now. Father said that the bedrock of a relationship is trust, and I don't know what to trust, so I don't know that I'm in a place where I can trust our relationship. Not just in what you say, but in how I feel."

Not a rejection. But the same honest expression of her heart that George had come to love about Flora.

He nodded. "I appreciate that. But I need you to let me say what I have to say, because I feel that as you weigh your feelings, you need to understand mine."

For a moment, Flora looked as though she was going to argue with him. But she gave him a tiny nod. "I suppose it's only fair that I hear you out."

"It's no secret that I care for you, as well. But just as you are trying to work out your feelings for me, I, too, am struggling. Things do not look good for me financially."

She gave him a look of understanding. "You've said as much."

"I know. But you need to know how important it is to me to have a woman willing to stand by me for better or for worse. For richer or poorer."

"I know all this," Flora said, an annoyed expression crossing her face.

George shook his head. "Let me finish. That's the problem with both of us. We keep assuming things without all of the information. And that's what I'm trying to say. I keep assuming that you won't have me if I lose everything. Or you'll be unhappy if I can't give you the life you're accustomed to. Just like I assumed you would act a certain way upon knowing who I was."

Recognition shone in her eyes. Like they were finally seeing things the same.

Perhaps there was hope for them, after all.

"I care for you. There are so many reasons why I respect and admire you, not the least of all being the fact that you are working so hard to know your heart and to be true to who God wants you to be. Even when you didn't know who I was, you showed me compassion and love, and for that, I will always be grateful. You are a good woman, Flora Montgomery, and I would stake my very life on that fact. Which I have done already, by revealing my true identity to you."

If anything could get through to Flora, if she would listen to any reason, it had to be based in complete truth.

George took a deep breath. "The explosion at the mine was not an accident, and I think you know that. We believe it was set to deter your father, only it had the opposite effect. I didn't get the chance to tell your father, but when I stopped by the sheriff's office to talk to Will about Herman Schmidt, I found out that the stagecoach George Bellingham was supposed to be on was robbed. The driver reported overhearing one of the robbers saying that the man they were looking for wasn't there. He couldn't see the picture they were looking at to compare to the passengers, but the bandits acted like it was someone important. We believe they were looking for me. To harm me."

Flora paled. He hadn't wanted to worry her, but she needed to know the people they were dealing with were dangerous.

He closed his eyes and took a deep breath, trying to find the words. Then he looked at her. "I hate that I am potentially putting you and your family in danger by being here. I can't ask you to risk your heart for me."

He swallowed. "But just know that if you do, if you find yourself willing to offer your heart to me, to stand by me no matter what happens, my heart will be irrevocably yours."

She nodded slowly, like she was trying to process the words. George didn't expect a response, not with so much at stake. Not when his heart was already accusing him of being a liar.

His heart wasn't to be given to Flora sometime in the future. As much as George hated to admit it, she already had it, whether she wanted it or not. But to tell her that now, with so many burdens already upon her, simply wasn't fair.

Or maybe that was just another excuse to protect the delicate pieces of himself he was desperately trying to keep together.

Chapter Fifteen

Dinner was a muted affair. Flora's mother had come down, but appeared subdued and morose. She barely looked at Flora, and had merely given George a curt nod. The only person who appeared to be normal was Pierre, who joyfully chatted about his day.

Will had stopped by shortly before dinner, and he'd closeted himself in her father's study with George and Flora's father. Since Will's departure, both Flora's father and George had been solemn.

Flora stole another look at George, whose gaze was firmly focused on his plate.

No man had ever offered his heart to her.

She'd kissed her share of beaux, a fact she should probably be ashamed of, but despite all of those freely given kisses, not one man had told her he loved her.

George hadn't said so, exactly, but his words had hit her far more deeply than any declaration of love. He saw her as his equal, a potential partner in life.

Flora glanced at her mother. According to her father, that's how their relationship had begun, as well. So, what had changed?

She shook her head. Her parents still loved each other. That wasn't the problem.

Agnes entered the dining room. "There are two unsavories at the back door, insisting on an audience with Mr. Montgomery and the miner. I told them you were having dinner, but they will not leave."

Her father looked up from his plate. "Send them in. And if you would, set places for the both of them. I'm sure they would appreciate a good meal."

"On my fine china?" Agnes looked as though she was about to have apoplexy.

"Yes, Agnes," Flora's mother said quietly. "It is our honor to have them in our home. And I believe it is *my* china."

"Well!" Agnes stomped out of the room.

Flora's father placed his hand over his wife's. "Thank you."

For the first time, she looked up, first at Flora, then at George. "I do not approve of this business, not at all."

Though Flora had always focused on what her father thought of the situation, she realized that she probably should have been worried more about her mother's opinion.

"Mrs.—" George began, but Flora's father shook his head.

George nodded and lowered his gaze back to his plate.

"No," her mother said. "You may speak. But first I will have my say. I cannot believe that all of you would deceive me so. You may have your reasons, but you have made me look and feel quite foolish. I am very hurt, and when this nonsense is over, I expect a full apology from each of you."

She turned to George, a tender expression on her face. "The son of my dear friend, and I did not know. You have no idea how much I have missed…"

Tears filled her eyes, and she threw her napkin on the table. "I believe I will go to my room and leave you to your guests. I find I have lost my appetite."

Before anyone had a chance to react, her mother left the room, nearly running into Agnes, flanked by two men.

One man was dressed in an odd assortment of furs, with hair so thick and matted, Flora wasn't sure where his hair ended and the fur began. The other man looked equally the worse for the wear, except he balanced on a crutch. When Flora looked down, she realized he was missing the better part of his leg.

The stench from both men was unmistakable, and Agnes's put-out expression equally so.

Flora's father stood. "Please, gentlemen, join us." He held his hand out to the grizzled man. "You must be Crazy Eddie."

Crazy Eddie nodded as he shook her father's hand.

Her father turned to the other man and did the same. "And I assume you're Herman."

With a gap-toothed smile, Herman said, "Yes sir."

Flora also stood. "Agnes, please get these men each a plate."

"That's all right, miss," Crazy Eddie said. "We wouldn't want to put you folks out."

"Nonsense," Flora said with a smile. "We're delighted to have you. I understand you were both acquainted with Pierre's father."

Pierre looked over at the men. Then he looked at

Flora and said in French, "They are my father's friends, but not mine. They scare me."

"It's all right," she told him. "If they were your father's friends, they must be nice. Perhaps they can help us find him."

Agnes returned with food for the men, and Flora was pleased to notice it was on her mother's fine china.

"Thank you, Agnes," Flora said, as her father helped the men get situated. "Could you please go to Will's house and let him know the guests we were expecting are here?"

Though Agnes muttered something under her breath, she nodded. Hopefully sending her for Will would calm her down. She didn't want to mention the law in front of these men and frighten them, but it would give Agnes peace of mind.

With a sigh, Flora mentally chided herself. Why should Will's status as a lawman make them feel any better about having strangers in their home, simply because they were obviously not of the same social station? How would Agnes react when she found out who George really was?

"Appreciate the hospitality, miss," Herman said.

Flora gave him a smile. "It's our pleasure. Please, what can you tell us about Pierre's father?"

"He would never willingly leave the boy," the man said.

Crazy Eddie nodded his agreement. "No, he wouldn't."

"I thought as much," Flora said. "Please, enjoy your meals while we wait for our other guest."

The men needed no further encouragement. In the past, Flora would have been horrified at the way they shoveled food into their mouths, but having been up at the camp, she'd become accustomed to the men eating like they hadn't had a meal in days and as if they thought this was the last one they'd ever have. Judging from the gaunt appearance of Herman, she imagined he likely hadn't been getting regular meals.

Fortunately, Will didn't live far from their home. He arrived just as Crazy Eddie and Herman were finishing their second helpings of supper. Agnes would be displeased, since she liked to use the leftover chicken in a soup for lunch the next day, but this was probably the first of many changes Agnes would have to get used to.

Introductions were made, and Flora noticed that Crazy Eddie shied away when Will let his status as a deputy be known.

"It's all right, Crazy Eddie, I know who you are," Will said. "You'll have no trouble from me."

Though Crazy Eddie looked slightly mollified, he also kept glancing toward the door, as though he would bolt at any second.

A clatter in the kitchen reminded Flora that they were not quite alone. Flora stood.

"If you'll excuse me, gentlemen, I'm going to check on Agnes."

As Flora entered the kitchen, her suspicion that Agnes had been listening in was confirmed. Agnes glared at her like she was angry at having been caught.

"It's a fine evening, isn't it, Agnes?" Flora said as she smiled at the woman, pretending that everything was fine. "I would like to go for a walk with Pierre. Father has asked that I not go out alone, so could you accompany us?"

Only a fool wouldn't think Flora was trying to get Agnes out of the house. But since George's secret had been discovered by Flora overhearing him talk, it seemed best to do her part to continue helping keep it.

"Strange goings-on here," Agnes muttered. "It's just not right."

"You are correct," Flora said with a smile. "And we're doing our best to make it right. So get your wrap, and I'll collect Pierre, and we'll be off so the men can have their privacy."

George couldn't help but admire the way Flora so easily handled the problem of Agnes. Though he knew the older woman was a loyal member of the household, it made him feel better to know that Flora was taking her and Pierre out on a walk, leaving the men to privately discuss the situation.

One more reason Flora was more of an asset than she gave herself credit for.

George turned his attention back to Will, who was asking Herman about the last time he'd seen Henri.

"He was upset," Herman said, shaking his head. "Kept saying in that funny way of his, 'Ezz not right!' He couldn't understand why Dougherty wasn't giving me any money after I got hurt."

The thought made George sick. Because of his work in the mine, Herman had lost most of his leg. And, based on the looks of things, would probably lose more—if not his life—if he didn't receive medical attention. Something a man like Herman, without assistance, wouldn't be able to afford.

"Could you tell us how you got hurt?" George asked, swallowing the disgust at knowing his part in the situation.

"Dougherty wanted me to explore a vein that had

previously been tapped out. Said that he thought we needed to go deeper and to the left. I told him that it looked like we'd be encroaching on another claim, but he said not to worry about that."

Herman shook his head. "Strangest thing. I know I placed that charge right, but somehow it was off, and I ended up getting caught in it. I got caught in the rock, and Dougherty just stood there, laughing. He left me to scramble out on my own."

Will leaned forward. "Why didn't you report it?"

"Report what?" Herman shook his head. "It was my word against Dougherty's. I know he left me to die, but I can't prove that. I managed to make my way out, but my leg…"

A deep expression of grief crossed Herman's face. "I was sharing a tent with Henri and Pierre. When I didn't come home, Henri came looking for me. He brought me to town and left me with a doctor. Said he'd return, but that was the last time I saw him."

Herman sighed. "He was torn up about it. Said it wasn't right. I suppose he was going to go talk to Dougherty, but to be honest, I wasn't thinking clearly. I still see him in my dreams, so angry about what happened to me. I don't think he understands. Those greedy mine owners don't care. They just want the silver, no matter what the cost."

Guilt tore at George's stomach. Of all the things he'd learned about his mine's poor business practices, this was the worst. Seeing a man who'd been left to die and would now be crippled forever.

Before he could talk himself out of it, George spoke. "I am so sorry for what happened to you. It's only fair that I tell you the truth about who I am. My name is

George Bellingham, and my family owns the mine. I had no idea what was happening. I am deeply sorry, and I will do everything in my power to make things right."

Will stared at him like he'd gone mad, but after being lectured by Flora's mother about his deception, and now face-to-face with a man whose life was ruined because of his family, George couldn't help himself.

Crazy Eddie pounded the table. "I knew you was a gent!"

"Yes, and I'm sorry for deceiving you," George said. "But if you gentlemen could please keep my identity a secret for the time being, I would appreciate it. We're still looking into what's happening at the mine, and it's easier if people don't know who I am."

He forced himself to look at Herman's mangled leg. "I can't replace your leg, but I will bear the expense of seeing to your care."

He turned to John. "That is, if you will help me."

As John nodded, George let out a long sigh. "I wish I could do more, but the truth is, our family is flat broke. I don't know what happened to our fortune, but we're trying to find out, and that's what I'm trying to make right. Please believe me when I say that I had no idea what was happening, and I'm so sorry for all the pain the mine has caused."

"Thank you," Herman said. "And at least now I know why Dougherty was trying to get me to tap into someone else's claim. The Pudgy Boy is pretty close to being played out, and it's no secret among us miners that if you don't find a new vein soon, you might as well close things up."

So there was no hope. Every option had been exhausted. Except stealing from someone else's mine, which was why Dougherty had left Herman to die.

"Why would Dougherty try to dissuade me from buying the mine?" John asked. "Wouldn't putting it into my lap and getting money for the Bellinghams be the solution?"

Herman shrugged. "It would if they'd had a chance to seed the mine. You're a smart man. If they simply took silver from another mine, you'd figure it out pretty quick, since you've got your fingers in just about every pot. But if they had silver from a vein in another claim that hadn't yet been developed…"

The wheels started turning in George's head. It would definitely be a large-scale fraud. "Dougherty's not smart enough to pull this off alone. He's too drunk most of the time. Besides, what does he care if I own the mine or if John does?"

"He doesn't," Herman said. "But there's someone above him putting the screws in him, that's for sure. He kept nervously mentioning the boss."

"And the boss is?" Will asked.

Herman shrugged. "I figured it was Bellingham, since he owns the mine." Then Herman looked at him. "But clearly not, since you're trying to figure it out instead of just having me killed."

Will turned to George. "Who in your family has all the information on the mine?"

"I've told you everything I know." George sighed. "I suppose Arthur, my brother-in-law, but he's family. He wouldn't put Julia and the children at risk. Robert Cooper has been our closest advisor, but I can't see him wanting to hurt our family. I mean, if this got out, it would ruin us more than we already are."

"Unless the sale made you even more wealthy," John said, letting out a sigh. "I thought the price they gave me was a bit steep."

"They?" Will looked at John expectantly.

"I'd been negotiating with Robert Cooper, but recently Arthur Eldridge has also been corresponding with me, since I asked to speak with a family member. I found it odd that neither volunteered George. When I asked about him, they both said he was too busy with his studies at Harvard to deal with family business. Honestly, it wasn't until I started digging deeper into the mine business that they started getting cold feet about selling. I think they knew that I'd discover their wrongdoing and expose it."

Though John had already told George all of this, and graciously allowed George to read the letters and telegrams, it still rankled to hear how easily they'd dismissed him.

Worse, they hadn't bothered to consult with George at all. He had a friend back at Harvard keeping his secret and passing on all correspondence. So far there had been nothing to indicate the situation with the mine or the dire condition of the family's finances. In answer to George's inquiries, they'd both said it was merely rumor and not to worry.

"Do you happen to have any claim maps we can look at, John?" Will asked. "I'd like to have Herman mark up the areas where he was setting charges, and where the claims are that they were encroaching on."

"Of course," John said. "I like to know what's what in our area. Pudgy Boy isn't the first mine to try taking silver from someone else's claim, so I pay close attention to who owns what and where."

When John left to get the maps, George turned to Herman. "I can't tell you how much I appreciate what you've done to help. I know nothing can bring your leg back, but I will do what I can to make things right."

Herman shook his head. "I know. I'm just sorry you're going to lose it all. I'd be honored to work for a man like you."

John returned with the maps, and they cleared the dishes to spread them out on the table. When Herman pointed out the areas where Dougherty had had him working, George's heart sank. It was the area Dougherty had been warning people was too dangerous to work. And now George had to wonder just who the danger would be to—the workers or Dougherty's secrets?

"I can take you there in the morning," Herman said, looking at the notations on the map. "The area where I blasted is hard to get to, and you'll need some ropes. But I can show you."

"No you won't," Will said. "That leg of yours needs attention. I'll see to it that you get to the hospital. The others can plan their excursion to the mine."

Herman shook his head. "We all know he can't pay. I've already accepted that I'm a goner. Let me do something good with the life left in me. Henri was my friend. I've no doubt that he probably went after Dougherty, trying to get justice for me, and Dougherty likely killed him. But if I can find evidence to show that Dougherty was up to something, at least I'll know my friend didn't die in vain. And that boy of his can know his father was a hero."

George reached into his pocket for the one thing of value he had left. He'd always hoped it would never come to this, but when he'd returned for his father's funeral, his sister had tearfully pressed their father's signet ring into his hand, telling him that their father would have wanted him to have it. She'd also cautioned him not to tell Arthur she'd given it to him. At the time, he'd thought it was because Arthur had wanted it for himself. But maybe there was a deeper reason.

Letting out a deep breath, George set the ring on the table. "I can pay. It's all I have left, but it's only right that I do this."

John placed his hand over George's.

"No, son. I'll pay. That ring…it meant so much to your father. And to me."

Putting his other hand on the table, John revealed a similar signet ring. "When we struck gold, we each gave ourselves, and our wives, a nugget to do with as we pleased. Elias and I had ours made into rings as symbols of the dynasty we'd create together. We promised to be there for each other always, and I intend to keep that promise to my friend, through his son."

With tears in his eyes, John looked at Herman. "I make a similar promise to you. Whatever it takes to make you well, I commit myself to doing. I promise to help you and anyone else wronged by this situation."

Then John let out a long sigh. "And, for the sake of my own mines and workers, I intend to make sure my people are similarly cared for. Until all of this, it never occurred to me that I'd lost sight of all Elias and I held dear. People thought him a fool for being too generous, but now I wonder if we all haven't been generous enough."

Crazy Eddie slapped his hand on the table again. "You're the finest gents I ever did meet. I'll take Herman's place. I know these mountains like the back of my hand. I can get you to the spot he's talking about."

"Thank you," George said. "I can never repay the debt we owe you for your assistance."

Crazy Eddie grinned. "You and that young lady of yours just give that little boy a good home and lots of brothers and sisters. That'll be payment enough."

As all the other men grinned and chuckled, George tried to smile, although he couldn't muster up the energy. He'd laid his heart on the line, but Flora seemed colder than ever to him. He knew she needed time and space, but he wasn't sure if it would eventually bring them closer or widen the gulf between them.

Chapter Sixteen

The next morning, Flora woke earlier than usual, hoping to catch the men before they left. The sun wasn't yet up, but Flora ran into George in the kitchen just as he was packing up to leave.

"You should let us come," Flora said, taking in every bit of his handsome features. She wished she could hug him tight and tell him to stay safe, but things were still too jumbled. Why get both of their hopes up?

"It's not safe," he said, looking at her with the same longing she felt in her heart.

"But if you find Pierre's father…"

"He's probably dead," George said solemnly. "We need to face it. The people who knew him all agree he would have never left his son willingly. We know he probably went after Dougherty, a man who tried to kill Herman rather than having his secrets be known."

Though Flora knew George was likely right, it still hurt to hear the words. "But Pierre…"

She willed herself not to cry at the thought of telling the little boy his father wasn't coming back. But that wasn't the only image that came to mind.

"If this man is willing to kill, what about your safety? What about my father's?"

"Will is bringing another deputy. Owen Hamilton helped investigate the explosion at the mine, and he's familiar with the area, as well. Between them and Crazy Eddie, we should be fine."

Despite her will, tears filled her eyes. "George…"

He shook his head. "Let's not do this now. You're afraid I'm going to die, and I'm telling you that I'm not. We'll be back before nightfall. Take care of Pierre. Go visit Herman in the hospital. Call on Rose. Will said that the ladies were asking about you."

All normal things. That hardly seemed right in light of the seriousness of the situation.

But how could Flora refuse him? She'd said she wanted to do her part. This was what they wanted her to do.

"All right," Flora said.

"Good."

For a moment, Flora thought that George was going to bend down and kiss her or at least hug her. But he shook his head and walked away.

After they left, Flora did her best to stay busy around the house, but her mother remained abed, pleading a headache, and Agnes was so irritated with her over everything, that it seemed pointless. Since it was still too early to politely call on anyone, Flora gathered Pierre and made her way to the hospital to visit Herman.

When they arrived at the hospital, they were directed to Herman's room. However, Herman was asleep.

"Oh! A visitor." The nurse smiled at her. "It will greatly help his recovery. You are most fortunate that he got medical attention when he did. The doctor says we caught the infection just in time."

"I'm so glad." Flora turned to Pierre and told him that the nurse said Herman was going to be all right.

Pierre smiled. Though the little boy was afraid of the other man, Herman had been his father's friend, and Pierre seemed concerned about the man.

"You might come back later. I expect he'll be sleeping for quite some time, and what he really needs right now is rest." The nurse looked apologetic, but given that Pierre was already squirming on Flora's lap, it sounded like a good idea.

"Thank you. I realize this is unusual, but is there any way you could have someone send a message to my home when Herman wakes up?"

"Of course, Miss Montgomery."

Flora stared at the woman. "You know who I am?"

"Oh, yes," the nurse said. "Everyone knows who you are, and the doctor made it quite clear that Mr. Schmidt is to get the finest care. Please don't worry yourself on his account."

Then the nurse looked at Herman with a soft smile on her face. "He's been asleep the whole time I've been here, but there's something kind about him in his face. I've always said that people with kindness in their faces are the best sort of people."

Unexpectedly, she turned her attention to Flora, confusion written on her face. "And I don't know why, because I've never had this feeling before, but I feel compelled to say that you have that same kindness on your face. Which is odd, because I've heard..."

The nurse shook her head. "I apologize. I'm speaking out of turn. I have no idea what came over me just now."

"No, please," Flora said. "It's all right. I wish to hear what you have to say."

"I suppose it's no secret that you aren't known for your kindness," the nurse said. "I mean no insult."

The woman looked as though she honestly feared Flora would say something to get her in trouble.

"Of course you don't," Flora said. "And you're right. I haven't been known for my kindness. But I hope that perception will change in time."

"With a face like yours, I can't imagine it not. It's so strange. I thought I caught a glimpse of you in the mercantile a few months back, and I can't say that I saw this in you. Something must have happened to change you greatly."

Something, indeed. "Thank you," Flora told the nurse. "What is your name? I should have asked sooner and I haven't. I apologize."

"Ida," she said, smiling. "And it's all right. You seem to have a lot on your mind."

"I do." Flora took a deep breath. "Speaking of things on my mind, I know that it's probably against the rules, but my friend Ellen Fitzgerald was brought in several days ago, and I've had no word of her condition. Is there anything you can tell me that wouldn't get you in trouble?"

Recognition dawned on the other woman's face. "Of course! Why didn't I realize it now? She's been asking for a Flora, but her family says she's being foolish. She's just down the hall. I'm sure it would be all right for you to have a short visit. I've just come from there."

Flora's heart lightened at the news. If Ellen was asking for her, that had to mean she was awake.

When Flora entered Ellen's room, Ellen turned her head to look at her. "Flora!"

Her voice was weak, but she still sounded like Ellen.

Flora dashed to her friend's bedside. "I'm so glad you're all right. No one would say."

Ellen gave a weak smile. "Mother got sick of all the vultures visiting the house, looking for gossip. I should have insisted she send word, but every time I told her we were friends, she said I must've hit my head harder than people thought."

"I'm sorry I haven't been a better friend to you," Flora said. "You were a good friend to me. I thought I'd never have the chance to tell you how grateful I am for you."

"Nonsense. We've only barely gotten to know each other. And when I'm well enough, I fully expect you to keep your promise to teach me how to make a hat the way you do."

"Of course." The thought of making hats sobered Flora. They'd planned on making hats with Diana. "But…"

"I know about Diana," Ellen said quietly.

Tears filled Flora's eyes. It seemed like all she did these days was cry, with all the tragedy surrounding them. "I just wanted to say, I'm so sorry. It should have been me. I shouldn't have traded places with you."

Ellen let out a long sigh. "I talked you into switching. This isn't your fault. You don't think I haven't lain here, wondering why Diana died and I lived? It's not our place to sort out who gets to live and who gets to die. Or even to ask why."

Then she smiled at Flora, looking so peaceful that Flora wished she knew Ellen's secret. "What I have learned is that God spared me for a purpose. Just as He spared you. The question is, what do we do with the gift of life we've been given? I believe you're already working out God's purpose, so don't give up on it, no matter how difficult it seems."

With what looked to be a painful motion, Ellen gestured at Pierre. "I see you still have this fine young man with you."

She closed her eyes briefly, then looked back up at Flora. "I can't stop thinking about how I told you to ignore your feelings for George. I was wrong. If I could change one thing about my past, I would have fought to stay in Boston, fought for the man I loved. If you love George, don't let anyone tell you not to."

Ellen took a deep breath and closed her eyes again. Before Flora could think of what to tell her friend, a woman entered the room.

"Ellen!"

Ellen gave a sigh and opened her eyes. "I'm fine, Mother. Flora was just stopping in to see how I was. Now will you believe me that we're friends?"

"Hello, Mrs. Fitzgerald. It's good to meet you," Flora said with a smile. Then she gestured at Pierre. "And this is Pierre."

"I heard you were caring for a child whose father is missing. I wish you the best." The woman patted her hat nervously, like she was worried about her appearance.

"Thank you. And may I say that your hat is quite lovely. Although I've promised Ellen lessons in how I decorate hats, I think she could learn a great deal from you. Perhaps we could all do it together once Ellen returns home?"

Mrs. Fitzgerald's eyes widened. "It would be a pleasure."

"Wonderful." Flora smiled at them both. "I know Ellen needs her rest, and I have likely overstayed my welcome. Promise you'll keep me updated on Ellen's condition. I have another friend here that I've been visiting, and I would love to stop in and say hello to Ellen whenever I'm here."

"Oh, please do," Ellen said. "I'm dying of boredom."

"I could bring you some books," Flora said brightly, feeling like she was finally gaining ground in establishing new friendships since she lost everything.

"Absolutely not." Mrs. Fitzgerald glared at Ellen. "I know she's longing to read again, but the doctor says the strain is too much for her until she recovers."

"But I miss my books," Ellen said, sounding less chipper than she had the entire time Flora had been there.

"Then it's settled." Flora leaned forward and patted her friend's hand. "I will come and read to you."

"That's very kind," Mrs. Fitzgerald said. "Thank you."

Pierre tugged at Flora's hand. "I suppose I'd best let this little one go outside and run around. But I will be back. I'm truly grateful for your recovery."

As Flora left, she couldn't help but feel a definite lightness in her spirit as she realized that the people she'd encountered today had commented on her kindness. Not her beauty or her fashions, but on the thing she'd most wanted people to notice. Her heart.

Which, as she thought about Ellen's words about George, still needed a great deal of sorting out. What was the truth about her feelings for him? Was it love?

Or was it some misguided emotion she hadn't been able to place?

And if it was love, was it strong enough to bear the hardship ahead?

Thanks to Crazy Eddie's help, they reached the place Herman had marked on the map easily. Even to George's untrained eye, the scattered rocks and boulders indicated a great deal of blasting had occurred in the area.

"There's the shaft," Will said, pointing to a narrow fissure in the ground.

"No wonder Herman nearly died," Crazy Eddie said. "Only a fool would try blasting here."

They lowered a lantern into the dark space, quickly illuminating their worst fear: a man's body.

George closed his eyes and said a quick prayer. Though he didn't want another death on his hands, he also couldn't bear to tell Pierre that his father was truly gone.

Crazy Eddie put a hand on his shoulder. "I'm so sorry."

They worked together to rig up some ropes to lower Owen into the hole. George had thought they'd argue with him about retrieving the body, but the others seemed to be thinking the same thing—Pierre's father deserved a decent burial.

When Owen reached the bottom, he called up to the others. "You aren't going to believe this."

George looked down at him. "What?"

"They found silver. Only it's not in the direction Herman thought. You'd need a surveyor to be certain, but this just might be part of your mine, George."

Owen shone the light around some more, then let it settle on the body. "Can anyone read French?"

"Just Flora," George said.

"Good. This man didn't die right away, and there's a knapsack and a journal lying next to him. I don't know any French, but I can clearly read the name Dougherty in these pages. If I didn't know any better, I'd say this man knew he was going to die and wanted to be sure his killer was brought to justice."

God hadn't answered George's prayers for Pierre's father to be found safe. But if there was a second thing George could have wished for on Pierre's behalf, it would have been justice for Henri.

The men quickly worked to pull the body up, then Owen followed with Henri's belongings. Owen and Will looked through the knapsack, speaking quietly between themselves, then turned to George.

"I don't think any of this will be needed as evidence," Will said. "It's good that the child will have a few things that were his father's."

Owen held up the journal. "But we will need to have Flora translate to confirm what we suspect this contains. If it does, we'll need to keep this until Dougherty and the other perpetrators can be brought to justice."

"Of course," George said, nodding. He took the knapsack Will handed him, holding it close. At least he had something to give Pierre.

As they returned to town, the deputies talked about the case and how they were going to proceed. George tried paying attention, but mostly he felt sick. How could anyone in his family have thought money so important that they'd destroy so many lives over it? Did they know the extent Dougherty had gone to so they could get rich?

George didn't know. But he had to trust that, somehow, they could bring justice to those who had been wronged. At this point, the weight of the reparations George would have to make felt so heavy, it was almost a relief to know that Flora hadn't declared herself to him. Though having her arms around him would lighten his burden, he couldn't imagine her having to bear it with him.

As it was, she would have the difficult task of breaking the news to Pierre about his father. She'd been upset at the hypothetical prospect, but now knowing it to be true, George wished he didn't have to add so much pain to their lives.

Chapter Seventeen

Flora didn't have to be told the results of their expedition when they returned. She knew as soon as she spotted them coming down the street.

The little boy had broken down in tears when they told him, and Flora had held him until he fell asleep, sobbing in her arms.

And now, as she sat in the parlor, struggling to focus on her embroidery, Flora was at a loss. The men were locked in her father's study, planning their next move.

George entered the room, holding a book. "We meant to ask you to do this earlier, but it didn't seem right with Pierre…" He let out a long sigh. "I still don't feel right about putting you through this pain. But I thought I should at least ask you."

"Ask me what?" Flora set down the sampler. All of the stitches would have to be torn out anyway because she'd made such a mess of things.

"Pierre's father left a journal. None of us can read it, because it's in French. We're fairly certain he writes about his dying moments, because he mentions the mine manager's name."

Flora stared at the book in George's hands.

"It's painful, I know, and if you'd rather, I'll ask Marie's father. He can do it, but I'm trying to let you choose for yourself."

"I'll do it." The lump in Flora's throat made it almost too painful to speak. George was right. Reading Henri's words would be difficult. But she needed to do this for his son.

George handed her the journal, then stood above her. "Should I?"

George gestured at a nearby chair. Flora nodded, then opened the journal.

At first, the pages contained only personal information, the man's descriptions of coming to America after the death of his wife and baby, hoping to make a better life for their son. Henri wrote of hardships, but with each one, he expressed an unwavering hope that things would be better. It felt like an intrusion, reading such things. But someday, Pierre would be glad to know about his father. Clearly, Henri Martin loved his son, and would do anything for the little boy.

Tears filled Flora's eyes. It seemed such a waste that a man who'd done so much could lose his life like this.

"Is everything all right?" George leaned forward.

Flora brushed away the tears. "Yes. I wish you could understand these words. Henri loved Pierre with all his heart. Everything he did was to give his son a better life."

"That matches everything we've heard about him."

She nodded, then turned her attention back to the journal, coming to the point where Henri wrote about Herman's accident. According to Henri, he'd gone to see Dougherty to demand that he pay for Herman to see a doctor. He'd left Pierre by a spot where they'd camped, thinking he'd be back in a few hours. He hadn't wanted to bring Pierre, because he'd seen small boys working the mine, and he wanted to shield his child from the sight. He never wanted Pierre to think he had to work to provide for them.

Dougherty had argued with Henri, saying the accident had not happened the way Herman said. He'd offered to take Henri to the place where it happened to show him. Herman had been drunk and made a mistake. That's why Dougherty wasn't paying for it. Henri hadn't believed Dougherty, but thought that he should play along. When they got to the spot, Dougherty had pushed him into the shaft, then set another charge to cover it up.

Henri played dead until Dougherty left, then vainly tried to make his way out. But the shaft was too deep, and Henri didn't have the right equipment to escape. So he spent his time writing about what had happened in hopes that someone would find his body and the truth would come out.

As Flora read the words to George, her father and the deputies entered the room. When she finished reading about Dougherty's deeds, she looked up at them.

"Is this enough to put the man in jail?"

Will nodded and took the book from her. "It's enough to arrest him."

"Could we have the parts about Pierre? He needs to know his father's love for him."

"I'll see what we can do," Will said.

Then Flora turned to her father. "Henri only wanted a good life for his son. There is no one else to care for him. Can you find out what I need to do to adopt him?"

For a moment, her father looked like he wanted to argue, but then he nodded.

Part of her felt completely numb. But she had to keep going for Pierre.

She turned to George. "I promised you would always be a part of Pierre's life. And I intend to keep that promise."

"Thank you." He leaned into her. "About—"

"Please don't ask. I have greater concerns than my own heart right now. There's a little boy upstairs who needs my full attention. I'm sure you can understand the need for space. You should be focused on doing what's right by your family."

George nodded slowly. "You're right."

Flora's mother entered the room and a greater heaviness descended upon her heart. She knew her mother had her own pain to deal with, but Flora wasn't sure she was ready to discuss anything with her.

"I understand the boy's father is dead," her mother said.

Flora nodded, not trusting herself to speak. She couldn't get into an argument with her mother, not now.

Her mother turned to George. "Will you be marrying my daughter?"

The tightness in Flora's chest threatened to choke her. Not the response she'd expected to hear, but at least it wasn't a demand to send the child to an orphanage.

"It's complicated," George said slowly.

"No, it's not." She looked from George to Flora. "I assume you intend to give the child a home. Will you not give him a father?"

Flora closed her eyes. Her mother was clearly still

fixated on their reputation. And Flora could no longer live that way.

"What of love?" Flora asked, finally looking her mother in the eye.

"If you need to ask that question, then I pity you," her mother said, shaking her head. Then she looked down at Flora. "Pierre is crying. You should go to him."

Flora rose, feeling everyone's eyes upon her. Well, she'd have to get used to it. In the past, she'd craved the attention, but only in a positive way. Then she'd come to dread it, hating the way everyone judged her. And now, as she went up to comfort the child who'd just found out his father was gone forever, she found she didn't care.

George watched Flora leave, wishing he could hold her or offer her some comfort. But with the way her mother glared at him, such a gesture was liable to find him at the business end of a shotgun.

"Mrs. Montgomery," he said slowly, trying to sound as gentle as possible, "I have nothing but the utmost amount of respect for your daughter."

She stared at him like he'd told her he wanted to hurt Flora in some horrible way.

"We have spoken at length about our circumstances," he continued, sending a pleading glance at John. "But Flora has made it clear that she needs time to search her heart to be certain of her feelings. I care too much for her to pressure her into something that will make her unhappy. Given the circumstances, I think it's only fair to give her the space she's asked for."

John stepped forward. "I appreciate you giving consideration to my daughter's feelings. But I hope you can understand the need for distance if you have not come to an agreement."

"I do. And I'm doing my best," George said. "Which is why I think we should talk about other things, such as how we're going to find out who Dougherty is working with."

"I agree." John turned to the other men. "I assume we can trust your discretion in the matter of my daughter."

"Absolutely," Will said. "I've seen nothing untoward between her and George, and I believe she handles herself admirably. I've never had cause to think George was acting inappropriately toward her. I hope my daughter grows up to meet a man who will treat her with the same respect."

The other man gave him a sympathetic look, as though he understood what it meant to be doing your very best to be honorable in a difficult situation.

A knock sounded at the door, and Flora's mother went over to open it. At the sound of the man's voice, George looked at John. "That's Robert Cooper. He'll recognize me."

John joined his wife at the door, while Will helped George get to the kitchen, where he would be shielded from view yet still able to hear the conversation.

"I'm here to talk to you about purchasing the mine," Cooper said, as John ushered him into his study.

George noticed that John left the door open a crack, giving him the ability to listen in on the conversation.

"I'm glad," John said. "My attempts at contacting your office have been unsuccessful."

Cooper made a sympathetic noise. "Yes. My apologies. We've been busy dealing with the other family holdings."

"We?" John asked.

"Arthur Eldridge and myself. We've been running the Bellingham family business since poor Elias's passing."

"Yes," John said. "My condolences. I've always regretted my rift with Elias."

"Thank you. The death of a friend, especially a former friend, always puts things in perspective, doesn't it?"

"Indeed it does. Which is why I feel the need to purchase the Pudgy Boy Mine. It seems only right to help the family out of a bind."

The two men sounded so cordial, it seemed almost impossible to believe that they suspected Cooper of mismanaging the funds.

"I can understand your desire. However, it is with great regret that I tell you the mine is no longer for sale. The family circumstances were much exaggerated, and we feel it's not prudent to dispose of such a valuable asset at this time. I'm sure you understand."

It seemed odd that Cooper would come all this way to tell John that the mine wasn't for sale. Especially since the man had been avoiding all contact with John up until now.

"Odd," John said smoothly. "That wasn't the impression George Bellingham gave me."

"What do you mean?"

George smiled at the panic in Cooper's voice.

"He's quite concerned about the family's circumstances, especially with the discrepancies I found in the mine records. He's coming to stay with me to get to the bottom of the situation."

"He is?"

It took considerable self-control not to laugh at the way Cooper's voice wavered.

"Indeed. Would you like to see our correspondence?"

George could hear rustling in the room, presumably to get the papers George had written and signed to make people like Cooper believe he'd been talking to John all along.

"I see," Cooper said. "But…"

"It's my understanding that only George can authorize the sale of the mine, is that not right?"

"Well, yes…"

"So, then, I don't believe we have anything else to discuss, do we, Mr. Cooper?" John's tone was incredibly patronizing, but if anything would set Cooper off, it was being talked down to like that.

"I…"

"Let me walk you out," John said.

He walked a rather bewildered-looking Robert Cooper to the door, and as soon as he left, John called in to the kitchen.

"What do you think?"

"Something's up," George said. "He was very nervous at the idea of George Bellingham having information about the mine."

"I think it's time for George Bellingham to finally make his appearance," John agreed.

"Definitely," Will said. "Now, if you gentlemen will excuse me, I'm going to make some arrangements."

Chapter Eighteen

George hated the feeling of being confined to the stuffy closet in the Montgomerys' guest room. After Dougherty's arrest several days ago, word had spread about the mismanagement at the mine, and John had been very careful to let people know that he expected George to arrive today.

John had spared no expense in setting up this ruse. He'd used his connections to get a private car in Denver for the train to Leadville, carefully making sure no one could see inside. Owen had donned fine clothing, covering up with a large overcoat, scarf and hat so no one could discern his features. Though it was too warm for such clothing, it had given him the air of being a wealthy man attempting to travel incognito. When John's carriage arrived at the station to pick up George Bellingham, the windows were carefully covered to protect Bellingham's identity.

The whole scene had created quite a stir in town, and from what George had gathered, everyone knew George Bellingham had arrived to sell his mine to John Montgomery and finally be rid of the stain of what was becoming a rather large embarrassment in the form of the Pudgy Boy Mine.

Which left them to wait. The Montgomery family had gone to the Tabor Opera House for an evening of entertainment, where they would regretfully inform their friends that Mr. Bellingham was too exhausted from travel to attend.

After the stagecoach robbery that seemed to be about harming George, Will and Owen were certain that whoever was behind the mine troubles would try again if they knew George Bellingham was home alone at the Montgomery house. Which left Owen in the guest bed, pretending to be George, and George hiding in the closet to identify the perpetrator.

However, as the hours seemed to tick by at an incredibly slow rate, George was beginning to think they'd misjudged the men behind the troubles. What if they'd been wrong in their calculations?

A rattle at the door alerted him.

"Are you sure this is it?" a voice asked quietly.

Owen gave a loud snore to make it sound like George Bellingham was asleep in his bed.

"Yes. Let's do this and be done with it."

George tried peering through the crack in the closet to see who was speaking, but the room was too dimly lit.

"No. Have to wait for the boss to verify it's him. Can't have another mistake like the stagecoach."

The other man groaned.

"Shh…you'll wake him."

Owen let out another loud snore.

Footsteps sounded across the room, and light briefly shone in as the curtains rustled at the window. Probably to signal the boss. George forced himself to remain calm. They were so close. And yet, as his heart thundered in his chest, he couldn't stop his racing thoughts from going over all the evidence. Everything said the man responsible was most likely Robert Cooper, but what if it wasn't?

More footsteps sounded in the hallway.

"Well?"

The impatient voice broke George's heart. Not Cooper. George closed his eyes and said a silent prayer. His brother-in-law.

George wanted to push open the door and demand to know how Arthur could do such a thing, but both Will and Owen had cautioned him to wait until they revealed themselves. They needed to get the men to actually attempt to kill the man they thought was George, and they needed to hear the boss admit involvement. The lawmen wanted an airtight case, which meant waiting as long as possible while the culprits spoke.

"Can we just get it over with?" one of the men asked. "We need to be gone before the family returns."

"They'll be a while." Another man chuckled. "Poor Mr. Montgomery is going to have some carriage trouble."

"Not another accident," Arthur said. "It'll be too suspicious for the Montgomerys to be killed the same night George was, the same way his father was."

The man who'd mentioned the carriage trouble made a sound. "Oh, I think it will make a lot of sense once these books are found in George's things. Poor man was into the moneylenders for quite a sum. Coming to Leadville to finalize the deal made him realize that it wouldn't be long before Dougherty talked and let Montgomery know Dougherty's been stealing from neighboring claims for a while now on his boss's orders. Not to mention the way he's been altering the financial records to cover up the embezzlement."

At least that was one more piece confirmed. George was grateful that he'd listened to the advice he'd been given and remained in the closet. He tried to peer through the crack to get a glimpse of the ringleader, but the angle wasn't right. Who was this mysterious man?

"Are you sure he hasn't?" Arthur asked. "Montgomery was doing an awful lot of digging. And with the mine being investigated? What if they found something?"

The ringleader snickered. "Dougherty got the right books out in time. Stupid drunk, nearly ruined it for us all, trying to scare Montgomery away with that explosion. All he was supposed to do was show Montgomery the books Robert made up so that Montgomery would go away and we could sell the mine to someone stupid enough not to know better. Now we've got a mess on our hands, which is why you're here to help clean it up."

The man was so sure of himself, so smug in how he thought he'd arranged it all. With no thought to the lives he'd destroyed in the process. Was still planning on destroying. It provided some comfort to know that Arthur obviously wasn't running the show, and that someone else was pulling the strings. But still, how could Arthur allow someone to hurt his family like this?

"But what if Dougherty talks?" Arthur asked, his voice wavering. "What if George hears us talking?"

"Dead men can't talk," the ringleader said.

As if Owen also wanted to keep the men speaking, he let out another snore.

"That's a lot of killing. Why do so many people have to die?" Arthur sounded scared. Like suddenly the man he'd been trusting wasn't quite so trustworthy.

"You know why. Under the terms of Elias's will, the only way that silly wife of yours gets more than a pittance is if George dies."

Though, over the past few days, George had questioned the wisdom of keeping his identity a secret, he was now grateful he'd done so.

Arthur murmured something incoherent.

"It's your own fault. You should have known Elias would figure out you were embezzling from the mine to cover your gambling debts. You're just fortunate that I got to him before he went to the law. Or told Julia."

George closed his eyes and fought the nausea rolling around in his stomach. The only good thing about hearing this discussion was that whoever this man was, he'd just admitted to killing George's father.

"Leave Julia out of this," Arthur said. "You promised you wouldn't tell her."

"And I won't," the other man said smoothly. "As long as you cooperate."

At least his sister wasn't involved. But the heartbreak she was about to endure…

Arthur let out a long sigh. "When's Robert going to get here? I want to get this over with."

"He's staying at the hotel to confirm that we were there with him all night. We needed you here to make sure we got the right man this time."

The more pieces that were put together, the more George hated knowing.

"Someone hold George down. And cover his mouth so he doesn't alert anyone. I heard the staff was off for the night, but we can't take any chances. We need some light so we can plant the evidence."

As footsteps echoed in the room, like whoever was ordered to hold "George" down was doing just that, George heard a struggle and muffled grunts.

From his vantage point in the closet, George couldn't be sure how events progressed. But when he emerged, he saw that Will, who'd been hiding under the bed, had somehow managed to get one man on the ground, and Owen had popped out of the bed and was holding the others at gunpoint.

"It was a trap?" The ringleader sounded incredulous as he stared at George.

"George?" Arthur sounded even more so as George came out of the closet.

"How could you?" George asked him, looking his brother-in-law in the eye for the first time. "Father gave you so much."

"He didn't leave me anything in his will, now, did he? When I married Julia, he told me I was expected to earn my keep, to actually participate in the family business instead of just reaping the benefits. Do you know how much money Julia spends?"

Considering Julia often asked George for money, he had a pretty good idea.

"So you killed him?"

Wild-eyed, Arthur turned in the direction of the ringleader. "No, he did. He said it was the only way. I'd lost so much at the tables, with no chance of ever paying it back."

George looked at the man Arthur blamed. His face was covered in scars, and George couldn't say he'd ever seen the man before, but there was something familiar about him.

"Hello, George," the man said, raising his pistol at George's face.

Owen jumped from his place by the bed and tackled the man, but not before he'd pulled the trigger. George ducked as the shot zinged across the room, shattering the window.

The man wrestled with Owen, and another gunshot rang out. Owen rolled off the man and stood. A patch of red spread out across the man's chest.

"Papa, *no*!" Arthur screamed as he ran to the man's lifeless body.

"Your father's been dead a long time," George said quietly.

"No..." Arthur began sobbing. "He faked his death because Elias had figured out Papa was stealing from him. We met again, a few years ago, at the gaming tables. I should have known Elias would have realized I was doing the same thing. I was just doing what my father told me to do. I can't go to jail. It's not my fault. Why did you kill my father?"

In a quick motion, Arthur pulled another gun out from under his vest. Owen started for him, but before he could get to Arthur, Arthur shot himself.

George turned away from the scene, noting that Will already had the other two men who were part of the plot in handcuffs.

"We're just the hired help," one of the men said, struggling against the restraints. "We didn't do anything."

Will pulled him toward the door. "Tell it to the judge

and jury. Until then, I've got a nice hard bed in the jail for you two."

Several other men ran into the room, guns drawn. "We heard gunfire," one of them said.

"It's over," Will said, pushing one of the men toward him. "Take this guy and his friend over to the jail. Bobby, can you get someone to come help with the bodies? Jim, go check on the Montgomerys at the Opera House."

Will pulled a watch out of his pocket. "They shouldn't be leaving for a while. Don't let them get in their carriage. Both the carriage and horses need to be inspected for sabotage before anyone uses them."

Then Will looked around the room. "Tell the ladies to stay at my house or with Rose tonight. Pierre's already at Rose's, so I'm sure that's where Flora will want to be."

George tried not to focus his gaze on the two lifeless bodies. "I don't know how I'm going to tell Julia."

Owen came and patted him on the back. "You'll do fine. And we're here for you. I don't know your sister, but I've got a pretty good idea that she's made of some strong stuff. I hate to speak ill of the dead, but she's better off without him."

A large bag sat by the door. George walked over and peered inside. "I guess these are the books they were going to plant to make it look like I was behind it all."

"Don't touch them," Will said. "We need to go over these for evidence. I doubt the two we sent to the jail are more than what they said they were—hired guns. But, just in case, I want to do this right. All these people deserve justice."

George nodded slowly. "I just can't believe they'd kill so many people to cover up their crimes."

"Ross Eldridge wasn't just accused of embezzlement," John said, entering the room. "I did some further digging into his life when I started to see similarities. There were rumors of people he'd had killed. It doesn't surprise me that he faked his death and was here tonight. Like I said the other day, a lot of this sounded like how he operated. I only wish Elias had realized it sooner."

John must have walked from the Opera House, or by the way he was breathing, ran. Fortunately, it wasn't a great distance, and the carriage was mostly needed to transport the women in their finery.

"I thought you were supposed to be at the show?" George asked.

"When Will's men came to warn me about the carriage, I couldn't stay. I asked one of the men to tell Anna, and I came straightaway. I couldn't let you deal with this alone. And Ross… How has he gone unnoticed all these years?"

Will looked down at the dead men. "He fits the description of a man known as the Steed. Runs a few moneylending and gambling outfits across the West. I can't wait to send a wire to let people know we got him. This man ruined a lot of lives."

Several other lawmen entered the room, carrying stretchers to take away the bodies.

"I'm sorry for your loss," John said, coming to George and putting his arm around him. "I know you cared for Arthur, and it's going to be difficult for your sister. I should have tried harder to repair my relationship with your father. Maybe none of this would have happened."

"It's not your fault," George told him. "My father was a stubborn man. And a proud one. He probably was too ashamed to face you, knowing you'd been right about…"

He couldn't even say the name. A man who'd been like family, two men, and they'd not only destroyed the family, but everything George's father had built.

"Whatever you or your sister need, we're here for you," John said. "It's the least we can do."

George shook his head. "As long as you're still willing to buy the mine. I know you'll give a fair price, and based on the fact that Dougherty had been wrong about that silver belonging to another mine, it should end up yielding you a tidy sum."

"I could lend you the money to get back on your feet," John said.

"No." George shook his head. "While I know you'd deal fairly with me, I can't end up beholden to someone like that, not knowing if I'd ever be able to repay you. That seems to be how all this mess started. I'll take the proceeds from the sale, take care of those who were wronged by Arthur's greed, and use whatever's left for my mother and sister. Then find honest work for myself."

George looked around the room. Even with the stench of blood and gunpowder, no one could mistake the opulence. "All I need is a roof over my head, food in my belly and a good, honest woman beside me. I don't want any of this, not with what I've seen it do to a man."

"What about Flora?" John looked at him intently.

"I laid my heart bare for her. She said she needed

more time. But you and I both know, given the scandal that's about to hit, she'd be a fool to accept me."

Then he remembered Pierre. "I'll still do right by Pierre. As long as Flora and whoever she ends up marrying will let me be there for him, Pierre can always count on me. But I'm finished pressing my suit."

The splendor of the Tabor Opera House was lost on Flora as she sat in one of the box seats, wearing a new silk gown her mother had bought specifically for Flora because it would attract attention. In the past, she'd have been preening and enjoying having so many eyes upon her. After all, it was the latest fashion from Paris.

As the intermission began, Flora didn't want to leave her seat. "You go say hello to everyone, Mother," she said. "I'm a bit fatigued, so I'm going to stay right here."

"But Mr. Lawson said we were to be sure everyone saw us here tonight so people knew we weren't at home."

Flora sighed. "I'm sure they can see us just fine in these box seats."

"Oh, they can, can they?" Flora's mother waved as one of her friends passed by. "It's just too bad you couldn't have come on the arm of George Bellingham."

"You know why he couldn't come," Flora said, trying not to sound irritated. Her mother meant well, and she was glad that the ruse was about to end. There'd be some explaining to do, but at least then everything would be out in the open.

Her mother let out a long sigh, like she still didn't like Flora's answer. "I suppose I should see where your father went off to. I can't imagine why he would disappear like that, when he was the one who said we had to be sure everyone saw us here."

As soon as Flora's mother left, Sarah slid into the chair she'd vacated.

"Enjoying the performance?"

Flora smiled. "Yes, thank you."

Was it so terrible that the last thing she wanted was to sit and make small talk with her former best friend? Honestly, if it wasn't so important that Flora be seen out in public tonight, she'd have stayed at Rose's with Pierre and enjoyed the popped corn Rose said they were making. Even though Milly didn't know French, she'd taken to following Pierre around, mimicking his words. Flora had promised to help Milly learn to speak with Pierre, and it felt good to know that even that relationship had been redeemed.

"So…" Sarah leaned in to her. "I hear George Bellingham is at your house now. Is he as handsome as everyone says?"

How was Sarah going to react when she learned that the heir she'd been swooning over was the same miner she'd been sneering at?

"I suppose," Flora said, sighing.

"Does he compare to your miner friend?"

Flora closed her eyes and willed herself not to make a nasty remark in return. How had she thought she wanted to restore this relationship?

Sarah put a hand over Flora's, and Flora opened her eyes to look at the other woman.

"I wasn't trying to tease," Sarah said softly. "I haven't been very nice to you, and I'm sorry."

Words Flora had never imagined hearing her say. "Thank you."

"At first, when you were an outcast, I was afraid," Sarah said. "If they all hated you, when would they turn on me? So I did everything I could to distance myself from you, and that was wrong of me. It's not what a true friend would do."

Flora examined the other woman's face, not sure who the person sitting beside her was.

"But as I've seen you change, and seen others respond to that change, I realized that I was the one in the wrong. I hated hearing how sorry you were. How you regretted your past behavior. It was like a spotlight was shining on me, asking me to do the same."

"I never meant to accuse you," Flora said softly. "I feared that's how you felt, and I wish there'd been some other way to make amends, but not in a way that made you feel bad."

Sarah nodded. "But I was guilty. Just as guilty as you. And I hated it. Every time we were nasty to you, you acted like it didn't matter. Which hurt, because I missed you so much, and I hated that you didn't miss me."

Tears welled up in Flora's eyes. "I did miss you." She shook her head as Sarah offered her a handkerchief. "In some ways, I still do, but I'm also not that person anymore. I find the amusements of my past don't bring me joy the way they used to."

"Anyone can see what a good mother you are. I was sorry to hear about Pierre's father."

"Thank you." Flora smiled at her. "I appreciate your kind words."

"I'm not just saying that," Sarah said. "I remember how horrified we all were at the thought of the women in our circle raising children themselves and not having a nanny, but the way you are with Pierre, and how happy you seem to be, I can understand why some women choose to raise their own children."

Sarah reached behind her for a small bundle. "In fact, that's really why I came to see you. I would have called on you, but I didn't want you to think it was an excuse to get a peek at the wonderful George Bellingham."

Flora unwrapped the bundle and saw that it was the shawl Sarah had chastised Pierre about.

"Everyone was right. It cleaned up just fine," Sarah said. "And I sprayed it with some of my perfume. I'd like Pierre to have it. If it gives him some comfort, it would make me most happy."

Turning the bundle over in her hands, Flora stared at it. "You should give it to him," Flora said, looking up at Sarah. "It would be good for him to see you doing a kindness for him."

"I couldn't intrude on your family during this time," Sarah said. "Not with George Bellingham visiting. Your mother has her heart set on your match."

Sarah let out a long sigh. "I know it isn't done to marry a miner, but I've always been envious of how you and George Baxter look at each other. If it weren't for the differences in your social stations, I'd say you were meant to be. The kind of love that we used to lie in our beds and giggle about until all hours. I suppose my jealousy over that was part of why I was so nasty to you."

"It sounds like you've been examining your own heart," Flora said, smiling at Sarah.

"Usually, when we want what someone else has, we go to the store and buy it." Sarah gave a wicked smile. "Well, *you and I* go buy something better, then flaunt it."

Her expression turned somber again. "But when you see someone else's happiness and you want it for yourself, you can only work to destroy it so that person isn't happy, which I'm learning makes you miserable. Being happy is something you have to learn to do on your own."

Tears shone in Sarah's eyes. "That's the lesson you've taught me, and why, even though I do not deserve to be your friend, I hope we can someday be so again."

Propriety said that she was supposed to say something kind and encouraging, then nod politely. But Flora was tired of being proper. She leaned over and gave Sarah a big hug.

"And so we are."

Tears streamed down both of their faces, and Flora knew they must look a sight. When the signal came that intermission was nearly over, they gave each other one final squeeze.

"Your mother is going to be horrified," Sarah said. "You look a fright."

"No I'm not," Flora's mother said, entering the space. "I'm glad the two of you are finally over your tiff."

Flora smiled up at her mother. "It was more than a tiff, and you know it."

"But it's over, and you're both smiling again, and that makes my heart happy."

A man approached and bent to whisper something in Flora's mother's ear.

"Oh, dear," she said, looking at Flora. "Something has happened at the house. We must go home at once."

"Ma'am," the gentleman said. "That is not what you were told. Mr. Montgomery specifically said—"

"And you repeated the message. But the men we love are in trouble, and I will not sit idly by."

"Mother!" Flora gaped at her mother.

"Oh, stop. I'm tired of you pretending that you don't love him. And if I have to create a scandal to force you to marry him, then I will."

Her mother turned and glared at Sarah. "But don't you think about starting any rumors. There's a lot you don't know, and if your mother is correct in telling me that you are truly contrite over your behavior, then you will keep your big mouth shut."

"Of course," Sarah said, a mixture of horror and wounded feelings crossing her face.

"Good." Flora's mother nodded. "You may call on us tomorrow at four. I believe things should be sufficiently settled by then."

"Thank you, I will," Sarah said. "And I will be praying for you."

When Sarah left, another woman approached Flora's mother and whispered something in her ear. Her mother paled, and stepped into an alcove to speak with the woman further. The women had a brief conversation, in which Flora's mother looked extremely agitated.

Her mother returned and held her hand out to Flora. "Come. Mrs. Harris said her husband heard gunshots at our house. If those men of ours got themselves shot, I will never forgive them."

Flora hid a smile as she followed her mother out of the Tabor Opera House. At least, until her mind finally processed her mother's words.

"Someone was shot?" Flora stopped and stared at her mother.

"Don't dawdle. And I don't know. I just know that guns were fired. You know how much I deplore firearms. Oh, the violence. Why can't men be more civilized? Don't think I'm going to let your father get away with bringing weapons into my home."

Flora started for their carriage, but her mother tugged at her arm. "The man your father sent said it wasn't safe for us to take the carriage, and we should walk to Rose's. Imagine that! Walking all the way there, in these shoes, when our house is half the distance? If I have to ruin my new shoes, then I'm certainly not going to sit in someone else's parlor, hoping for news. That father of yours has clearly underestimated us, and if there are ruffians in my home, then I'll be by his side protecting it. Gunshots indeed!"

As her mother prattled on about how irresponsible people were with guns, she dragged Flora through the streets. Fortunately, their home wasn't far from the Tabor Opera House, but every step seemed like a mile.

George could be dead.

Which was when all the confusion in Flora's heart disappeared.

Had he hidden the truth from her? Yes. But he'd also explained his reasoning, the very same reasoning Flora's father had used in keeping the truth from Flora's mother. And though that decision had been just as ill-advised as George's, Flora's mother clearly forgave her husband. George had also made it clear that he was trying to learn from that mistake, to let Flora be a part of the decisions affecting her.

George had done everything in his power to admit

he had been wrong, and show he'd changed, but Flora had still held him at arm's length. How was that any different from how people treated her? If she wanted people to accept her changes, then she needed to also accept George's.

Perhaps Flora still had a few lessons to learn about what it meant to love someone.

When they reached the house, the women pushed past the deputies standing outside.

"Where is my husband?" Flora's mother demanded.

The two men were walking down the stairs, unaware that the women were present. They spoke somberly, and George's clothes had some blood on them.

But they were safe.

Flora ran up to George and threw her arms around him. "George!"

Before he could answer, she reached up and kissed him. And kissed him. Because, finally, she could kiss the man she loved.

At least, until her father cleared his throat.

"Now you most certainly will be getting married," Flora's mother boomed. "Even if I have to drag you to the altar myself."

Flora turned and smiled at her mother. "That won't be necessary. I'd be delighted to walk on my own."

Then she looked up at George. "That is, if you'll still have me."

"Always," he said, bending down and kissing her again.

"That is enough kissing," Flora's mother said, stomping her foot on the floor. "At least until after the wedding. I'm going to have a hard enough time explaining these unusual circumstances. Do not bring further scandal upon the family."

George looked up and grinned. "Then you should probably ask the preacher to come quickly. Because I have no intention of letting Flora go."

He started to embrace her again, but Flora's father put his arm between them. "I believe my wife has spoken on this issue."

Flora looked down at her mother, who wore a broad smile as she said, "And there will be a wedding. It will be written up as the finest event of the season. I've already picked out the dress."

George led Flora down the stairs and into the parlor. "You should have stayed away."

"I had to know you were all right."

They sat on a sofa, and George smiled at her. "I don't want to sound like I'm trying to dissuade you from marrying me, but I also want to be honest with you. The situation for my family is more dire than it first appeared. I'm not sure we'll weather the scandal. You won't be marrying a miner, but one of the scandalous Bellinghams that people whisper about on the street."

George explained what had happened while Flora was out. She hated the sadness on his face as he described the betrayal of his brother-in-law. She wanted to take him in her arms and hold him, but she was well aware of her parents' eyes on them as they spoke on the other side of the room. Only Flora's mother could simultaneously have a discussion with her father and very intensely observe her at the same time.

The more serious George's expression grew, the more Flora thought that her mother's intense gaze was mostly about being worried Flora would see his words as a reason not to marry him than she was that Flora and George would act inappropriately.

George concluded his explanation by saying, "I know I told you that our life might be more along the lines of the 'for poorer' part of the wedding vows. But that is all I have to offer you. I know your father is being more than generous in his purchase of the mine, but I've told him that I won't marry your money. It's what destroyed my brother-in-law, the greed for our wealth. As part of the sale of the mine, your father offered me a job managing the mine, and I've accepted. If you marry me, you're marrying the manager of the Pudgy Boy Mine, who lives in a cabin on the property. The pay isn't terrible, but it's only enough to keep food on the table, a roof over our heads and a little to set aside for rainy days."

"It sounds wonderful," Flora said, squeezing his hands.

"The cabin's got dirt floors, and I'm pretty sure, just like the one at the camp, the roof leaks."

Flora tried not to grimace.

George smiled at her. "I'll do what I can to fix the roof, and as I have time, I'll work on putting some planks down on the floor."

He gestured at the room around them. "But there won't be any of this."

"I don't need it," Flora said. "The funniest thing happened to me at the Tabor Opera House. Usually, it's thrilling to be there, at the center of everything. But all I could think about was how much I wished I could be at Rose's house, popping corn with her and the children."

With a grin, George brought her hand up to his lips

and kissed it. "I think we can afford some corn for popping."

"Then we'll have all we need. Now, let's go get our son." Flora stood and held out her hand to him.

As he took her hand, she felt no trepidation about the future. No, it wasn't the life she'd planned for herself. But for the first time in a long time, she didn't question what she was thinking. Rather, her heart had spoken loud and clear.

Epilogue

One year later

The spring air was still crisp this time of morning as Flora stepped out of their cabin by the mine. Her parents were visiting, and George was taking the day off to spend it with them.

"Maman!" Pierre came running up to her, clutching a bouquet of flowers. "I mean, Mama. Look what I found for my grandmother. She will like?"

"She will." Flora bent down and kissed him on top of his head, then pointed to the trail leading up from the main road. "Look! They're coming!"

Pierre needed no further encouragement to run to greet her parents. George stepped out of the cabin and joined her on the porch.

"Do you think they've guessed our news?" he asked, wrapping his arms around her and placing his hand over her stomach.

"I'm sure you just let them know." Flora turned and kissed him. "But that's all right."

Her mother ran up to them. "Is that what I think it is?"

"Yes. We're expecting a baby."

"Oh! Honoria will be so pleased!" Flora's mother hugged them tight to her.

In the weeks that followed the horrible ordeal at Flora's parents' house, the Montgomerys and Bellinghams had reestablished their friendship and Flora's mother spent time in Denver visiting George's mother. The two matriarchs had giggled like schoolgirls as they planned their children's wedding. Though George's mother had still not fully recovered from the accident, she could walk short distances with a cane, and Flora hoped that soon they could have her in their home for a visit.

She turned to stare at the room George had been adding on in his spare time. It wouldn't be as fine as George's mother was used to, but there was something very satisfying about looking at the touches they'd added to their home and knowing that they'd built it together.

George's sister had settled in a small house in Leadville that George purchased for her out of the proceeds from selling the mine. Though Flora wasn't able to get down to Leadville as often as she liked, she was glad to have Julia nearby so Pierre had cousins to play with.

Not that Pierre had any trouble finding children his age to entertain him. In honor of Pierre's father, Flora had begun a small school for the miners' children. Even those who were too young for regular school were welcome. Flora's main concern was having a safe place for the children to be while their parents worked. No child should have to suffer the way Pierre had.

And, in the evenings, they invited the miners and anyone else who was interested to come in to learn to read for themselves so they wouldn't be tricked by another Dougherty.

Flora's father joined them on the porch, Pierre on his shoulders. "So, I see Pierre is going to be a big brother."

"Oui," Pierre said, puffing out his chest. "I cannot wait to tell my friends at the French gathering."

As part of their decision to continue honoring Pierre's background and birth family, they took Pierre down to Leadville once a month to get together with the French families. Though Pierre could speak better English, Flora wanted him to maintain his native language and preserve some of his traditions.

The shawl Sarah had given Pierre now hung proudly above his bed—except on some nights when he felt particularly lonely for his birth parents. Sarah occasionally visited, bringing her perfume to refresh the scent.

Smiling from the very depths of her heart, Flora looked around at her family. Was it wrong to be so happy with such simplicity?

"I'm sure your friends will be quite pleased for you," Flora's father said, putting the boy down with a measuring eye. "You're getting heavy. Growing."

Pierre puffed out his chest. "I eat all my vegetables, so I can be strong, like *Père*. Strong enough to bring in all the fish. You are taking me fishing later?"

Giving the little boy a squeeze, he said, "Don't I always when I come up? Let me visit with your parents a little while longer, then we'll find Peanut and see if he wants to join us."

Though the other miners had been disappointed to find that George had misled them, when the full story of how eager his brother-in-law's associates had been to kill him came out, they'd all been horrified. And given that George now worked right alongside them, not just as their boss, but as a man committed to helping them better their lives, the friendships that had begun were now blossoming.

"I am hearing good things about your work here at the mine," Flora's father said, turning to George. "I can't believe how much the profit margin has improved over the past year."

"It's like my father always said, if you treat your people well, your business will thrive." George gave Flora a squeeze. "But I wouldn't have been able to do it without Flora. She's the one who had the idea to help with the children so the parents could work. The ministry is coming again to spend the summer, and Flora is hoping to convince Pastor Lassiter to build a regular place of worship. We've been having Bible studies here at the cabin, but I think poor Flora would like her house back."

He smiled down at her, and even in this simple glance, Flora felt deeply loved.

"Especially with the baby coming," he said, giving her a kiss. "I don't know how to count my blessings, because they keep multiplying faster than I can count."

"Then I suppose you'll need to hire some help for the calculations," Flora's father said, holding his arm out to Flora's mother.

"We've been talking, and though I support your decision to be your own man and make your own way in the world, you've also been a good steward of my mine." With a smile, Flora's father pulled a paper out of his jacket.

"Which is why I've made you both owners of the Pudgy Boy Mine."

Flora stared at him. "I don't understand…"

"Sir, you're too generous," George said.

"None of that." Flora's father held up a hand. "The profits have more than doubled since you took over, and when I purchased the mine, I fully expected to barely break even, based on the numbers I'd seen and what I knew of the new vein. I only purchased the mine to honor a dear friend's memory."

Then he gave Flora a look of such love, it warmed her heart more than she thought possible. "And because I wanted my daughter to have a roof over her head."

Her father turned his attention back to George. "You've done that and more. And, from what I hear, you have even greater plans, serving the men who've been injured in mine accidents at other mines. Those plans take money. Owning a thriving mine will give you the money you need for that, and so much more."

"And you can use the money to take Flora and Pierre to Denver to visit your mother," Flora's mother said. "It's a disgrace how seldom Honoria gets to see you. Plus, with the way Flora's figure is changing, she's going to need a whole new wardrobe."

Flora shook her head. "Mother, I don't—"

"Nonsense! Just because you're a mother doesn't mean you can't be fashionable. I will not have my daughter and grandchildren dressed in rags. Speaking of which, if your father will go down to the carriage, I've brought some new things for Pierre."

She turned and gave her husband a look, and he shook his head and smiled.

"Fine," her mother said, holding out a hand. "Pierre, come help your grandmother."

Flora's father turned back to them. "You know she's not going to bend on the new wardrobe."

Sighing, Flora nodded.

"And I'm not going to bend on the mine. The papers have been signed. Even if you refuse, it's still in your name."

Flora looked up at George. "What do you think?"

"I think all the good we've been hoping to do is about to get done."

Bending down to kiss her again, George asked, "Now that you've been married to me 'for poorer,' do you think you can handle the 'for richer' part?"

"I'm sure I'll find a way to suffer through it," Flora said, grinning up at him as she kissed him.

* * * * *

If you enjoyed Flora's book, pick up the stories of Flora's friends and neighbors, also set in Leadville, Colorado:

ROCKY MOUNTAIN DREAMS
THE LAWMAN'S REDEMPTION
SHOTGUN MARRIAGE
THE NANNY'S LITTLE MATCHMAKERS
FOR THE SAKE OF THE CHILDREN

Available now from Love Inspired!

Find more great reads at www.LoveInspired.com

Dear Reader,

We all know Flora was the nemesis of a lot of our Leadville ladies. Why couldn't I have left well enough alone and let her be the horrible woman everyone hated? Because, as a good friend and I discussed, it's in my nature to want to redeem everyone. I want to believe that someone like Flora, whom everyone hates, has something good in her, and that God can transform all those bad places to reveal that beautiful thing inside her no one else has seen.

Can everyone be redeemed? I believe, with all of my heart, that if you want to be redeemed, and you seek God's guidance, then you absolutely can and will find redemption.

My prayer for you is that if you find yourself far from God, regretting mistakes of your past, that you will turn your face toward Him, and you will realize the light of His love shining upon you.

I always love hearing from my readers, so feel free to connect with me at the following places:

Website: http://www.danicafavorite.com/
Twitter: https://twitter.com/danicafavorite
Instagram: https://instagram.com/danicafavorite/
Facebook: https://www.facebook.com/
DanicaFavoriteAuthor

Abundant blessings to you and yours,

Danica Favorite

THE BRIDE'S MATCHMAKING TRIPLETS
Lone Star Cowboy League: Multiple Blessings
by Regina Scott

When mail-order bride Elizabeth Dumont arrives in Little Horn, Texas, to find her groom already taken, she stays on as nanny to the orphaned triplets in the town's care. But after she falls for the babies, the only way to adopt them is by agreeing to marry minister Brandon Stillwater—her former sweetheart.

A TAILOR-MADE HUSBAND
Texas Grooms • by Winnie Griggs

Giving up hope that Sheriff Ward Gleason will ever return her affections, seamstress Hazel Andrews plans to head East for a fresh start. When the handsome sheriff finds an abandoned little girl, Hazel can't say no to Ward's request for help. But can their temporary arrangement turn into a forever family?

MAIL ORDER SWEETHEART
Boom Town Brides • by Christine Johnson

Lumberjack Sawyer Evans is drawn to Fiona O'Keefe, who needs a husband to help support her and her orphaned niece. But if Sawyer tells her the truth—that he's a railroad-empire heir—will he ever be sure she loves *him* and not his wealth?

TAKING ON TWINS
by Mollie Campbell

Back in his hometown to train with the local doctor, Jake Hadley becomes stand-in dad to orphaned twins. And offering to help him with the children is the one person he never planned to spend time with again—Coralee Evans, the woman he once loved.

SPECIAL EXCERPT FROM

Love Inspired HISTORICAL

*Elizabeth Dumont came to town to be a mail-order bride...
but arrived to find her would-be groom marrying someone
else! With nowhere to go, she's grateful for a temporary job
caring for foundling triplets, even if it means interacting
with her ex-sweetheart, pastor Brandon Stillwater.
But when Brandon offers a marriage of convenience that
will allow her to adopt the babies she's come to love, can
they let go of their painful past to build a future—and
a family—together?*

Read on for a sneak preview of
THE BRIDE'S MATCHMAKING TRIPLETS,
the sweetly satisfying conclusion of the series
**LONE STAR COWBOY LEAGUE:
MULTIPLE BLESSINGS.**

"What did you say?" she asked.

"I asked you to marry me. I can see that you genuinely
care for Jasper, Theo and Eli. Just as important, they care for
you. If we married, we could petition the Lone Star Cowboy
League to adopt them." His voice softened until she could
hear the yearning in it. "We could be a family."

A family. She could be mother to those three darling babies,
see them grow into the fine men she was sure they could be.
She could stay in Little Horn, deepen her friendships with
Louisa, Caroline, Fannie, Annie and Stella. She would finally
have a home to call her own. All she had to do was give up on
love. For he hadn't offered that.

She must have taken too long to answer, for his shoulders
slumped.

"Have I offended you?" he murmured, face so worn he
wanted to reach out and stroke the lines from beside his eyes.

"No, of course not." She brushed at her skirts, anything to keep her hands too busy to touch him. "It was very kind of you, Brandon, but we both know your heart wasn't in it."

His mouth quirked, more pain than smile now. "It seemed like the perfect plan for us both. I've come to care about the boys, but I'm not in a position to adopt them. And I was under the impression you wanted to stay in Little Horn."

She did. Outside her aunt's home, she had never felt so welcome anywhere, until those vicious rumors had started.

"And there are those rumors," he added as if he had heard her thoughts.

She fought a shiver. Rumors. Gossip. How easily they tainted a life. If people in Little Horn thought her of poor character, she might well find it impossible to secure a position in the area. And how would the people of Little Horn react if those rumors tarred their pastor with the same brush?

Heat flamed through her. "You're concerned about what people will say about us. You're worried for your reputation."

He colored. "My reputation will survive. I'm more concerned about yours."

She put her hands on her hips. "Oh, so now you agree that I'm some kind of fortune hunter?"

"No." He puffed out a breath. "Elizabeth, please. Consider my offer. You and the boys would have a secure home, a place in the community. I can protect you. But if marrying me is unthinkable, even under those terms, I'll understand."

David McKay had offered her a similar arrangement, and she'd accepted. But this was Brandon. Brandon, who had once claimed her heart.

Brandon, who had abandoned her when she needed him most.

Don't miss
THE BRIDE'S MATCHMAKING TRIPLETS
by Regina Scott, available June 2017 wherever
Love Inspired® Historical books and ebooks are sold.

www.LoveInspired.com

LIHEXP0517

*Will a pretend courtship fend off matchmaking mothers,
or will it lead to true love?*

Read on for a sneak preview of
THEIR PRETEND AMISH COURTSHIP,
the next book in **Patricia Davids**'s
heartwarming series, **AMISH BACHELORS**.

"Noah, where are you? I need to speak to you."

Working near the back of his father's barn, Noah
Bowman dropped the hoof of his buggy horse Willy, took
the last nail out of his mouth and stood upright to stare
over his horse's back. Fannie Erb, his neighbor's youngest
daughter, came hurrying down the wide center aisle,
checking each stall as she passed. Her white *kapp* hung
off the back of her head dangling by a single bobby pin.
Her curly red hair was still in a bun, but it was windblown
and lopsided. No doubt, it would be completely undone
before she got home. Fannie was always in a rush.

"What's up, *karotte oben*?" He picked up his horse's
hoof again, positioned it between his knees and drove in
the last nail of the new shoe.

Fannie stopped outside the stall gate and fisted her
hands on her hips. "You know I hate being called a carrot
top."

"Sorry." Noah grinned.

He wasn't sorry a bit. He liked the way her unusual violet eyes darkened and flashed when she was annoyed. Annoying Fannie had been one of his favorite pastimes when they were schoolchildren.

Framed as she was in a rectangle of light cast by the early-morning sun shining through the open top of a Dutch door, dust motes danced around Fannie's head like fireflies drawn to the fire in her hair. The summer sun had expanded the freckles on her upturned nose and given her skin a healthy glow, but Fannie didn't tan the way most women did. Her skin always looked cool and creamy. As usual, she was wearing blue jeans and riding boots under her plain green dress and black apron.

"What you need, Fannie? Did your hot temper spark a fire and you want me to put it out?" He chuckled at his own wit. He along with his four brothers were volunteer members of the local fire department.

"This isn't a joke, Noah. I need to get engaged, and quickly. Will you help me?"

Don't miss
THEIR PRETEND AMISH COURTSHIP
by Patricia Davids, available June 2017 wherever
Love Inspired® books and ebooks are sold.

www.LoveInspired.com